INTERIM SITE

W9-CZR-460

3 1192 00296 4375

DATE DUE

TO READ AND TO TELL

ALSO EDITED BY
NORAH MONTGOMERIE

More Stories to Read and to Tell

This Little Pig went to Market

TO READ & TO TELL

An anthology of stories for children chosen and edited by

NORAH MONTGOMERIE

with drawings by
MARGERY GILL

THE BODLEY HEAD

LONDON SYDNEY

TORONTO

EVANSTON PUBLIC LIBRARY
CHILDREN'S DEPARTMENT
1703 ORRINGTON AVENUE
EVANSTON, ILLINOIS 60201

To Catherine Mary Brooks

All rights reserved
This collection © The Bodley Head Ltd 1962
Illustrations © The Bodley Head Ltd 1962
ISBN 0 370 01048 5
Printed and bound in Great Britain for
The Bodley Head Ltd
9 Bow Street, London WC2E 7AL
by Redwood Burn Limited
Trowbridge & Esher
First published 1962
Reprinted 1963, 1965, 1967, 1971, 1974

Contents

II. STUFF AND NONSENSE

III. ANIMAL FABLES

IV. STORIES ROUND THE YEAR

SPRING

SUMMER

8 CONTENTS

VI. ONCE UPON A TIME

Introduction

Great-grandmother lived with us until I was seven. I remember her vividly and how she eyed me if I toyed with food. 'Take it or leave it' was her maxim. So was: 'Don't give children paps, give them something they can chew!' And this seemed to be the principle she applied also to story-telling.

What a talent she had, with her sense of the dramatic, her ear for the rhythm of story-telling phrase and repetition! Her repertoire was large and I cannot remember a time when we were considered too young to listen. However, I do remember that first favourites were the cumulative stories, full of repetition, like 'The Little House' and 'The Enormous Turnip', and stories like 'The Three Bears' and 'The Three Pigs', with their repetitive patterns making them easy to remember. Young children have a nice sense of ritual and these stories give frequent opportunity to prompt and join in. We laughed at the nonsense stories and later enjoyed the snippets of terror that are in so many traditional folk tales.

Great-grandmother also read to us from Grimm and from the collections of Joseph Jacobs, Andrew Lang and many others; but she disliked our sentimentally pretty story-books and the dolled-up versions of nursery tales. Nothing would persuade her to read them to us. 'Paps' is what she called them!

A book is no substitute for a good story-teller but good story-tellers are rare. Many have the position thrust upon them and it is for them—the mothers and the infant-teachers —that this book has been made. For the true story-teller, a book may be a source of inspiration, for the rest of us it is a tool.

Many of the stories in this book are versions of well-known folk tales with recurring themes in world literature and there are many from the East as well as from Europe, such as 'The Stone Monkey' and 'The Rat Princess'. Animal fables have been collected from as many different native sources as possible, and there are unusual variants of popular nursery tales, for example, a Scottish version of 'The Three Bears', and the Americanised 'Stupid Cries' of Joseph Jacobs—here called 'Soap! Soap! Soap!'.

Children like stories of real life, but simply-told stories of household heroes are often difficult to find. It was only after much searching that I found 'Little Abe Lincoln' and 'Appleseed John'—the story of an unusual man which has a special appeal for children. They also enjoy stories with references to season or festival, like 'The Easter Hare', 'Persephone' and 'Babushka and the Three Wise Men', and these have been gathered under the appropriate headings.

I have included some stories by modern authors and I should like to thank them for allowing me to do so. Their names are attached to their stories. They all have that rare quality, the story-teller's ear, and have given me hours of pleasurable 'reading aloud' to children. The other stories, traditional tales, fables and biographical tales, I have retold myself— either from memory or from original sources. I hope they will read as if they were being told.

Last, but not least, I should like to thank so many librarians, teachers and friends for their generous help and advice in the making of this book.

NORAH MONTGOMERIE

I

FIRST TALES TO TELL

Traditional and Modern

The Cock and the Bean

A Cock was pecking about the farmyard, peck, peck, peck and he picked up a bean. He tried to swallow it but choked, and stretched out full length on the ground. He lay there, hardly able to breathe.

The Hen saw him and ran up to him.

'Oh, Cocky, Cocky!' she said. 'Why are you lying there like that? Can't you breathe?'

'I've choked myself with a bean,' said the Cock. 'Go to the Cow! Ask her for some butter to help me swallow the bean!'

Off ran the Hen to the Cow, tippity-tippity-tip.

'Please, Cow, give me some butter,' said she. 'The Cock is lying on the ground. He can't breathe. He's choked himself with a bean.'

'First, go to the Farmer and ask him for some grass!' said the Cow.

Off ran the Hen to the Farmer, tippity-tippity-tip.

'Please, Farmer, give me some grass!' said she. 'I want some grass for the Cow so that she can give me some butter. The butter is for the Cock. He's lying still on the ground, he can't breathe. He's choked himself with a bean.'

'First, go to the Oven and ask for some bread!' said the Farmer.

Off ran the Hen to the Oven, tippity-tip-tip-tip.

'Oven, please, give me some bread!' said she. 'The bread is for the Farmer so that he'll give me some grass. The grass is for the Cow so that she can give me some butter. The butter is for the Cock. He's lying still on the ground and can't breathe. He's choked himself with a bean.'

'First, go to the Woodcutter and ask him for some wood!' said the Oven.

Off ran the Hen to the Woodcutter, trip-trip-trip.

'Woodcutter,' said she, 'please give me some wood! It is for the Oven so that the Oven can give me some bread. The bread is for the Farmer so that he'll give me some grass, and the grass is for the Cow so that she can give me some butter. I need the butter for the Cock. He's lying still on the ground and can't breathe. He's choked himself with a bean.'

'First, go to the Smith,' said the Woodcutter. 'Ask him for an axe!'

Off ran the Hen to the Smith, triptrip, triptrip.

'Please, Smith, give me an axe!' said she. 'It's for the Woodcutter so that he can chop me some wood. The wood is for the Oven so that it can give me some bread. The bread is for the Farmer so that he'll give me some grass, and the grass is for the Cow, so that she can give me some butter. I need the butter for the Cock, who is lying still on the ground, unable to breathe. He's choked himself with a bean.'

'Well,' said the Smith, 'just you go to the wood and fetch me a bit of burning charcoal!'

Off went the Hen to the wood, tippity t-i-p-p-i-t-y t-i-p. And there she found a nice bit of burning charcoal.

She took the charcoal to the Smith and he gave her an axe.

She took the axe to the Woodcutter and he gave her some wood.

She took the wood to the Oven and it gave her some bread.

She took the bread to the Farmer and he gave her some grass.

She took the grass to the Cow and she gave her some butter.

And tippity-tippity, tip-tip-tip, she took the butter to the Cock. The Cock ate the butter and down slipped the bean. Then he jumped up and crowed and crowed:

'Cock-a-doodle-doo!

COCK-A-DOODLE-DOO!'

Russian Folk Tale

The Three Bears

Once upon a time, there were three Bears and they lived in a big house in the middle of the forest. One was a great big Bear, and one was a middle-sized Bear and one was a little wee Bear.

One day the three Bears went for a walk while their porridge was cooking, and while they were away who should come along but the young rascal of a Fox!

When he saw the Bears' great big house, he wondered if he'd find anything good to eat in it. He looked this way and that to see if anyone was about, then he tip-toed quietly to the front door, and pushed, very gently. What a bit of luck! The door was not even shut properly, so he pushed again and put his nose inside. There wasn't anyone there, so he pushed again and put one paw in, then he put another paw, and another paw, and another paw, and there he was, right inside the three Bears' house. He looked around and sniffed with his long sharp nose. He was now quite sure there was no one at home.

So that rascal Fox prowled about the room and he saw three chairs set round a table all laid for the three Bears' breakfast. There was a great big chair, a middle-sized chair and a little wee chair.

'I'll sit down and rest,' said he.

He sat on the great big chair, but it was much too hard; so he sat on the middle-sized chair, but it was too slippery and he soon slipped off. Then he tried the little wee chair. It was so comfortable he settled himself down for a nice long rest when, all of a sudden, the little wee chair broke and that rascal Fox fell on the floor, and he could not mend the chair however hard he tried.

Then he saw three bowls of cream the three Bears had set on the table to eat with their porridge. There was a great big bowl, a middle-sized bowl and a little wee bowl.

'I like cream,' said he.

So he took a sip out of the great big bowl, and turned up his nose. It was much too sour! He took a sip of the middle-sized bowl, but it was much too sweet. He tried the little wee bowl. It was so delicious that he drank it *all* up and licked the bowl clean.

Then that rascal Fox thought he would like to go upstairs. So up the stairs he went, and at the top he found a great big room, and in the room were three beds—a great big bed, a middle-sized bed and a little wee bed. The Fox climbed into the great big bed, but it was much too hard, and he soon climbed out again. Then he climbed into the middle-sized bed, but it was so lumpy that no matter which way he turned he just couldn't make himself comfortable, so he rolled right off on to the floor. Then he tried the little wee bed. It was so soft and warm he curled up under the bedclothes and went fast asleep.

When the three Bears returned from their walk, the great big Bear went over to his great big chair and said, in his great big voice:

'WHO'S BEEN SITTING IN MY CHAIR?'

The middle-sized Bear said in her middle-sized voice:

'Who's been sitting in my chair?'

The little wee Bear said in his little wee voice:

'Who's been sitting in my chair and broken it all up?'

Then they looked at the table and their nice bowls of cream, and the great big Bear said in his great big voice:

'WHO'S BEEN EATING MY CREAM?'

The middle-sized Bear said in her middle-sized voice:

'Who's been eating my cream?'

The little wee Bear said in his little wee voice:

'Who's been eating my cream and eaten it all up?'

The three Bears were very angry and, after looking round their house downstairs, they stumped up the stairs in very bad tempers.

'STUMP, STUMP, STUMP!' went the great big Bear.

'Stump, stump, stump!' went the middle-sized Bear.

'Stump, stump, stump!' went the little wee Bear, following close behind.

When they got upstairs the three Bears looked at their beds. They grew angrier than ever, and the great big Bear roared in his great big voice:

'WHO'S BEEN SLEEPING IN MY BED?'

The middle-sized Bear shouted in her middle-sized voice:

'Who's been sleeping in my bed?'

The little wee Bear wailed in his little wee voice:

'Who's been sleeping in my bed? Look, there he is!'

Just then, that young rascal of a Fox woke up with a start. He looked up and there he saw THREE ANGRY BEARS staring down at him and saying, all together:

'WHAT SHALL WE DO WITH HIM?'

The great big Bear roared in his great big voice:

'I'LL SIT ON HIM AND SQUASH HIM!'

The middle-sized Bear said in her middle-sized voice:

'I'll cut off his long red tail!'

But the little wee Bear said in his little wee voice:

'Let's throw him out of the window!'

So without further ado, the three Bears took that rascal Fox and dragged him to the window. The great big Bear took his forelegs, the middle-sized Bear took his hind legs, while the little wee Bear said: 'One! Two! Three! Throw!'

That rascal of a Fox went flying out of the window, and landed with a BUMP! on the ground below. Wasn't he frightened! He thought all his bones were broken! First he tried one leg, and it wasn't broken! Then he tried his second leg, and it wasn't broken. Then he tried his third leg and it wasn't broken! Then he tried his fourth leg, and stood on his four good legs and not a single bone broken! But he didn't turn to wave to the three Bears, he just trotted home to his

den at the edge of the forest, and never bothered the three
Bears again.

Scottish version of this Folk Tale

The Wee Bannock

Once upon a time there lived an old man and an old wife
beside a stream. They had two cows, five hens and a cock, a
cat and three kittens. The old man looked after the cows while
the old wife span. The kittens liked to claw at the old wife's
spindle as it danced over the hearth.

'Shoo, shoo,' she said, 'go away!'

One day, after porridge time, she thought she would like
a bannock. So she baked two oatmeal bannocks, and set them
by the fire to toast. After a while, the old man came in, sat
down by the fire, took up one of the bannocks and snapped it
through the middle. When the other bannock saw this, it
ran off as fast as it could, and the old wife after it, with the
spindle in one hand and the distaff in the other.

But the wee bannock went away, out of sight, and ran
until it came to a great big house, and in it ran till it came to
the fireside. There were three tailors sitting on a long table
stitching, and when they saw the wee bannock, they jumped
up and hid behind the goodwife, who was busy beside the fire.

'Don't be frightened,' said she, 'it's only a wee bannock.
Catch it, and I'll give you a mug of milk to drink with it.'

Up stood the three tailors and chased the wee bannock,
but it dodged them and ran about the fire-place. One tailor
threw his sleeve board and another tried to snip it with the
shears, but it was no use. The bannock escaped, and ran till
it came to a wee house at the roadside. In it ran, and there
was a weaver sitting at a loom and his wife winding wool.

'Tibby,' said he, 'what's that?'

'Oh,' said she, 'it's a wee bannock.'

'It's welcome,' said he, 'for our porridge was thin to-day Catch it, wife, catch it!'

'Ay,' said she, 'if I can. That's a clever wee bannock. Catch it, Willie, catch it!'

But the bannock ran round about, across the floor and off over the hill. On it ran to the next house, and in to the fireside, where the goodwife was making butter.

'Come away, wee bannock,' said she. 'I'm having cream butter and bread to-day.'

But the wee bannock ran round the churn, the wife after it, and in the hurry she nearly overturned the churn with all the cream in it. Before she had set it right again, the wee bannock was off, down the hillside to the mill, and in it ran.

The miller was sifting meal and, looking up, he smiled at the wee bannock.

'Ay,' said he, 'it's a sign of plenty when you're running about, and nobody looking after you. Come in, and I'll give you a bed for the night. I like bannock and cheese.'

But the wee bannock would not trust itself with the miller and his cheese. So it ran and it ran till it came to the blacksmith's. In it went, and up to the anvil. The smith was making horse-nails.

'I like a mug of ale and a well-toasted bannock,' said he. 'Come away in.'

The wee bannock was frightened, when it heard about the ale, and ran off as hard as it could. The smith ran after it, and threw his hammer at it. But the bannock whirled away and was out of sight in an instant. It ran till it came to a farm-house. In it went to the fireside, where the goodman and the goodwife were working.

'Janet,' said the goodman, 'there's a wee bannock. I'll have the half of it!'

'Well, John, I'll have the other half. Hit it over the back!'

But the bannock played tig and was too clever for them.

Off and up the stream it ran to the next house and whirled in to the fireside. The goodwife was stirring the porridge and the goodman plaiting ropes for the cattle.

'Hey, Jock,' said the goodwife, 'come here! You're always crying for a bannock. Here's one. Come, hurry now! I'll help you catch it!'

'Ay, wife, where is it?'

'See, there, over to that side!'

But the wee bannock ran behind the goodman's chair and Jock fell among his ropes. The goodwife threw the porridge stick after it, and the goodman threw a rope, but it was too clever for either of them. It was off and out of sight in an instant, through the gorse, and down the road to the next house. In it went to the fireside just as the folk were sitting down to their porridge, and the goodwife scraping the pot.

'Look,' said she, 'there's a wee bannock come to warm it-self at our fireside!'

'Shut the door,' said the goodman, 'and we'll try to catch it!'

When the bannock heard this, it ran into the kitchen and they after it with their spoons, and away it ran out of the back door.

On and on it ran till it came to another house, and in it went just as the folk were going to their beds. The good-man was taking off his trousers and the goodwife was raking the fire.

'What's that?' said the goodman.

'Oh,' said the wife, 'it's a wee bannock!'

'I could eat the half of it for all the supper I had,' said he.

'Then catch it!' said his wife, 'and I'll have a bit too. Throw your trousers at it!'

So the goodman threw his trousers at it, and nearly smothered it. But it wriggled out and ran, the goodman after it without his trousers. There was a rare chase up the yard,

over the field and in among the gorse. There the goodman lost
it, and had to go trotting home half naked. But it had grown
dark, and the wee bannock couldn't see. It went through a
gorse bush, and right into a fox's hole. The fox had had no
meat for two days and was very hungry.

'Welcome, welcome,' said the fox, and snapped it in two.
And that was the end of the wee bannock.

Scottish Folk Tale from *The Well at the World's End* by Norah and
William Montgomerie

The Cat and the Mouse

The Cat and the Mouse
Lived in a wee house.

The Cat bit the Mouse's tail off.
'Please, Puss, give me back my tail.'
'No,' said the Cat, 'I'll not give you your tail, till you go
to the Cow and fetch me some milk.'

First she ran, and then she leaped,
Till she came to the Cow,
Then she cheeped:

'Please, Cow, give me some milk to give the Cat, so she'll
give me back my tail.'
'No,' said the Cow, 'I'll not give you milk, till you go to
the Farmer and fetch me some hay.'

First she ran, and then she leaped,
Till she came to the Farmer,
Then she cheeped:

'Please, Farmer, give me some hay to give to the Cow, so she'll give me some milk to give to the Cat, so she'll give me back my tail.'

'No,' said the Farmer, 'I'll not give you hay, till you go to the Butcher and fetch me some meat.'

> First she ran, and then she leaped,
> Till she came to the Butcher,
> Then she cheeped:

'Please, Butcher, give me some meat to give to the Farmer, so he'll give me some hay to give to the Cow, so she'll give me some milk to give to the Cat, so she'll give me back my tail.'

'No,' said the Butcher, 'I'll not give you meat, till you go to the Baker and fetch me some bread.'

> First she ran and then she leaped,
> Till she came to the Baker,
> Then she cheeped:

'Please, Baker, give me some bread to give to the Butcher, so he'll give me some meat to give to the Farmer, so he'll give me some hay to give to the Cow, so she'll give me some milk to give to the Cat, so she'll give me back my tail.'

> 'Well,' said the Baker, 'I'll give you some bread,
> But don't eat my meal or I'll cut off your head.'

The Baker gave the Mouse some bread which she took to the Butcher, who gave her some meat which she took to the Farmer, who gave her some hay which she took to the Cow, who gave her some milk which she took to the Cat, and the Cat gave the Mouse her own tail again.

Scottish Folk Tale

The Little Red Hen

There was once a little Red Hen who lived in a house all by herself. Now, over the hill, in a dark den, lived a fox with his old, old mother. This rascal of a fox thought that the little Red Hen would make a good dinner, and he wondered how he could get hold of her. He thought and he thought until he grew so thin there was nothing left of him but skin and bone. But he could not catch the little Red Hen for she was too clever for him.

Every time she went out she locked the door behind her, and every time she went in she locked the door behind her, and put her key in her pocket where she kept her scissors and her piece of sugar candy.

At last the rascal of a fox thought of a way to catch the little Red Hen. Early one morning he said to his old mother, 'Have a pot boiling when I come home to-night, for I'll be bringing the little Red Hen home for supper.'

Then he slung his bag over his shoulder, and away he went till he came to the little Red Hen's house. The little Red Hen was just coming out of her door to gather firewood. So that rascal of a fox hid behind the woodpile, and as soon as she bent down to pick up the wood, he slipped into the house, and hid behind the door.

When the little Red Hen came in, she shut the door and locked it, and put the key into her pocket with her scissors and sugar candy.

And then she saw that rascal of a fox standing there with his bag slung over his shoulder.

Whuff! What a surprise! She was so scared she dropped her bundle of wood and flew straight up to the beam across the ceiling. There she sat, quite out of breath, and peered down at the fox below.

'You may as well go home,' said the little Red Hen, 'for you'll not get me up here!'

'Ho! ho! ho!' said the fox. 'Can't I though!'

And what do you think he did? He stood on the floor, just under the little Red Hen and whirled and whirled in a circle after his own tail. He whirled, and whirled, and as he whirled faster and faster the poor little Red Hen got so dizzy she had to let go of the beam. Down she fell, and that rascal of a fox just picked her up and popped her into his bag.

Away he went up the hill, while the little Red Hen was still so dizzy inside the bag she did not know where she was. But as they went on the dizziness wore off, and she began to wonder what she could do to escape from the fox. She remembered the scissors in her apron pocket. Snip! She cut a wee hole in the bag, and then she poked her head out to see where she was. As soon as the fox stopped to have a rest, she cut the hole a little bigger and jumped out. A big stone was lying there, so the little Red Hen picked it up and popped it in the bag, quick as a wink. Then she ran as fast as she could till she came to her own wee house. She ran inside and locked the door. Goodness! Was she glad to get home!

Now, that rascal of a fox carried the stone in his bag and never knew the difference. He was pretty tired by the time he reached his den, but he was so pleased with himself, thinking of the fine supper he was going to have, that he did not mind at all.

'Have you got that pot boiling?' he called to his mother.

'Sure I have,' said she. 'Have you got the little Red Hen?'

'I have,' said the fox, 'and as soon as I open the bag, you take the lid off the pot so that I can drop her straight in. Then pop the lid back on, before she can jump out.'

'I'll do that,' said his old mother, and she stood close to the boiling pot, ready.

The fox lifted the bag up till it was over the pot, and gave it a shake. Splash! Plonk! Splash! In went the stone and out splashed the boiling water, all over that rascal of a fox and his greedy old mother. They were so badly scalded that they never went after hens again.

As for the little Red Hen, she lived happily ever after in her own wee house.

Irish-American Folk Tale

The Little House

Once upon a time a box fell off a farmer's cart and rolled to the side of the road. A little Mouse came running along. He saw the box lying there and thought what a nice little house it was, and he wondered who lived there.

So the little Mouse said: 'Little house, little house, who lives in the little house?'

Nobody answered. So the little Mouse looked in and found no one there!

'Well, then,' said he, 'I shall live here myself.'

So he settled himself in the wooden box.

Along came a Frog hopping and said, 'Little house, little house, who lives in the little house?'

'I, Mr Mouse. I live in the little house, and who are you?'

'I am Mr Frog.'

'Then come inside, and let us live together.'

Then a Hare came running along the road, and saw the box.

'Little house, little house,' said he, 'who lives in the little house?'

'Mr Frog and Mr Mouse. Who are you?'

'I am Mr Hare who runs over the hills. May I come in too?'

'Yes, you may. Come inside and live with us, there's plenty of room for three.'

Then the Fox came running by, and said, 'Little house, little house, who lives in the little house?'

'Mr Hare and Mr Frog and Mr Mouse. Who are you?'

'I'm Mr Fox.'

'Then come inside and live with us.'

So the Fox got into the box too, and all four lived together in the little house. One day a Big Brown Bear came out of the Forest and said in a Big Gruff Voice: 'LITTLE HOUSE, LITTLE HOUSE, WHO LIVES IN THE LITTLE HOUSE?'

And they all said: 'Mr Fox and Mr Hare and Mr Frog and Mr Mouse. And who are you?'

'I am Mr BEAR-SQUASH-YOU-ALL-FLAT!'

And the Big Brown Bear sat down on the box and squashed it flat.

Russian Folk Tale

The Bear and the Little Girl

Once upon a time there was a little girl called Mary, who lived with her mother and father on the edge of a forest.

One day Mary went with her friends to gather berries.

Mary found a large bush covered with ripe berries, but by the time she had picked every berry off the bush, she found that her friends were nowhere to be seen. She called, but there was no answer, so she wandered on and on till she was quite lost.

At last she came to a little house and knocked on the door, but no one came. She turned the handle and opened the door.

'Is there anyone at home?' she called.

There was no reply so she went in and warmed herself by the fire.

Presently the Big Brown Bear who lived there, returned home. He was delighted when he saw the little girl.

'What is your name, little girl?' said he.

'Mary,' said the little girl, who thought the Bear was very BIG.

'That is a nice name,' said the Big Brown Bear. 'I need a little girl to cook my meals, wash and mend my clothes and keep my little house neat and tidy, so you can just stay. Now you are here I will never let you go.'

Mary began to cry, but what could she do? She just had to stay with the Big Brown Bear.

So she cooked and she washed, and she kept his house clean, while the Big Brown Bear was in the forest all day.

'If you run away,' said he, as he left the house each morning, 'I shall catch you, and eat you all up!'

Mary tried to think how she could escape from the Bear. She thought and she thought, and then she made a plan.

One day she said, 'Bear, please will you take a present to my mother and father?'

'I'll do that,' said the Bear.

So Mary baked some tarts. Then she got a great big basket, and she said to the Bear: 'Look, I'll put the tarts in the basket so that you can carry them to my mother and father. But don't you eat a single one of the tarts, mind! I'll climb on to the roof and watch you!'

Now, while the Big Brown Bear went outside to light his pipe, Mary quickly climbed into the basket, and hid under the tarts. Back came the Bear. He saw the basket was ready, heaved it up on to his back and set off for the village where Mary's parents lived. On and on he went till he grew tired and said:

'On this tree stump I'll make my seat,
And a lovely tart I'll eat.'

But Mary cried out from the basket:

'I spy! I spy!
That tree stump shan't be your seat,
And a tart you must NOT eat!'

The Big Brown Bear looked round and said:

> 'My word, she is sly!
> There she sits up on high,
> And on me she can spy!'

So he picked up the basket and went on his way. On and on he went till he came to another tree stump, and said:

> 'On *this* old stump I'll make my seat,
> And a lovely tart I'll eat!'

Then Mary called out again from the basket:

> 'I spy! I spy!
> Get up, Bear, upon your feet,
> That old stump shan't be your seat,
> Not a single tart you'll eat!'

The Big Brown Bear was afraid, and said:

> 'Goodness gracious, she is sly,
> There she sits up on high,
> And on me she can spy.'

So he got up and ran off as fast as he could, till he came to the house where Mary's mother and father lived. He knocked at the door and said, 'Hi, good folks, open the door! I've brought you a present from your little girl!'

But the dogs smelt the Bear and they rushed at him. The Bear was very frightened. He put down the basket, and ran off as fast as he could into the forest.

Mary's mother and father took the basket and opened it. There was Mary sitting inside, smiling at them.

Russian Folk Tale

The Cock and the Hen

A Cock and a Hen lived together. One day they went to the wood to look for nuts. They saw a Hazel tree and the Cock climbed up to pick the nuts, while the Hen stayed on the ground to gather them up.

The Cock threw down a nut, and it hit the little Hen on her head.

This hurt the little Hen very much and she went away crying. A man, driving by in a cart, saw her and said, 'Little Hen, little Hen, why are you crying?'

The little Hen said, 'The Cock threw a nut and it hit me, crack, on the top of my head.'

So when the man drove past the Cock who was still picking nuts, he called up to the Cock, 'Little Cock, little Cock, why did you throw a nut, and hit the Hen right on her head?'

'Because the Hazel tree tore my trousers,' said the Cock.

So the man went on till he came to the Hazel tree. 'Hazel tree, Hazel tree, why did you tear the little Cock's trousers?' said he.

'Because the Goats ate my bark,' said the Hazel tree.

So the man drove on, and when he saw the Goats, he said, 'Goats, Goats, why did you eat the bark of the Hazel tree?'

'Because the Goat-herds didn't look after us,' said the Goats.

So the man drove on, and when he saw the Goat-herds, he said, 'Goat-herds, Goat-herds, why did you not look after the Goats?'

'Because the Farmer's wife didn't give us pancakes,' said the Goat-herds.

And the man drove on till he met the Farmer's wife.

'Farmer's wife, Farmer's wife, why didn't you give the Goat-herds their pancakes?'

'Because the Pig spilled my batter,' said the Farmer's wife.

When the man saw the Pig, he said, 'Pig, Pig, why did you spill the batter?'

'Because the Wolf carried off my Piglet!' said the Pig.

So when the man met the Wolf he said, 'Wolf, Wolf, why did you carry off the Piglet?'

'Because,' said the Wolf, 'I was HUNGRY!'

So the man ran off as fast as he could in case the Wolf was still hungry.

Russian Folk Tale

The Three Pigs

There was once an old Sow who had three little Pigs. One day she thought it was time they went out into the world to seek their fortunes. So she gave each a bag of food and some money, and waved them good-bye.

'Remember to build your house with bricks,' said she, 'and look out for the big bad Wolf!'

'We'll remember,' said the little Pigs, and away they went, each by a different road.

Now, when the first little Pig met a man with a cartload of straw he forgot all that his mammy had told him, and said, 'Man, man, give me some straw to build a house.'

So the man gave him some straw, and he built himself a nice little house.

Along came the Wolf, knocked on the door, and said, 'Little Pig, little Pig, may I come in?'

'No, no, by the hair of my chiny chin chin!'

'Then I'll huff and I'll puff, and I'll blow your house in!'

And the Wolf huffed and he puffed, and he blew the house in, and he ate the little Pig ALL up.

Now, when the second little Pig met a man with a barrow

full of sticks, he too forgot what his mammy had told him and said, 'Man, man, give me those sticks to build a house.'

So the man gave him the sticks, and he built himself a nice little house, but he had no sooner built it than along came the Wolf, and said, 'Little Pig, little Pig, let me come in!'

'No, no, by the hair of my chiny chin chin!'

'Then I'll huff, and I'll puff, and I'll blow your house in!'

The Wolf huffed, and he puffed, and he puffed and he huffed. At last he blew the house in, and ate the second little Pig ALL up.

Now, the third little Pig, remembering what his mammy had told him, waited till he met a man with a cartload of bricks, and said, 'Man, man, give me some bricks to build a house.'

So the man gave him the bricks, and he made some mortar, and he built himself a fine strong house, with a chimney, a window and a door that locked. When the house was ready he went inside and locked the door.

Presently, along came that big bad Wolf, knocked on the door and said, 'Little Pig, little Pig, please let me in.'

But the little Pig said, 'No, no, by the hair of my chiny chin chin, I'll NOT let you in!'

'Then I'll huff, and I'll puff and I'll blow your house in!' So he huffed and he puffed, and he puffed and he huffed, and he huffed and he puffed, but he could NOT blow that house in. And when he found he could not blow the house in by huffing and puffing, that big bad Wolf said in his very best voice, 'Little Pig, I know where there is a lovely field of turnips.'

'Do you,' said the little Pig, 'where is that?'

'Down by Farmer Brown's. If you'll be ready to-morrow morning early, I'll call for you, and help you carry back some turnips for your dinner.'

'Very well,' said the little Pig, 'what time do you want to go?'

'At six o'clock,' said the Wolf.

Well, the little Pig got up at five o'clock, went down to Farmer Brown's field, fetched the turnips and had them in the pot before the Wolf called at six.

'Little Pig, little Pig, are you ready?'

And the little Pig said, 'Ready! Why I've been, and the turnips are all ready in the pot.'

The big bad Wolf was very angry indeed when he heard this. He was just going to march off in a huff when he had an idea.

'Little Pig, I know where there is an apple tree full of fine rosy apples,' said he in his best voice.

'Where?' asked the little Pig.

'In Mr Black's garden, and if you'll be sure to wait for me this time, I'll call for you at five o'clock, and we'll get some of those fine rosy apples.'

Next morning the little Pig was up at four o'clock. Off he went for the apples, but they tasted so good that he ate as he picked, and stayed longer than he should, and so, just as he was climbing over the garden wall with his sack full of apples, who should he see coming down the road but that big bad Wolf! Goodness, he did get a fright.

'Good morning, little Pig, so you've got here before me! Did you find any good apples?' said the Wolf.

'I did, I did,' said the little Pig. 'Here's some for you!' And he threw them so far, that while the Wolf went after them to pick them up, the little Pig was able to jump down off the wall, and run off home before the big bad Wolf had time to catch him. The Wolf was angrier than ever, but next day he came again and said, 'Little Pig, there's a Fair down in the village, would you like to go?'

'I'd like to go,' said the little Pig. 'What time will you be ready?'

'I'll be here at four,' said the Wolf.

But the little Pig got up at three, and away he went to the

Fair, and bought himself a butter-churn. He was just rolling it home, when who should he see coming down the road but the big bad Wolf, who had got up earlier that morning. This time the little Pig was so frightened that he hid inside the butter-churn and as he did so, the churn began to roll, and it rolled and it rolled all the way down the hill. This frightened the Wolf so much that he ran off home without going to the Fair at all.

By now, the Wolf was determined to catch the little Pig and eat him up, somehow. At last he decided to climb down the little Pig's chimney, and catch him that way. So he climbed on to the little Pig's roof. But when the little Pig saw him, he guessed what he was up to. He put lots of logs on the fire until it was blazing. Then he filled his biggest pot full of water and put it on the fire. Just as the big bad Wolf was coming down the chimney, the little Pig took the lid off the pot, and in fell the Wolf, PLUNK! Then the little Pig put back the lid, boiled up the Wolf, and ate him for supper. That was the end of the big bad Wolf, and the third little Pig lived happily ever after in his own little house.

English Folk Tale

The Enormous Turnip

Grandpapa planted a turnip. It grew and it grew and it grew and the time came to pull it up. It was enormous.

Grandpa took hold of it and pulled and pulled, but he could not move it. It was stuck fast in the ground.

'Grandma, come and help me pull this turnip!' he cried.

So Grandma went and pulled Grandpa, and Grandpa pulled the turnip. They pulled and they pulled and they pulled, but they could not move it. It was stuck fast.

Grandma called to Mother, 'Come and help us pull this turnip!'

So Mother went and pulled Grandma, while Grandma pulled Grandpa and Grandpa pulled the turnip. But it was no use, they could not move it. It was stuck fast.

'Little Daughter, Little Daughter,' called Mother, 'come and help us pull this turnip!'

So Little Daughter ran as fast as she could and pulled Mother. Mother pulled Grandma, while Grandma pulled Grandpa and Grandpa pulled the turnip. They pulled and they pulled and they pulled, but they could not move it. It was stuck fast.

'Puppy, Puppy,' called Little Daughter, 'come and help us pull this turnip!'

So Puppy ran and pulled Little Daughter, Little Daughter pulled Mother, Mother pulled Grandma, Grandma pulled Grandpa and Grandpa pulled the turnip. They pulled and they pulled and they pulled, but they could not move it. It was stuck fast.

Then Kittycat ran from her place in the sunshine. Miew! Miew! She pulled Puppy. Puppy pulled Little Daughter, Little Daughter pulled Mother, Mother pulled Grandma, Grandma pulled Grandpa and Grandpa pulled the turnip. They pulled and they pulled and they pulled, but they could not move it. It was stuck fast.

Then Tiny Mouse ran out of her little hole. Weet! Weet! She pulled Kittycat, while Kittycat pulled Puppy, Puppy pulled Little Daughter, Little Daughter pulled Mother, Mother pulled Grandma, Grandma pulled Grandpa and Grandpa pulled the turnip. They pulled and they pulled and they pulled, but they could not move it. It was stuck fast.

So little Black Beetle went and pulled Tiny Mouse. Tiny Mouse pulled Kittycat, Kittycat pulled Puppy, Puppy pulled Little Daughter, Little Daughter pulled Mother, Mother pulled Grandma, Grandma pulled Grandpa and Grandpa pulled the turnip.

They pulled and they pulled and they PULLED. And they pulled that turnip right out of the ground! WHO-OO-OUMP!

The ENORMOUS TURNIP fell on Grandpa, Grandpa fell on Grandma, Grandma fell on Mother, Mother fell on Little Daughter, Little Daughter fell on Puppy, Puppy fell on Kitty-cat, Kittycat fell on Tiny Mouse, and it was a good thing that little Black Beetle ran away before Tiny Mouse could fall on her!

And they all had turnip for dinner that day.

Russian Folk Tale

The Fox and his Sack

A Fox was digging behind a tree and there he found a bumble-bee. The Fox put the bumble-bee into his sack and went on his way.

The first house he came to the housewife was feeding her hen, and the Fox said to her, 'May I leave my sack here while I go to What-chuma-call-it's?'

'Certainly,' said the woman.

'Be careful not to open the sack,' said the Fox.

But, as soon as the Fox was out of sight, the woman took a little peep in the sack and out flew the bumble-bee. Buzz, buzz, buzz! The hen caught the bumble-bee and ate it up.

When the Fox returned he looked inside his sack and saw there was no bumble-bee. He was very angry and said to the woman, 'Where is my bumble-bee?'

'I just untied the sack and out flew the bumble-bee. The hen caught it and ate it up.'

'Very well,' said the Fox, 'I must have the hen.'

So he put the hen in his sack and went on his way, till he came to another house. Here the goodwife was feeding her pig.

'May I leave my sack here,' said the Fox, 'while I go to What-chuma-call-it's?'

'Certainly,' said the woman.

'Be careful not to open the sack while I'm away,' said the Fox.

But as soon as the Fox was out of sight the woman took a little peep in the sack, and out flew the hen. Cluck! cluck! cluck! The great big pig caught the hen and ate her up.

When the Fox came back he looked inside his sack and saw there was no hen. He was very angry and said to the woman, 'Where is my hen?'

'I just untied the sack and out flew the hen. The great big pig caught her and ate her up.'

'Very well,' said the Fox, 'I must have the pig.'

So he put the pig in his sack and went on his way, till he came to another house. He went in and said to the housewife, 'May I leave my sack here while I go to What-chuma-call-it's?'

'Certainly,' said the woman.

'Be careful not to open the sack while I'm away,' said the Fox.

But as soon as the Fox was out of sight, the woman took a little peep inside the sack, and out jumped the pig. Grumph! Grumph! Grumph! The woman's little boy chased the pig away over the fields.

When the Fox returned he looked inside the sack and saw there was no pig. He was very angry and said, 'Where's my pig?'

'I just untied the sack and out ran the pig. My little boy chased it away over the fields.'

'Very well,' said the Fox, 'I must have the little boy.'

So he put the little boy into his sack and went on his way.

When he came to the next house he went in and said to the woman, 'May I leave my sack here while I go to What-chuma-call-it's?'

'Certainly,' said she.

Now the woman was baking a cake and when she took it, hot and ready, out of the oven, her children gathered round her.

'Oh, Mother, please give me a piece,' said one. 'Just a wee piece,' said another. 'Please, please,' they all begged.

The little boy in the sack smelt the lovely hot cake, stopped crying, and called, 'Please give me a piece too!'

'Goodness!' said the woman, 'there must be a child in the sack.'

She untied the sack and helped out the little boy. Then she put the fierce house-dog into the sack and tied it fast, just as the Fox had left it. The little boy sat up at the tea table and had some cake with the other children.

When the Fox returned, he looked at the sack and saw that it seemed to be just as he had left it. So he put it on his back and went on his way. On he went till he came to a wood, where he untied his sack. Out jumped the fierce house-dog and ate him ALL up!

American Folk Tale

The Pedlar and his Caps

Once upon a time there was a Pedlar who sold caps. On top of his head he wore his old brown cap. On top of the old brown cap he put his yellow caps. On top of his yellow caps he put his blue caps. On top of his blue caps he put his green caps. And on the very top he put his red caps. Then he would go into a village, walking up one street and down another, calling, 'Caps for sale! Caps for sale!'

One day nobody wanted to buy a cap, not even a red one.

'Well,' thought the Pedlar, 'this will be a good day to take a rest.' So he walked off to the edge of the village, where he found a large tree. He settled himself down by the tree and went sound asleep.

He slept a long time. When he woke up, the first thing he did was to feel for his caps. All he could find was his old brown cap.

He looked to the left of him. No caps.

He looked to the right of him. No caps.

He walked all round the tree. No caps.

Then he looked up in the tree. There he saw monkeys and every monkey had a cap on.

'You monkeys, you!' he shouted, 'you give me back my caps!'

But the monkeys only shook their fingers back at him and shouted, 'Tsk! Tsk! Tsk!'

'You monkeys, you!' shouted the Pedlar, shaking the finger of his other hand at them, 'you give me back my caps!'

But the monkeys only shook their fingers back at him and shouted, 'Tsk! Tsk! Tsk!'

'You monkeys, you!' he shouted again, stamping his right foot, 'you give me back my caps!'

But the monkeys only shouted back at him, 'Tsk! Tsk! Tsk!'

'You monkeys, you,' pleaded the Pedlar, as he stamped his left foot, 'please give me back my caps.' But the monkeys only answered, 'Tsk! Tsk! Tsk!'

Then the old Pedlar was so angry that he took his old brown cap off his head and threw it on the ground.

Every monkey took his cap off and threw it on the ground. So the old Pedlar gathered all his caps together again. On top of his head he put his old brown cap. On top of his old brown cap he put his yellow caps. On top of the yellow caps he put his blue caps. On top of his blue caps he put his green caps. And on the very top he put his red caps.

Then he went back to the village, up one street and down another, calling, 'Caps for sale! Caps for sale!'

Folk Tale retold by Ruth Tooze

The Red Hat

Once upon a time there was a little fish swimming in the sea with a lot of other little fishes. All down below him the water looked dark, and the deeper he went the darker it got. But when he looked up he could see the blue sky and a red hat. 'I would like that red hat,' he thought.

So he said good-bye to the other fishes and swam up and up and up till he got to the top of the water and all around him was the sea and big ships, and above him was the blue sky and large white clouds and the red hat.

He tried to swim higher but no matter how hard he tried he couldn't get higher than the top of the water.

So he called out to a seagull that was flying just overhead, 'Oh, Mr Seagull, please fly up high and bring me down that lovely red hat. I'd like to wear it.'

But the seagull said, 'You'd better go away, little fish, or I'll eat you for my breakfast.' And he dived down at the little fish and tried to catch him in his big sharp yellow beak, but the little fish swam under the water and got away.

Then he saw a fisherman in a boat with a great long fishing line with a hook on the end of it. So he looked out of the water and he said, 'Oh, please, Mr Fisherman, will you try and catch that red hat in the sky for me with your long line and hook?'

'You'd better look out,' said the fisherman, 'or I'll catch
YOU!'

And he twirled the fishing line around his head three times
and sent the hook spinning towards the little fish, but he just
missed him and the little fish swam away.

Presently the little fish came to a river and there on the
bank he saw an elephant who was singing a little song to
himself:

> 'The elephant is large and fat,
> He eats so much of this and that,
> He likes to sit and gorge and cram
> On hay and grass and strawberry jam.'

The little fish called out, 'Will you please stretch out your
long trunk and fetch me down that red hat from the sky?'

So the elephant stretched out his trunk as far as he could.
He stretched and he stretched and he stretched but he
couldn't reach the red hat.

'I'll tell you what I'll do,' he said. 'I'll pick you up in my
trunk and throw you as high as I can right into the sky and
you can fetch down the hat for yourself.'

So he picked up the little fish and threw him high into
the air, higher than the clouds, right up into the blue sky,
and the little fish looked and he saw that it wasn't a red hat
in the sky, it was the sun.

Then he fell right back into the sea with the biggest splash
you've ever seen.

All the other little fishes swam round him and said, 'Why
haven't you brought back the red hat?'

'It isn't a red hat,' he told them, 'it's the sun.' And they
all laughed at him. 'Don't be silly,' they said, 'of course it's
a red hat!' and away they swam laughing and playing.

From *Next Time Stories*, by Donald Bisset

A Growing Tale

There was once a tiny boy called Tim.

He was smaller than his sister Sally and smaller than his brother Billy. He was the smallest person in the house, except the kitten and the canary, and you can't count them.

Tim was so tiny he could only just walk, he could only just talk and he only had one candle on his birthday cake. So you can guess how small he was.

He couldn't wash himself, he couldn't dress himself, and he couldn't blow his own nose. His mother had to do almost everything for him. She gave him a tiny chair to sit on, and a tiny bed to sleep in every night.

He didn't know his right foot from his left foot. He didn't know what was red and what was blue. He couldn't say what one and one makes. He was much too small to count.

He was very good at shouting, at banging and at bawling. He was very good at throwing, at grabbing and at crawling. Tim was so very tiny he could walk beneath the table and never bump his head!

But he wished and he wished he could see over fences, and turn door handles all by himself.

He grew and he grew until he was two, he grew and he grew until he was three, and he grew and he grew and then he was FOUR. And when he was four, Tim was a Great Big Boy. He had four candles on his birthday cake.

He could see over fences and what was on tables. He could now turn door handles, all by himself.

He was MUCH too big for his tiny little chair, he was much too big for his tiny little cot, so he slept in a real bed of his very own. He could wash himself, dress himself, and blow his nose on a great big pocket handkerchief. He put his left shoe on his left foot, his right shoe on his right foot, and he tied both the laces in a very tidy bow. He knew what was red and what was blue, so he didn't bother bawling and he didn't bother crawling. He was much too big for that!

Tim was now so BIG, he went to the Nursery School. What do you think of that?

He was still much smaller than his sister Sally, and he was still much smaller than his big brother Billy. For they had grown too!

Norah Montgomerie

The Travels of Ching

In the land of China a dollmaker made a little doll. The doll's name was Ching.

The dollmaker stuffed Ching with the best stuffing and glued him with the best glue. He sewed him with the best thread. Then he sold him.

He sold him to a toyshop where everything was very expensive. For a long time Ching sat in the toyshop and waited. He was waiting for somebody who wanted him.

Now there was a little Chinese girl who came by the toy-shop. This little girl wanted Ching. But she was poor. She wanted Ching more than anything. But she had no money to buy him.

So Ching was sold to a rich tea merchant who drove away with him in his rickshaw.

But the tea merchant did not want Ching. He only bought him to give to somebody else.

He took Ching to the Post Office and sent him far, far away.

He sent Ching down a mountain on a donkey, and down a river in a sailing boat and across the ocean on a steamship, all the way to AMERICA.

There he was put on a train and sent across America to a city, where the postman delivered Ching to a little girl who lived in a beautiful flat.

But the little girl did not want Ching. She already had more dolls and dresses and things than she knew what to do with.

She took Ching to the terrace and left him sitting right on the edge of the balustrade. It was a very careless thing to have done.

Ching fell off.

Luckily he floated down.

He landed on a small tree in a small back yard—and hung there. Then he dropped into a flower bed—and sat there.

When it rained, Ching got wet.

When it snowed, Ching got cold.

At last, in the spring, an old gentleman found him sitting in the flower bed. He was a nice old gentleman and took Ching inside.

But the old gentleman did not like Ching. What he liked was old chairs and old tables and old pieces of bric-à-brac.

He did not care for a dirty little doll.

So the old gentleman gave Ching to his cook. But the cook did not like Ching. Her kitchen was very neat and she did not like it cluttered.

She threw Ching into the rubbish bin.

Many people went by. But nobody wanted Ching. He was too dirty.

Early in the morning the dustman came and dumped Ching into his dust cart.

But the dustman did not want Ching. What he wanted was old bones and old rags and old paper and old tin cans.

The dustman took Ching to his rubbish yard, but he had to put him in a separate place all by himself.

One day a Chinese laundryman came by and bought Ching. All the dustman charged for him was sixpence. IMAGINE!

The laundryman took Ching to his laundry and combed his hair. He washed his robe and ironed it. He went to a lot of trouble.

But the laundryman did not want Ching. He only bought him to give to somebody else.

He took Ching to the Post Office and sent him far, far away.

He sent Ching across America on a train, and across the ocean on a steamship, and up a river in a sailing boat, and up a mountain on a donkey, all the way to his little niece in CHINA!

And this little girl DID want Ching!

She had always wanted Ching, more than anything, ever since she saw him in a toyshop.

Do you remember?

She put him in her little cart and took him for a nice ride over her favourite bridge.

In the evening she and Ching had supper in the cosy kitchen.

Then they went to bed.

Outside a wise old Chinese owl looked in and the moon shone. The cat slept on the sill.

The little girl put her arm around Ching because she was so glad to have him.

From the picture-book *The Story of Ching* by Robert Bright

The Good Hen and the Bad Hen

Once upon a time there were two hens. One was a good little hen and the other was a bad hen. It wasn't so much that the Bad Hen wanted to be bad—she didn't. She thought herself a very amiable character. But she was stupid and lazy, and this meant that she was just as much trouble to everyone as if she had set out to be wicked.

Well, these two hens lived side by side in a pleasant country place and were well off and contented. But two or three dry seasons ruined the harvest so the food grew scarce and the hens did not have enough to eat.

One day the Bad Hen saw the Good Hen packing all her belongings on to a little cart and preparing to go away.

'Where are you going?' said she.

'I am going to travel until I find a place where there is a good rainfall and enough to eat,' said the Good Hen. 'Will you come with me?'

'Oh yes!' said the Bad Hen, 'I will come at once.'

'But won't you need a few things for the journey?' asked the Good Hen.

'Oh, no. I won't bother,' said the Bad Hen. 'We are sure to find somewhere soon and I can't be bothered to pack and sort. No, much better to make a fresh start once and for all.'

So as the Good Hen was now ready the two hens set out.

It was not long, however, before they began to feel the heat of the midday sun, and the Good Hen stopped and took a shady hat from her little cart and put it on.

But the Bad Hen had nothing and she began to grumble and complain.

'Oh! I wish I had my big shady hat,' she cried. 'Now why ever didn't you remind me to bring it with me? You must have known I should need it.'

The Good Hen felt sorry for the Bad Hen even though she thought it unfair she should be blamed for her friend's discomfort, so she agreed to share her hat turn and turn about.

And so they went on till evening, and although they had not yet reached a fertile place where food would be plentiful they decided to settle for the night.

The Good Hen laid out a few blankets and pillows which she had thoughtfully stowed in her cart.

'What a lot of fuss and bother,' said the Bad Hen scornfully. 'The night is warm. What do you need with all that
paraphernalia?'

But the Good Hen finished her arrangements, laid herself
down and was soon asleep.

After some time the Bad Hen, who had perched herself in a
tree, began to feel cold. She at once woke up the Good Hen
and began to scold and complain.

'You're a fine friend, you are, indeed! You should have
told me the nights on the road would be cold and then I, too,
could have made myself cosy with blankets and pillow.'

So the Good Hen moved over and made room for the Bad
Hen to creep in beside her, but in truth neither of them slept
well after that for they were too confined, and the Bad Hen
woke up in a very bad temper. They began to peck about for
their breakfast, but there was little enough to be found, so
the Good Hen took up the bedding and prepared to go upon
their way. As she stored the things away the Bad Hen came
and watched her.

'What is that little sack down there in the corner?' she
asked.

'My friend,' replied the Good Hen, 'in that sack is all the
corn I had left when the drought began. I have not eaten any
of it, hard-pressed though I have been by hunger. When we
reach a fertile valley I will plant it, and then in time I shall
have an abundance of grain both to eat and to store. It will be
a lean time till the first harvest, but it is worth suffering a
short time to enjoy a good living in the end.'

'Oh! What nonsense,' cried the Bad Hen. 'Here am I
starving at this very moment. I can go no further without a
mouthful of food, that is certain. I shall be dead by the roadside, a monument to your stinginess if I do not have a bite.
We will open it quickly and have a good breakfast and then
we shall go on so fast we will all the sooner reach a land of
plenty.'

But the Good Hen wouldn't do this, and they argued and quarrelled, and the sun rose and the day advanced until at last the Good Hen said, 'It is no good quarrelling. At this rate we will never reach our journey's end. I will tell you what I will do. I will divide the contents of my sack and you may do what you will with your share, but at least, then, you must leave me be with mine.'

So the Good Hen divided the precious grain into two piles, and the Bad Hen pranced about in excitement, not having seen so much food for months.

When the corn was divided the Good Hen at once returned her part to the sack and quickly fastened it up and stowed it away at the very bottom of her cart.

But the Bad Hen with her share began to peck and peck, clucking with pleasure and giving no thought to the future but only rejoicing in the good fortune of the moment.

When she could eat no more she put what remained in a bag which she carried over her shoulder so that she might easily dip into it when hunger assailed her. And then, in silence, the two hens continued their journey.

When evening came they reached a valley through which ran a river ending in a vast lake.

It was quite apparent that here there would never be a lack of water and much relieved the Good Hen declared that this should be her home. The Bad Hen agreed that they could do no better than this, and to celebrate their arrival she ate up all the rest of her corn—not a grain was left.

Again the Good Hen shared her bed with the Bad Hen, and next day she got up early leaving the Bad Hen still in bed, and setting to work in earnest she soon had built herself a little house, had dug and planted a field of corn, and had then unloaded her treasures from the cart, and by the evening she was so comfortably settled in she might have been there all her life.

The Bad Hen on the other hand, having come with nothing, found herself at a disadvantage.

'Oh, well,' she said, 'until I can gather a few things together you can't possibly begrudge me a corner of your house.'

And the Good Hen agreed.

The next day the Good Hen went foraging around to find grubs and grass to eat until her corn should be ready. But the Bad Hen lolled about in the porch and went paddling in the lake, and said she was not hungry when the Good Hen remarked on what she did.

But when the Good Hen was busy that evening trimming the lamps and preparing for the night the Bad Hen declared she was stuffy in the house and would like a stroll by the river. Out she went, and just think what she did!

She went to the little field planted with the Good Hen's corn and scratched about and pecked up a whole row of seed, and then returned well fed at little trouble to herself.

And this went on all through the winter.

Whilst the Good Hen got thinner and thinner, the food she was able to find growing scarce in the hard weather, the Bad Hen seemed to put on flesh and her friend wondered at it.

'You need not be so surprised,' said the Bad Hen. 'Everyone knows the contented grow fat, and I am not always bothering and worrying. You should copy me, my dear.'

But the real reason was that every single evening she paid a visit to the cornfield and there dug up and ate a row of the precious grain.

At last came the first signs of spring and the very last row of corn was eaten.

The Good Hen, all unaware of this, went out to her field to see if the corn was sprouting, but no sign did she see and she was disappointed, for it had been a bad time for her all the winter and now she hoped to have the promise of plenty.

But when days passed and still no sign of her corn she was

seriously troubled and began to dig about and poke in the earth to discover what had happened to it. A field mouse saw her and cried out to her in passing, 'Oh, you needn't go digging about there. Your friend has been before you and eaten it all up.'

At this news the Good Hen burst into tears.

Through the spring and the summer she might manage on the food to be found growing wild, but another winter like the last, with no store of grain to sustain her, she would never survive.

'Alas and alas!' she upbraided the Bad Hen. 'What a thing to have done. Had you shown a little forbearance we might have ended our days here in prosperity. But now we shall have to go travelling again and hope to find people to employ us and feed us until we save enough to set up on our own.'

'Pooh!' said the Bad Hen. 'What a fuss you make. There's the whole spring and summer before us and something is sure to turn up.'

'I will fly to the top of a tree,' said the Good Hen, 'and see in which direction we had better go.'

And she did.

On the far side of the great lake she espied hills laid out in fields and under cultivation.

'It is there we must go,' she told the Bad Hen on descending. 'But the dear Lord knows how we shall get across the lake.'

They went to the water-side and saw driftwood floating by.

'We must make a boat,' said the Good Hen. And she waded in and brought some wood ashore.

But when they came to load up the boat with all the Good Hen's possessions it was found that it would only take the Good Hen besides, and that only because she was so small and light from her winter of fasting.

'Oh, leave your precious rubbish,' said the Bad Hen. 'We

will borrow possessions as well as food from the people on the other side.'

But this the Good Hen would not do.

'No,' she said, 'I will help you to build another little boat, and then we will sail across together.'

But the Bad Hen was too impatient for this new adventure. 'Oh, no!' she cried. 'I won't be put to all that bother. I'm not so cluttered up with things as you are. I will go across on a raft. This will be the very thing.' And she dragged a flat piece of wood to the shore.

The Good Hen tried to dissuade her, but as the Bad Hen then declared that she would sail ahead without her the Good Hen argued no more, but embarked in her own boat and they both pushed off from the shore.

And now the Bad Hen got what she deserved. If she had not been so fat on the corn she had eaten all the winter the raft might have borne her safely. But so heavy as she was she had no sooner got into deep water than the raft began to sink beneath her weight and she fell into the lake and would certainly have drowned had not the Good Hen thrown her a rope, and turning her boat back to the shore dragged her companion to safety.

'Oh, my friend!' said the Good Hen, whose natural anger about the corn had been forgotten as soon as she saw her friend in danger. 'I blame myself for not insisting on your making yourself a little boat like mine. We will set about it this minute.'

'Oh, no we won't!' said the Bad Hen. 'You won't catch me gallivanting about on the water. Why can't you stay here? I am sure we shall manage to get along.'

'We should manage through the summer,' said the Good Hen. 'But we would perish in the winter.'

But nothing would persuade the Bad Hen to take the Good Hen's advice and entrust herself again to the water.

So at last the Good Hen set sail without her and soon

reached the farther shore where she found good employment, worked hard and grew prosperous.

But the Bad Hen remained on the other shore eking out a very meagre living in the greatest discomfort, for since her wetting she suffered from the rheumatics—but in my opinion this was no more than she deserved.

From *William and the Lorry* by Diana Ross

The Riddle-me-Ree

'In marble walls as white as milk,
Lined with a skin as soft as silk,
Within a fountain crystal clear,
A golden apple doth appear.
No doors there are to this strong-hold,
Yet thieves break in and steal the gold.'

Little Tim Rabbit asked this riddle when he came home from school one day.

Mrs Rabbit stood with her paws on her hips, admiring her young son's cleverness.

'It's a fine piece of poetry,' said she.

'It's a riddle,' said Tim. 'It's a riddle-me-ree. Do you know the answer, Mother?'

'No, Tim,' Mrs Rabbit shook her head. 'I'm not good at riddles. We'll ask your father when he comes home. I can hear him stamping his foot outside. He knows everything, does Father.'

Mr Rabbit came bustling in. He flung down his bag of green food, mopped his forehead, gave a deep sigh.

'There! I've collected enough for a family of elephants. I got lettuces, carrots, wild thyme, primrose leaves and tender shoots. I hope you'll make a good salad, Mother.'

'Can you guess a riddle?' asked Tim.

'I hope so, my son, I used to be very good at riddles. What is a Welsh Rabbit? Cheese! Ha ha!'

'Say it again, Tim,' urged Mrs Rabbit. 'It's such a good piece of poetry, and all.'

So Tim Rabbit stood up, put his hands behind his back, tilted his nose and stared at the ceiling. Then in a high squeak he recited his new riddle:

> 'In marble walls as white as milk,
> Lined with a skin as soft as silk,
> Within a fountain crystal clear,
> A golden apple doth appear.
> No doors there are to this strong-hold,
> Yet thieves break in and steal the gold.'

Father Rabbit scratched his head, and frowned.

'Marble walls,' said he. 'Hum! Ha! That's a palace. A golden apple. No doors. I can't guess it. Who asked it, Tim?'

'Old Jonathan asked us at school to-day. He said anyone who could guess it should have a prize. We can hunt and we can holler, we can ask and we can beg, but we must give him the answer by to-morrow.'

'I'll have a good think, my son,' said Mr Rabbit. 'We mustn't be beaten by a riddle.'

All over the common Father Rabbits were saying, 'I'll have a good think,' but not one father knew the answer, and all the small bunnies were trying to guess.

Tim Rabbit met Old Man Hedgehog down the lane. The old fellow was carrying a basket of crab-apples for his youngest daughter. On his head he wore a round hat made from a cabbage leaf. Old Man Hedgehog was rather deaf, and Tim had to shout.

'Old Man Hedgehog. Can you guess a riddle?' shouted Tim.

'Eh?' The Hedgehog put his hand up to his ear. 'Eh?'

'A riddle!' cried Tim.

'Aye. I knows a riddle,' said Old Hedgehog. He put down

his basket and lighted his pipe. 'Why does a Hedgehog cross
the road? Eh? Why, for to get to t'other side.' Old Hedgehog
laughed wheezily.

'Do you know this one?' shouted Tim.

'Which one? Eh?'

'In marble walls as white as milk,' said Tim loudly.

'I could do with a drop of milk,' said Hedgehog.

'Lined with a skin as soft as silk,' shouted Tim.

'Nay, my skin isn't like silk. It's prickly, is a Hedgehog's
skin,' said the Old Hedgehog.

'Within a fountain crystal clear,' yelled Tim.

'Yes, I knows it. Down the field. There's a spring of water,
clear as crystal. Yes, that's it,' cried Old Hedgehog, leaping
about in excitement. 'That's the answer, a spring.'

'A golden apple doth appear,' said Tim, doggedly.

'A gowd apple? Where? Where?' asked Old Hedgehog,
grabbing Tim's arm.

'No doors there are to this strong-hold,' said Tim, and now
his voice was getting hoarse.

'No doors? How do you get in?' cried the Hedgehog.

'Yet thieves break in and steal the gold.' Tim's throat was
sore with shouting. He panted with relief.

'Thieves? That's the Fox again. Yes. That's the answer.'

'No, it isn't the answer,' said Tim patiently.

'I can't guess a riddle like that. Too long. No sense in it,'
said Old Man Hedgehog at last. 'I can't guess 'un. Now here's
a riddle for you. It's my own, as one might say. My own!'

'What riddle is that?' asked Tim.

'Needles and Pins, Needles and Pins,
  When Hedgehog marries his trouble begins.'

'What's the answer? I give it up,' said Tim.

'Why, Hedgehog. Needles and Pins, that's me.' Old Man
Hedgehog threw back his head and stamped his feet and

roared with laughter, and little Tim laughed too. They laughed and they laughed.

'Needles and Pins. Darning needles and hair pins,' said Old Hedgehog.

There was a rustle behind them, and they both sprang round, for Old Hedgehog could smell even if he was hard of hearing.

Out of the bushes poked a sharp nose, and a pair of bright eyes glinted through the leaves. A queer musky smell filled the air.

'I'll be moving on,' said Old Man Hedgehog. 'You'd best be getting along too, Tim Rabbit. Your mother wants you. Good-day. Good-day.'

Old Hedgehog trotted away, but the Fox stepped out and spoke in a polite kind of way.

'Excuse me,' said he. 'I heard merry laughter and I'm feeling rather blue. I should like a good laugh. What's the joke?'

'Old Man Hedgehog said he was needles and pins,' stammered poor little Tim Rabbit, edging away.

'Yes. Darning needles and hair pins,' said the Fox. 'Why?'

'It was a riddle,' said Tim.

'What about riddles?' asked the Fox.

> 'Marble milk, skin silk,
> Fountain clear, apple appear,
> No doors. Thieves gold,'

Tim gabbled.

'Nonsense. Rubbish,' said the Fox. 'It isn't sense. I know a much better riddle.'

'What is it, sir?' asked Tim, forgetting his fright.

'Who is the fine gentleman in the red jacket who leads the hunt?' asked the Fox, with his head aside.

'I can't guess at all,' said Tim.

'A Fox. A Fox, of course. He's the finest gentleman at the hunt.' He laughed so much at his own riddle that little Tim Rabbit had time to escape down the lane and get home to his mother.

'Well, has anyone guessed the riddle?' asked Mrs Rabbit.

'Not yet, Mother, but I'm getting on,' said Tim.

Out he went in the opposite direction, and he met the Mole.

'Can you guess a riddle, Mole?' he asked.

'Of course I can,' answered the Mole. 'Here it is:

> 'A little black man in a hole,
> Pray tell me if he is a Mole,
> If he's dressed in black velvet,
> He's Moldy Warp Delvet,
> He's a Mole, up a pole, in a hole.'

'I didn't mean that riddle,' said Tim.

'I haven't time for anybody else's riddles,' said the Mole, and in a flurry of soil he disappeared into the earth.

'He never stopped to listen to my recitation,' said Tim sadly.

He ran on, over the fields. There were Butterflies to hear his riddle, and Bumble-bees and Frogs, but they didn't know the answer. They all had funny little riddles of their own and nobody could help Tim Rabbit. So on he went across the wheatfield, right up to the farmyard, and he put his nose under the gate. That was as far as he dare go.

'Hallo, Tim Rabbit,' said the Cock. 'What do you want to-day?'

'Pray tell me the answer to a riddle,' said Tim politely. 'I've brought a pocketful of corn for a present. I gathered it in the cornfield on the way.'

The Cock called the Hens to listen to Tim's riddle. They

came in a crowd, clustering round the gate, chattering loudly.
Tim Rabbit settled himself on a stone so that they could see
him. He wasn't very big, and there were many of them,
clucking and whispering and shuffling their feet and shaking
their feathers.

'Silence!' cried the Cock. 'Silence for Tim Rabbit.'

The Hens stopped shuffling and lifted their heads to listen.
Once more Tim recited his poem, and once more here it is:

> 'In marble walls as white as milk,
> Lined with a skin as soft as silk,
> Within a fountain crystal clear,
> A golden apple doth appear.
> No doors there are to this strong-hold,
> Yet thieves break in and steal the gold.'

There was a silence for a moment as Tim finished, and then
such a rustle and murmur and tittering began, and the Hens
put their little beaks together, and chortled and fluttered
their wings and laughed in their sleeves.

'We know! We know!' they clucked.

'What is it?' asked Tim.

'An egg,' they all shouted together, and their voices were
so shrill the farmer's wife came to the door to see what was
the matter.

So Tim threw the corn among them, and thanked them for
their cleverness.

'And here's a white egg to take home with you, Tim,'
said the prettiest hen, and she laid an egg at Tim's feet.

How joyfully Tim ran home with the answer to the riddle!
How gleefully he put the egg on the table!

'Well, have you guessed it?' asked Mrs Rabbit.

'It's there! An egg,' nodded Tim, and they all laughed and
said, 'Well, I never! Well, I never thought of that!'

And the prize from Old Jonathan, when Tim gave him the

answer? It was a little wooden egg, painted blue, and when Tim opened it, there lay a tiny carved hen with feathers of gold.

From *The Adventures of Tim Rabbit*, by Alison Uttley

Too Timid, Too Bold and Just About Right

Once upon a time there were three mice. One of them was Altogether Too Timid, and the other was Altogether Too Bold, but as for the third he was neither too timid nor too bold, he neither fled from danger nor rashly sought it out. He was in fact Just About Right.

The hole where the three mice lived was under the dresser. To reach the larder they had to cross the whole length of the kitchen floor, for the larder opened out of the kitchen most conveniently. And as for being the other side of the floor that did not worry them a bit. For every morning early before the Cook was up, one, two, three, Hippity Hop Hop, the three little mice ran across to the larder and there ate for their breakfast anything they could find. As soon as they heard the Cook come down the stairs, CLOMP, CLOMP, CLOMP, one, two, three, Hippity Hop Hop, they ran back home and sat down to wash their whiskers.

And they repeated this performance in the evening, as soon as the Cook had shut the kitchen door and they heard her footsteps going up the stairs, then one, two, three, Hippity Hop Hop, across to the larder they went and this time there was no need to hurry for the whole long night was before them, and how they poked and pried into every dish and saucer; and nibbled their way into paper bags and cardboard boxes, and tried, but without success, to get the good things from tins and earthenware jars. But, indeed, even without these there was always enough, and more than enough, for their supper.

But there you are! This peaceful, regular life at last came to an end.

For one day as they dozed in their hole remembering breakfast and wondering about supper . . .

MIAOW, MIAOW, and then louder, MIAOW, MIAOW.

'There, there, Pussy. Don't be frightened. Look, she's jumped out of the basket.'

'Oh! Mother, isn't she a darling?'

'Yes, and more than a darling. Here, Cook, take her, she is yours. At all events until she's cleared the kitchen of mice.'

'MIAOW, MIAOW,' said Pussy, and they heard her run this way and that.

Oh dear, oh dear, oh dear! A CAT had come to the house.

'Well, I don't care,' said Too Bold, peering out of the hole to get a good look at her. 'I'm not afraid of a CAT! Why, the silly things spend all their time in sleeping. Who's afraid of the old Tom Cat?'

'I am,' said Too Timid in a very small voice. 'And besides it isn't a Tom. It's a She, and everyone knows that they are worse than Toms. And besides they have kittens, and then there's no end to it. Oh dear, oh dear, oh dear! Whatever will become of us? Either we shall starve to death in our hole or the very first time we venture out the Cat will kill us.'

'Well,' said the third. 'It is certainly a nuisance. I don't like cats and they complicate existence. But if we take care and are prudent we need not come to any harm. Life was perhaps too easy before and this will put us on our mettle.'

And they did not go to sleep all the rest of that day, but stayed awake listening to the unfamiliar sounds in the kitchen; how the cat miaowed and was given some milk, and how she lapped it up, and then began to purr.

'Oh dear, oh dear!' cried Too Timid. 'Did you ever hear the like of it? The whole house is trembling at the sound!'

Then at last night came, and Cook was going to bed, and this was the time when they used to be so happy, hungry for their supper, and excited as to what it would be.

But now, 'Good night, Pussy,' they heard Cook say. 'Mind you earn your dinner. If you cannot catch a mouse in this kitchen you couldn't catch a cold in the Arctic.'

'Miaow, miaow,' answered Pussy.

Then the Cook shut the door and CLUMP, CLUMP, CLUMP, upstairs she went, and left the mice to get their dinner as best they might.

'Well,' said Too Bold, yawning and stretching. 'Nothing like a little sport for improving the appetite. I'll take a look at this monster on the way to my supper, and if you don't come with me, why, then, all the more for me!'

And without the slightest care or precaution this foolish mouse ran out of his hole, Hippity Hop Hop, across the kitchen floor as gay as you please, saying 'Cats,' to himself. 'Well, I'm not afraid of a CAT.'

No sooner had he spoken than Ploump!

Miss Pussy had sat watching him prancing so gaily across the kitchen floor, and with one bound had seized him in her jaws, and too late he cried, 'Help! Help!'

'So you're not afraid of a CAT! Well, you'll taste none the worse for that.' And snip, snap, snorum.

She ate him up for her supper.

'Oh dear, oh dear! It is just as I feared,' cried Too Timid in a fit of hysterics. 'Whatever will become of us? Our brother is eaten and we shall be eaten too! Oh! why was I ever born that such a thing should happen?'

'Nonsense,' said the other. 'You must keep your wits about you. I am sorry, too, that our brother has been eaten. But really he tempted Providence, the foolish way he adventured. But if we take care we may yet live in peace and comfort. It seems to me we must move our home. I have long observed a crack in the floor-boards of the larder, which should make quite a reasonable hole with a good night's gnawing. If we make the venture but once, we need cross the kitchen floor no longer, but can live in peace in the larder and take our meals when the fancy takes us. They will never put a cat in the larder for she would prove as big a thief as we.'

'Oh dear, oh dear,' cried Too Timid. 'I shall never be able to move from our hole. Just think how wide the kitchen floor is! Why, my heart turns to water at the very idea of it.'

'Your fear runs away with you,' said the other. 'But if you will come with me there will be little danger. We will wait for the very moment when Cook comes down the kitchen stairs in the morning, for then Pussy will run to the door to meet her. Having been shut up all night she will be miaowing for milk and anxious to go out. Then will be the time for us to make our dash, and if it does not succeed, well, at least we die bravely, and not by slow starvation in our hole.'

But Too Timid only sighed and groaned.

'We'll never be able to do it,' he sobbed. 'Oh dear, oh dear, I wish I had not been born.'

However, the night passed, and in the morning, CLOMP, CLOMP, CLOMP.

Here was Cook as usual coming down the kitchen stairs.

'Now,' said Just About Right. 'Wait for Pussy to miaow at the door, and then be brave, be quiet, and run for all you are worth.'

And as soon as he heard Pussy miaow, and scratch at the door Just About Right DASHED from the hole, and ran, Hippity Hop Hop Hop, and was safe in the larder by the time Cook opened the door.

He looked round, breathless, for his brother. But oh! dear me.

Too Timid had started to follow, had reached the middle of the floor but suddenly thinking, 'Heavens! Here I am alone on the kitchen floor in full view of a CAT,' the thought so frightened him he gave a little squeak of dismay, started to run back, and then again ran forward, but as you can imagine, all this squeaking and scurrying to and fro was quickly noticed by Miss Pussy who with one leap, MIAOW, MIAOW, seized him in her jaws.

So when Cook came into the kitchen, 'Well, well, well. What a fine cat it is. Catching the little villains under my very nose. Your breakfast to-day shall be mouse and milk.'

And Cook went into the larder to get the jug. But by that time the other little mouse had quickly climbed up to the highest shelf, and was waiting quietly behind some bags of rice for the larder to be empty so that he could start gnawing his new hole.

So that is how it was.

Too Bold was caught by Pussy for his foolishness and daring. Too Timid was caught by Pussy for not being daring enough.

And as for the other mouse, he lived for many years in the larder growing sleek and fat, and not at all put out by Miss Pussy.

From *Nursery Tales*, by Diana Ross

II

STUFF AND NONSENSE

The Greedy Cat

Once upon a time a man and his wife had a cat and she was so big, and such a one to eat, they couldn't keep her any longer. Before they sent her away the Goody gave her a bowl of porridge and a saucer of cream. She ate them up and jumped through the open window. Outside stood the Goodman threshing.

'Good-day, Goodman,' said the Cat.

'Good-day, Puss,' said the Goodman. 'Have you had your food?'

'I have, but I'm still hungry,' said the Cat. 'It was only a bowl of porridge and a saucer of cream—and now I think of it, I'll have you too!' So she took the Goodman and gobbled him up.

After that she went into the byre where the Goody sat milking.

'Good-day, Goody,' said the Cat.

'Good-day, Puss,' said the Goody. 'Have you eaten up your food yet?'

'I have, but I'm still hungry,' said the Cat. 'It was just a bowl of porridge, a saucer of cream, the Goodman—and, now I think of it, I'll take you too!' So she took the Goody and gobbled her up.

'Moo-oo-oo!' cried the Cow when she saw the Goody disappear altogether.

'Good-day, Daisy the Cow,' said the Cat.

'Good-day, Pussy,' said the Cow. 'Have you eaten to-day?'

'I have, but I'm still hungry,' said the Cat. 'I only had a bowl of porridge, a saucer of cream, the Goodman, the Goody and—now I'll have you!' So she took the Cow and gobbled her up.

On she ran into the forest and there she saw Reynard Sly Fox prowling about.

'Good morning, Reynard Sly Fox,' said the Cat.

'Good morning, Mrs Pussy, have you eaten to-day?'

'I have, but I'm still hungry. I only had a bowl of por-ridge, a saucer of cream, the Goodman and the Goody, Daisy the Cow and, now I come to think of it, I'll have you!' So she took the Fox and gobbled him up.

Then she met a Wolf.

'Good morning, Greedy Greylegs Wolf,' said the Cat.

'Good morning, Mrs Pussy. Have you eaten to-day?'

'I have, but I'm still hungry. I only had a bowl of porridge, a saucer of cream, the Goodman and the Goody, Daisy the Cow, Reynard Sly Fox and—now I'll have you!' So the Cat gobbled the Wolf all up.

Then she went farther than far into the forest and met a Bear Cub.

'Good morning, Bear Cub,' said she.

'Good morning, Mrs Pussy,' said the Bear Cub. 'Have you eaten to-day?'

'I have, but I'm still hungry. I only had a bowl of porridge, a saucer of cream, the Goodman and the Goody, Daisy the Cow, Reynard Sly Fox, Greedy Greylegs Wolf, and now I'll have you!' So she gobbled the Bear Cub all up.

Then she met Mother Bear, who was tearing away at a tree till the splinters flew, she was so angry at losing her cub.

'Good morning, Mother Bear,' said the Cat.

'Good morning, Mrs Pussy, have you eaten to-day?'

'I have, but I'm still hungry. I only had a bowl of porridge, a saucer of cream, the Goodman and the Goody, Daisy the Cow, Reynard Sly Fox, the Wolf, Bear Cub, and now I'll have you!' And she gobbled the Mother Bear all up.

Then the Cat met Father Bear.

'Good morning, Father Bear,' said she.

'Good morning, Mrs Pussy, have you eaten to-day?'

'I have, but I'm still hungry. I only had a bowl of porridge, a saucer of cream, the Goodman and the Goody, Daisy the Cow, Reynard Sly Fox, the Wolf, Bear Cub, Mother Bear, and now I'll just have you!' And the Cat gobbled Father Bear up too.

Then the Cat went on and on, and farther on, till she came to the end of the wood, and into a village. There she met a Bridal Procession walking down the road.

'Good morning, you Bridal Procession on the road,' said the Cat.

'Good morning, Mrs Pussy. Have you eaten to-day?'

'I have, but I'm still hungry, for it was only a bowl of porridge, a saucer of cream, the Goodman and the Goody, Daisy the Cow, Reynard Sly Fox, the Wolf, Bear Cub, Mother Bear, Father Bear, and now I come to think of it I'll have you too!' And the Cat gobbled up the whole Bridal Procession, the Bride and Bridegroom, their friends and relations, with the cook and the fiddler, the horses and all.

Farther along the road the Cat met a Funeral.

'Good afternoon, Funeral you,' said she.

'Good afternoon, Mrs Pussy. Have you eaten to-day?'

'I have, but I'm still hungry, for I only had a bowl of porridge, a saucer of cream, the Goodman and the Goody, Daisy the Cow, Reynard Sly Fox, the Wolf, Bear Cub, Mother Bear and Father Bear, a Bridal Procession, and now I'll have you!' So the Cat gobbled up the Funeral with all the mourners —even the body and the bearers.

Now, when the Cat had the body inside her, she was taken up into the sky, and there she met the Moon.

'Good evening, Mrs Moon,' said the Cat.

'Good evening, Mrs Pussy. Have you eaten to-day?'

'I have, but I'm still hungry,' said the Cat. 'I only had a bowl of porridge, a saucer of cream, the Goodman and the Goody, Daisy the Cow, Reynard Sly Fox, the Wolf, Bear Cub, Mother and Father Bear, a Bridal Procession, a Funeral, and now I don't mind if I have you too!' So the Cat seized the Moon and gobbled her up.

In the morning the Cat met the Sun.

'Good morning, you Sun in the Heavens you,' said she.

'Good morning, Mrs Pussy. Have you eaten to-day?'

'I have, but I'm still hungry, for I just had a bowl of porridge, a saucer of cream, the Goodman and the Goody, Daisy the Cow, Reynard Sly Fox, the Wolf, Bear Cub, Mother and Father Bear, a Bridal Procession, a Funeral, the Moon, so now I may as well have you!' So the Cat seized the Sun in the Heavens and gobbled him up.

Then the Cat went on and on and on till she came to a bridge and there she met a Billy-goat.

'Good morning, Billy-goat on the bridge.'

'Good morning, Mrs Pussy. Have you eaten to-day?'

'Oh, I've had a little to eat, but I'm still hungry, for I only had a bowl of porridge, a saucer of cream, the Goodman and the Goody, Daisy the Cow, Reynard Sly Fox, the Wolf, Bear Cub, Mother and Father Bear, a Bridal Procession, a Funeral, the Moon, the Sun in the Heavens, and now I'll have *you*!'

'We'll soon see about that. You'll have to fight me first,' said the Billy-goat, and he butted the Cat till she fell over the bridge into the river. There she BURST!

Out they came, one after the other, as good as ever, and went on with their business, all those the Cat had gobbled up: the Goodman with his threshing, the Goody in the byre with Daisy the Cow, Reynard Sly Fox, Greedy Greylegs Wolf, the the little Bear Cub, Mother Bear and Father Bear, the whole Bridal Procession, the Funeral, Lady Moon in the Sky, and the Lord Sun in the Heavens.

Norse Folk Tale

Soap! Soap! Soap!

One time there was a woman fixin' to wash clothes and she found out she didn't have no soap, so she hollered for her little boy and told him to go to the store for soap. Says, 'Don't you forget now—*soap*.'

So he headed for the store, a'runnin' along and sayin', 'Soap! soap! soap!'—so he wouldn't forget. Come to a slick place in the road and he slipped and fell. Got up again, went on, tried to think what it was his mommy sent him for and he couldn't remember. So he walked back to where he slipped, says, 'Right there I had it.'

Walked on a few steps, stopped, says, 'Right there I lost it.'

Walked back—'Right there I had it.'

Walked on again—'Right there I lost it.'

Kept on walkin' back and forth sayin', 'Right there I had it—Right there I lost it'—till he had him a regular loblolly there in the road—had mud mired plumb right over the tops of his shoes. Man come along directly and heard what he was sayin'. Asked him, says, 'What ye lost?'

> 'Right there I had it—
> Right there I lost it.'

'What ye lost? I'll help ye find it.'

> 'Right there I had it—
> Right there I lost it.'

So the man thought he was crazy and started on by, and he slipped in the boy's loblolly and like to fell. Says, 'That blame mud! It's slick as soap.'

'Soap! soap! soap!' says the boy and started off again. And that man thought the boy was mockin' him so he stepped

over and grabbed him and shook him, says, 'You say you're
sorry and won't do it again, or I'll whip you good.'

> 'Sorry I done it; won't do it again—
> Sorry I done it; won't do it again.'

So the man turned him loose and the boy run on; but he
started in sayin' that and couldn't think of the soap. Got
down the road and come across an old woman had fell in
the ditch and broke all the eggs she had in her basket.
She was gettin' up about the time that boy come along—

> 'Sorry I done it; won't do it again—
> Sorry I done it; won't do it again.'

And the old woman thought he was makin' fun of her, so
she grabbed him and boxed his ears, and then she pushed him
in the ditch, says, 'I'm out and you're in.'
And when he got out of the ditch he went on, sayin':

> 'I'm out and you're in.
> I'm out and you're in.'

Come to where a man had one wagon wheel mired way
down in a mudhole and was tryin' to get it out—

> 'I'm out and you're in—
> I'm out and you're in.'

The man grabbed him, says, 'You oughtn't say that.
One's out and now you come here and help me get the other'n
out—or I'll whup you good.'
So the boy had to help him, and when they got it out, on
down the road he went—

'One's out; get the other'n out—
One's out; get the other'n out.'

And a one-eyed man come along and that boy went past him—

'One's out; get the other'n out—
One's out; get the other'n out.'

So the one-eyed man grabbed him and he just smoked that boy's britches. Says, 'You oughtn't say sech a thing to me. You might a said "One's in anyway!"' Turned him loose, and on the boy went—

'One's in anyway—
One's in anyway.'

Come to where a woman was washin' clothes at her washin' place in the creek 'side the road. Her two least young 'uns was runnin' around there playin' and one of 'em had slipped and fell in the creek. The woman ran to get it out and just about that time there was that boy—

'One's in anyhow—
One's in anyhow.'

So she jerked the young 'un out of the creek, and then she went after that boy and grabbed him, and she was about to give him a good paddlin' for makin' fun of her and her young 'uns but when she saw how dirty he was where he'd been in the mud so many times and been cryin' and wipin' his face with his muddy hands, she took pity on him and turned him loose, says, 'You run on back home and tell your mommy to take some soap and wash that black face.'

Time he heard 'Soap' he lit out down the road—

'Soap! Soap! Soap!—
Soap! Soap! Soap!'

And that time he got to the store and got the soap and run on home with it and handed it to his mommy. And she give him one look and then she took him by the ear and marched him down to her wash-place and soused him in the creek—clothes and all. Then she soaped him all over—with his britches and his shirt right on him. Soused him ag'in, till she got all the mud and dirt off him.

Then she took two clothes-pegs and hung him up on her clothes-line by his shirt-tail, and left him there to dry while she got the rest of her washin' done.

From *Grandfather Tales*, collected and retold by Richard Chase

Lazy Harry

Harry was lazy. He had nothing to do except look after his goat, yet he moaned and groaned from morning to night.

'It's hard on a chap,' he said, 'looking after a goat, day after day, when I could be having a nice snooze. You can't close your eyes with a goat to look after. You can never tell what a goat will be up to, nibbling young trees and tearing up folk's plants. It's a hard life, I can tell you!'

He sat down and wondered how he could get out of doing so much work. He was just about to fall asleep, when he had an idea.

'I know what I'll do,' said he, 'I'll marry fat Lena. She has a goat too. She'll be able to take my goat out to the field with hers, and I'll not need to bother myself.'

So Harry got up and went across the street to visit Lena. He was glad she lived so near.

'Good-day,' said Harry to her mother and father, when they opened the door, 'I've come to ask if I can marry your industrious and beautiful daughter.'

The parents looked surprised, but they did not take long to make up their minds.

'Certainly,' they said, and added (under their breath), 'Birds of a feather flock together.' But Lazy Harry didn't hear that.

So Fat Lena became Lazy Harry's wife. Every day she took both the goats to pasture, while Harry lay in bed until midday to rest himself from the long sleep of the night before.

'It's a waste of time to get up too early!' he said.

Now, Lena was as lazy as her husband.

'Harry, dear,' she said one day, 'why should we work so hard? There is no need for it. Our two goats wake us far too early each morning. Wouldn't it be better if we exchanged them with our neighbour for one of his beehives? Then all we'd have to do would be to put the hive in a sunny place and leave the bees to look after themselves. They don't have to be taken to a field every day. They fly off, collect their honey and find their way home without any bother at all.'

Harry sat up in bed.

'You are clever, Lena,' he said. 'We'll take the goats to our neighbour to-day. You know, Lena, honey is much nicer than milk, and it keeps much better. It doesn't go sour in hot weather, and it's very good for you!'

The neighbour was only too willing to give them a beehive in exchange for two goats.

Lazy Harry and Fat Lena put the hive in a sunny place, and went back to bed. While they slept, the bees flew in and out, back and forth, from morning to night, and soon filled the hive with the most delicious honey.

In the autumn there was so much honey, Lazy Harry was able to fill a great big jar with it. He and Lena were afraid someone would come and steal it while they were asleep, so they put it on a shelf just above their bed, and kept a strong stick beside them to drive off any thief without stirring themselves too much. Weren't they lazy?

Well, one morning, as Lazy Harry lay on his feather bed with the sun streaming in, resting after his long sleep, he said to Lena, 'I know you're always tasting the honey when I'm not looking so I think we should exchange the honey for a goose and goslings before you eat it all up.'

'Not before we have a son to look after them for us,' said Lena, as she lay on the feather bed. 'Why should I have to look after a lot of little geese?'

'Ha! ha! Do you really think a son of ours would herd geese for us?' said Harry.

'I'd see he did as he was told, or else I'd take a stick to him, like this. Just like this!' And she took the stick they kept by the bed, raised it above her head, and in her excitement waved the stick so vigorously that it knocked down the jar of honey. The jar broke into little pieces and the honey spilled all over the floor.

Lazy Harry leaned over the side of the bed and looked at it.

'Ah, well,' he sighed, 'that's that! There goes our flock of geese! They won't need anyone to look after them now!' Then he noticed there was still a little honey left in one of the larger pieces of jar.

'There's a little left, my dear,' said he. 'We'll eat it after we've had a rest. What excitement! It doesn't matter if we get up later than usual.'

'There's plenty of time,' said Fat Lena, 'and haste will get us nowhere.'

'We'll just take it easy,' yawned Harry, as they both got under the bedclothes and went to sleep.

Retold from Grimm

The House that Suits You will not Suit Me

A man wanted to build a house, but didn't know how.

'I will go along the road and ask whoever I meet. Some-one will certainly tell me how to do it.'

So he went along the road and met with a worm.

'Good morning,' said he.

'Good morning,' said the worm.

'Can you tell me how to build myself a house?'

'Easy enough,' said the worm, 'come along and I will show you.'

The worm led him to the other side of the road.

'Find a nice earthy bank, and it's better after rain; fortunately it rained last night, so it won't be so hard for a beginner. Find a place that is not too stony, set your head at the earth, wriggle, shove, burrow and turn, and soon enough you will be in your house.'

And the worm did as he advised and within a minute was inside the bank and a nice little house all round him.

'Nothing is done without trying,' said the man, and knelt down and put his head to the bank.

He wriggled, he shoved, he burrowed, he turned. Mud in his hair, mud in his eyes, mud in his mouth and mud in his nose. He scraped with his hands and broke his finger-nails. He shoved with his nose and stung it on a nettle.

Pebbles and earth fell down the back of his neck. Oh dear! and oh dear! what a sight he looked, and he hadn't even begun to build himself a house in the bank!

'The house that suits you will never suit me,' he said at last.

'Just as you please,' said the worm.

So the man got up and went on his way.

The next thing he met was a bird.

'Good morning,' said he.

'Good morning,' said the bird.

'Can you tell me how to build myself a house?'

'Easy enough,' said the bird. 'Come, and I will show you.' And he led the man into the midst of the thicket.

'Find a bush not too high and not too low, not too thick and not too thin. Gather together grass, sticks, hair and wool, line it with moss and then you will have a home to be happy in.'

'Nothing is done without trying,' said the man. And he began to look around for sticks and grass and hair and wool and moss, and as for mud, if he wanted to use it there was plenty of that still about him.

When he had got his materials together he made a little pile underneath a tree. It happened to be a thorn tree and the bird was sitting in it, and seemed to think it was quite the right place for building a nest.

So he made a bundle of his sticks and tied it to his back and began to climb the tree.

First he caught his clothes in the branches: then the bundle of twigs was pulled off his back; then the thorns ran into his hands and pulled so much of his hair out he had quite enough for lining a nest.

And when at last he got near the top and had chosen a fork on which to build his nest, the wind blew. CRACK! CRASH! BUMP! The bough broke and down he fell, tearing his jacket to ribbons and skinning his hands and knees.

'The house that suits you will never suit me,' said the man.

'Just as you please,' said the bird.

So up he got and went on his way.

He came to a river and across it was a bridge. He stopped on the bridge and looked into the water.

'What do you want?' asked a fish. 'You make me uncomfortable, staring at me like that.'

'I did not see you,' said the man. 'I did not know that you were there. But since you are, perhaps you can help me. Can you tell me how to build myself a house?'

'Easy enough,' said the fish. 'Come down here and I will show you.'

So the man went down and knelt on the river bank.

'Find a big fat stone where the weeds grow thickest, wriggle yourself in the gravel till you are right underneath it, and there you are at home, safe and comfortable, and not much trouble into the bargain!'

'Nothing is done without trying,' said the man. And he jumped into the water. WHOO! How cold it was!

He found a big flat stone and down he lay and wriggled into the sand, but long before he wriggled underneath the stone he came bursting up to the surface for air. Phoo! Phoo! and the water bubbled up all round him.

'The house that suits you will never suit me,' said the man.

'Just as you please,' said the fish. 'I have always found it satisfactory.'

So the man went back on the road, his clothes hanging about him, his boots squelching, even his pocket handkerchief soaked through in his pocket.

As he stood there the very picture of misery, another man came by.

'Mercy on us! Whatever has happened?'

'I wanted to know how to build myself a house. The worm showed me and I was covered with mud. The bird showed me and I tore my clothes. The fish showed me and I nearly drowned. And still I don't know how to build myself a house.'

'Come,' said the man, 'and I will show you. Cut down a tree and saw it into planks.'

So they cut down a tree, chop, chop, chop; you should have seen the chips fly.

They sawed it into planks. SHH, SHH, SHH, they sawed and sawed.

'Get nails and a hammer and nail the planks together.'

Bang, bang, bang, they were hammering the whole afternoon.

And at the end they had a little wooden house with wooden walls and a wooden roof and a stout wooden door that opened and shut.

'Is this the way to build myself a house?' asked the man.

'Only one way,' said the other.

'Well, this little house will certainly suit me, so if there are other ways I won't be bothered to learn them.'

And he went indoors and shut the door behind him, and as he had made no windows in his house what he did after that I'm afraid I cannot say.

From *The Golden Hen*, by Diana Ross

The Miller, his Son and their Ass

One day a Miller decided to sell his Ass, so he and his young son set out to drive the Ass to market.

They had not gone far when they passed some farm labourers who, when they saw the Miller and his son driving the Ass before them, shouted, 'Hi, you fellows! Why do you walk when you could ride?'

So the Miller told his young son to get on to the Ass's back.

'You can ride, son. I prefer to walk,' he said.

The boy rode while his father walked happily beside him. They had not gone far when they passed a group of old men gossiping in the morning sunshine.

'Look at that,' they cried. 'The boy rides, while the poor old man has to walk. Get off that Ass, you lazy young rascal, and let your old father ride!'

So the boy got down off the Ass and helped his father to mount.

The Miller was most uncomfortable for he was far too fat

to ride, but there he sat and away they went, the Miller trying hard not to fall off the Ass and the young son walking by their side.

They had not gone far when they passed some women and children picking blackberries by the roadside. The women shouted after them, 'Hey, there, Miller! Aren't you ashamed of yourself? A great big man like you, riding, while your son has to walk. Take the lad up on the Ass beside you!'

So the good-natured Miller told his son to get up behind him. The boy found there was not much room left for him and, as for the Ass, it was all it could do to carry such a load.

On they went till they came to the outskirts of the town. There they met a gentleman who stopped them and asked, 'Is that your own Ass, sir?'

'It is,' said the Miller, 'we're taking it to market.'

'By the way you've overloaded it, I doubt if you'll get there,' said the man. 'Why, you're more able to carry the poor beast yourselves!'

'Well, sir, we'll carry it if you think that is the correct thing to do,' said the Miller. And he and his young son got down off the Ass.

They tried to lift the Ass, who did not like it at all, and kicked at them, hard. So they tied its legs together to keep them from kicking, and after a great struggle, they managed to hoist the poor beast on to their shoulders, and slowly trudged into town.

The three of them looked so funny as they crossed the bridge, that all the children ran after them, and people followed them, laughing and shouting, 'Ha, ha, ha! Which is the Ass now!'

The Ass, who was even more uncomfortable than his masters, was very frightened by all this commotion. He struggled this way and that till he broke the rope, then bounded over the bridge, and into the river below.

Before anyone could rescue it, the poor animal was drowned.

So the Miller and his son were left to return home alone.

'Serves me right!' said the Miller. 'I tried to please everyone, but pleased no one, and lost my good Ass into the bargain!'

Retold from Æsop

The Wise Men of Gotham

1. *How they took the cheeses to market*

There was once a man of Gotham who was going to sell cheeses at the market in Nottingham. As he was going down the hill to Nottingham Bridge, one of the cheeses fell out of his basket and rolled down the hill.

'Ah, so you can run to market on your own, can you?' said the man of Gotham. 'Then I'll send all the others after you. It would be stupid of me to carry them if they can go by themselves.'

So he put down his basket, and took out the cheeses, and he rolled them down the hill, one after another.

'Mind you meet me near the market place,' he called after them, as they rolled away down the hill and out of sight, some into one bush and some into another.

When the man of Gotham reached the market place the cheeses were nowhere to be seen.

'Has anyone seen my cheeses?' he asked all his friends and neighbours.

'Who is bringing them for you?' they asked.

'They're coming on their own. They know the way well enough,' said he. 'They were running so fast they've probably run past the market, darn them. They'll be almost at York, by now, I shouldn't wonder!'

So he hired a horse and rode to York, but he didn't see them on the way, nor were they at York when he got there. No one had seen them and he never saw them again.

2. *How they drowned an eel*

When Good Friday came, the men of Gotham put their heads together to decide what they were going to do with their white herrings, their red herrings, their sprats and their other salt fish. At last they decided to throw all their salt fish into the pond in the middle of the town, so that the fish would breed and they would have twice as many fish and more next spring.

'I have many white herrings,' said one.

'I have many sprats,' said another.

'I have many red herrings,' said a third.

'I have any amount of salt fish,' said yet another. 'Let us throw them all into the pond, then we'll eat like lords next year.'

At the beginning of the next year, the men went and dragged the pond for their fish, but there were no fish there. Only an enormous eel.

'Darn this eel,' they said, 'it has eaten up all our fish. What shall we do with it?'

'Kill it,' said one.

'Cut it up into pieces,' said another.

'No,' said the third, 'we'll just drown it.'

'Agreed,' said all the others. So they took the eel to another pond, threw it in and left it to drown.

3. *How they counted to twelve*

One day twelve men of Gotham went fishing. Some waded in the water. Some stayed on dry land.

When they were going home, one of them said to the others, 'We've been messing about in the water so much, I hope none of us were drowned.'

'Could be,' said the others. 'We'd better count ourselves.'

So they each counted the company, but each one forgot himself, and so could only count eleven.

'Goodness, gracious,' they said, 'one of us *must* have been drowned.'

Then they went back to the brook where they had been fishing, and sadly they searched and searched and searched.

A horseman came riding by.

'What is the matter?' said he.

They told him their sad tale.

'Well,' said the horseman, 'what will you give me if I find you the twelfth man?'

'Sir,' said they, 'all the money we have.'

'Agreed,' said the horseman. Then he gave one of them a blow with his riding crop. 'Here is the first.' And he did this to each one of them, numbering them, second, third, and so on, until he came to the last man, and he said, 'Here is the twelfth man!'

'Thank you, Sir, and bless you,' they all said. 'You have found our neighbour!' Each one emptied his pockets and gave the horseman all the money they had.

4. *How they argued about sheep*

There were two men of Gotham, and one of them was going to Nottingham to buy sheep. The other was coming from the market, and they passed each other on Nottingham Bridge.

'Where are you going?' said the one who came from Nottingham.

'I'm going to Nottingham,' said the other, 'to buy sheep.'

'Buy sheep? And which way will you bring them home?'

'I'll bring them over this bridge.'

'By Robin Hood,' said the man from Nottingham, 'you shall not!'

'But I will,' said the one who was going to Nottingham.

'You will not,' said the other.

'I will.'

'You will not.'

And they each beat the ground with their sticks and got red in the face with rage.

'Hold on,' said the one. 'There won't be any bridge for my sheep to cross if you carry on like this!'

'I'll not allow your sheep to cross anyway,' said the other, beating the ground with his stick harder than ever. 'They'll not come this way!'

'Oh, yes they will!'

'They will not.'

'They will.'

And so they went on and on, and they did not notice another man of Gotham who had come up to the bridge with his horse, a sack of meal on its back.

'You're a fine pair, I must say, fighting about sheep, and not a single sheep between you. Come and help me pull this sack on to my shoulders.'

So the two men stopped quarrelling and helped the man pull the sack from his horse's back to his own. Then he went to the side of the bridge and tipped all the meal out of the sack into the river.

'Now, how much meal is there in my sack?' said he.

'None at all,' said the others.

'Right,' said the man, 'and there are as many brains in your two heads as meal in my sack!'

English Folk Tales

Clever Lisa

There was once a girl called Clever Lisa. She was a plain girl but she did try to use her brains as well as she could.

When she grew up, her father said, 'It's high time our Clever Lisa got married.'

'Yes,' said her mother. 'If only someone would come along and want to marry her.'

At last, along came a lad called Hans.

'I'll marry Clever Lisa,' said he, 'if she is as smart as you say she is!'

'Oh,' said the father, 'our Lisa's smart enough!'

'Aye, that's true!' said the mother.

'Well,' said Hans, 'if she's really smart, I'll have her.'

So they invited Hans to stay and have dinner with them. When they were all seated at table, the mother said, 'Lisa, go down to the cellar and fetch up some beer.'

So the clever girl took a jug, and trotted down the cellar stairs. There she sat down on a stool beside the cask of beer, set the jug in place and turned on the tap. While she waited for the jug to fill, she did not want to waste time, so she looked around her. Now, what did she see, right above her head, but a pickaxe! Suddenly she burst into tears.

'If I marry Hans,' she thought, 'and have a child, and he comes down here to fetch beer, the pickaxe may fall on him and kill him, then what shall I do! OOoooooo!'

And she cried and cried at the very idea.

Upstairs, her parents and Hans waited for her, but she did not come.

'Wife, you go down and see what has happened to our Clever Lisa,' said the father to the mother.

When the mother found Lisa crying, she said, 'What is the matter?'

'Well,' sobbed Lisa, 'if I marry Hans and we have a child, and he comes down here for beer, the pickaxe may fall on his head and kill him. Then what shall I do? OOoooooooooooo!'

'What things you think of!' said her mother. 'It all comes of being so clever. You've made me cry as well! OOoooo!' And she too sat down and cried and cried.

Upstairs, time passed, and Hans and the father wondered what had happened to the two women.

'I'll have to go down myself,' said the father, 'and see what is keeping them so long.'

So the father went down to the cellar and saw them both sitting and crying bitterly. When he heard why they were crying, he sat down and cried too!

Hans, in the meantime, was waiting in the kitchen, and when no one returned, he said to himself, 'Perhaps they're waiting for me down there. I'd better go and see what they're doing.'

As he went down the cellar stairs he could hear them crying, and he wondered what he would find.

'What has happened?' he asked, when he saw them sitting there, the tears streaming down their faces.

'Oh, dear Hans,' said Lisa. 'If you and I marry, and have a child, and we send him down here to fetch beer, that pick-axe up there may fall on his head and kill him! And then what shall we do?'

'Well,' said Hans. 'I think it's very smart of you to think all that out! And, since you're such a clever girl, I'll marry you right now!'

So he grabbed her by the hand and took her upstairs, and they were soon married.

Retold from Grimm

The Woodcutter's Three Wishes

There was once a Woodcutter who went into the forest to cut down trees. He found a fine old oak and raised his axe to make the first cut when a wood sprite jumped out.

'Don't cut down this tree. It's my home!' cried the Wood Sprite.

'All right, I'll leave it then,' said the Woodcutter. He was a little afraid of wood sprites.

'Thank you, Woodcutter, and now your next three wishes shall be granted.'

That night, as he sat with his wife in front of the fire, the Woodcutter felt very hungry.

'That was thin cabbage soup we had for supper, wife,' said he. 'I wish I had some nice fat black puddings to eat.'

As soon as he said that, down fell a string of black puddings at his feet.

'Good gracious!' cried his wife. 'Where did they come from?'

'I don't know. They were just what I'd wished for,' said the Woodcutter. Then he remembered what the Wood Sprite had said about wishes. (Not that he'd believed a word of it!)

So he told his wife all that had happened in the forest that morning.

'And you go and waste a wish on a string of black puddings! You must be daft. You know we need a cow and a horse and cart—and—and all *you* can manage to wish for are black puddings!'

'Black puddings. Black puddings,' cried her husband. 'How I wish they'd stick to your nose and keep you quiet!'

No sooner had he said this than, sure enough, the black

puddings flew up and stuck on the end of his wife's nose, making it impossible for her to speak.

The Woodcutter tried to pull them off, but no matter what he did, he could not move the puddings at all. He was afraid to cut them off, for they now appeared to be part of his wife's nose. On the other hand he could not leave them where they were.

'I'll just have to use my last wish,' said he, 'and don't you dare say I wasted it.'

His wife shook her head and looked so miserable that he at once wished the black puddings would disappear altogether. As soon as he wished they vanished completely, and with them all the riches his wish might have brought him and his old wife.

English Folk Tale

Some Strange Adventures of Baron Munchausen

There was once a nobleman called Baron Munchausen. He travelled far and wide, and had the most extraordinary adventures. In fact, if he had not written down, in black and white, all the remarkable things that had happened to him, I am sure no one would have believed they were true. Here are three of his adventures, just as he wrote them down in his memoirs.

1. *How he shot a stag*

I, Baron Munchausen, was out on a hunting expedition. I had been shooting all day and had finished all my shot, when I saw a fine stag. Well, I charged my gun with powder, then added a handful of cherry stones. (I had eaten several pounds of the fruit during the hunt.) Then I shot the stag and hit him just between his antlers. He staggered, but managed to run off into the forest.

A year or two later, when I was hunting in the same forest, I saw a fine stag with a full-grown cherry tree, about ten feet high, growing between his antlers. I remembered the stag I had shot with the cherry stones, and I was sure this was the same animal. So I aimed my gun and brought him to the ground with one shot.

That night we had cherry sauce with venison at supper— for the tree was covered with the richest fruit, better than I had ever tasted before.

2. *How he cleared the road*

When I left Russia, I travelled by a comfortable carriage drawn by a pair of fine black horses. As we travelled down a narrow lane I told the boy to sound his horn, to warn any oncoming traffic. He blew with all his might, but not a sound came, which was rather unfortunate, for we met a coach and pair coming the other way. There we stood, neither able to move.

So I got out of my carriage and hoisted it, wheels and all, on to my head. Then I jumped right over the other carriage (which was quite difficult considering the great weight of my carriage). I went back for the horses, and, placing one on my head, and the other under my left arm, I jumped with them to the front of my carriage.

Thus we were able to continue our journey until we came to an Inn. There my servants and I refreshed ourselves. The boy hung his horn on a hook by the fire, while I sat on the other side of the hearth to warm myself.

Suddenly we heard a loud 'Peeep! peeepeeep! peeep!'

We looked round, and then we realized why the boy had not been able to sound his horn. The notes had been frozen up in it! Now that the horn was warmed up, the notes thawed and came out. So it was not the boy's fault after all! To show us his skill, he played us a number of merry tunes like 'The Grand Old Duke of York', and 'Over the Hills and Far Away', all without putting his mouth to the horn.

3. *How he accidentally visited the moon*

While I was on a sea voyage a hurricane lifted our ship up into the sky, and we went up to a height of about one hundred miles above the sea. A fresh gale filled our sails, and we travelled along at great speed above the clouds for six weeks.

At last we saw a round, bright and shining island in the sky. It was the Moon. We spotted a good harbour and managed to sail our ship into it. Far, far below us, we saw a bright globe, with sea, mountains, rivers and forests. We guessed that it was the earth we had left behind. However we didn't waste any more time looking at it. Instead we went ashore on the Moon.

This new world, the Moon, was inhabited. We saw huge figures riding on enormous vultures with three heads. Instead of riding on horses as we do on earth, the inhabitants of the Moon flew about on these birds.

Everything was ENORMOUS! An ordinary flea, for instance, was larger than one of our sheep, and not one of the natives was less than thirty-six feet high. They didn't waste time eating, they just opened their left side, put in enough food to last them one month, then closed it up again. They left it closed until the same date on the next month, when they had their next meal, or 'fill-up'. They never ate more than twelve times a year, which was really very practical when you come to think of it. They had one finger on each hand with which they managed to do everything perfectly.

Usually, the inhabitants of the Moon carried their heads under their right arm; but when they travelled they left their head at home, and when they played games they usually left it in a safe place. They could get on quite well without it, for they could consult their head at any distance, and they could take their eyes out and put them in, just as they pleased. Luckily they could see with them in their hand quite as easily as in their head. Which was just as well when they had to leave their heads at home so often! And do you know, if they lost or damaged an eye they could always buy or borrow another. Of course, there was a great range of colours to choose from—yellow, green, blue. In fact you could have whatever colour of eyes you fancied.

I know all these things must seem very strange, but if you don't believe me, you should go there yourself, and then you will know that everything is just as I have described it to you.

Retold from Raspe's *The Marvellous Travels of Baron Munchausen*

Timothy Titus and his Tottie

Timothy Titus went to see his best girl-friend, Tottie, and she gave him a present of a beautiful bright silver penknife. He was very pleased and he stuck the penknife in the hay cart and drove home.

'Where have you been?' said his mother.

'To see my girl-friend, Tottie. She gave me a penknife.'

'Then, where is it?' said his mother.

'In the hay cart,' said Timothy.

'Timothy Titus! What a place to put a penknife! Don't you know you should keep a penknife in your pocket?'

'I'll know next time,' said Timothy.

Next day, Timothy Titus went to see his girl-friend, Tottie, and what do you think she gave him? A nice little kid. So Timothy Titus stuffed the kid in his pocket, and when he got home the poor kid was dead, for it had not been able to breathe in a pocket.

'What's that you've got in your pocket?' said his mother.

'A kid, my girl-friend, Tottie, gave me. It's pretty sick now, it couldn't breathe at all in my pocket.'

'Timothy Titus! What a place to put a kid! Don't you know you should put a rope round a kid, and lead it home?'

'Ah, well,' said Timmy, 'I'll know next time!'

Next day he went to see his girl-friend, Tottie. This time she gave him a really nice back gammon of ham for his mother, so he tied a rope round it, and led it home, just as his mother had told him.

As he went all the dogs of the village followed after, and ate up all the ham, every scrap. When he got home all he had was a long piece of rope.

'Well,' said his mother, 'what did Tottie give you this time?'

'A nice piece of back gammon for you, Ma,' said Tim. 'I

tied a piece of rope round it, just like you said, but as I was leading it home all the dogs came and ate it up.'

'Timothy Titus! Timothy Titus! You must be the stupidest boy I know! You should have wrapped that ham in butter muslin and carried it on your head if it was too heavy to carry under your arm. Just you remember that the next time you're given a nice piece of ham!'

'I'll remember next time, Mother,' said Timothy Titus.

So, next day, when he went off to visit his best girl-friend, Timothy Titus stuffed a piece of butter muslin in his pocket, just in case! When he got to her house, what do you think Tottie gave him? A great big slab of fresh butter she had just churned herself.

'I can't go wrong this time,' thought Timothy Titus, 'for butter muslin must be for butter!' So he thanked Tottie for the butter, then he wrapped it up in the butter muslin, tied it on to his head, and off he went home, whistling and feeling very pleased with himself.

But unfortunately it was a hot day and the sun shone right down on that great slab of butter. The butter began to melt and trickle down Timothy's face, neck and back.

'Goodness, carrying butter is hard work! I've never sweated as much as this!' said Timothy Titus, mopping his face with his big pocket handkerchief.

'Goodness gracious me!' cried his mother, when he went into the house. 'What have you been doing to yourself? Did you fall in a vat of oil or something? Why have you got that dirty greasy rag tied to your head? I hope you didn't go and see Tottie looking like that!'

Poor Timothy could scarcely speak or see. He had butter in his ears, his eyes and his mouth, and he felt very, very uncomfortable. At last he managed to speak.

'Tottie gave me a great slab of fresh butter to bring home, so I did just as you said, I wrapped it up in butter muslin, tied it on my head, and it should be there still!'

'Really, Timothy Titus! You haven't a single brain in your head! I've never heard of anyone as stupid as you, as sure as I'm born! If you'd had any sense at all you'd have wrapped that butter in a water-proof bag, tied it up and put it in the cool stream. Then you could have fetched it home in the evening, when the sun was down.'

'I'll remember next time,' said Timothy Titus.

But next day, when he went to visit Tottie she had nothing to give him. He looked so disappointed that she said, 'You can just take ME home!'

'You'll do fine, Tottie,' said Timothy Titus. And what do you think that stupid boy did? He wrapped poor Tottie up in his old water-proof cape, tied her up, and put her into the cool stream.

'I'll come back for you when the sun is down,' said he.

When he told his mother what he had done, she dropped all the dinner plates she was carrying. She got such a fright!

'Away you go and pull her out before she drowns, you ——!'

But Timothy didn't wait to hear what she called him. He ran as fast as he could to the stream to rescue Tottie. As he ran he thought how kind and brave she'd think he was to rescue her from drowning and how pleased she'd be to see him.

But when he got there, Tottie was nowhere to be seen, and when he went to her house, her door was locked and she refused to open it. She was so angry. Poor Timothy Titus could not understand why his best girl-friend, Tottie, married that stupid loon, Tommy Topper, in the spring.

English Folk Tale

Two of Everything

Mr and Mrs Hak-Tak were rather old and rather poor. They had a small house in a village among the mountains and a

tiny patch of green land on the mountain side. Here they grew
the vegetables which were all they had to live on, and when
it was a good season and they did not need to eat up everything as soon as it was grown, Mr Hak-Tak took what they
could spare in a basket to the next village which was a little
larger than theirs, and sold it for as much as he could get.
Then he bought some oil for their lamp, and fresh seeds, and
every now and then, but not often, a piece of cotton stuff to
make new coats and trousers for himself and his wife. You
can imagine they did not often get the chance to eat meat.

Now, it happened one day that when Mr Hak-Tak was
digging in his precious patch, he unearthed a big brass pot. He
thought it strange that it should have been there for so long
without his having come across it before, and he was disappointed to find that it was empty; still he thought they
would find some use for it, so when he was ready to go back
to the house in the evening he decided to take it with him. It
was very big and heavy and, in his struggles to get his arms
round it and raise it to a good position for carrying, his purse,
which he always took with him in his belt, fell to the
ground, and, to be quite sure it was safe, he put it inside the
pot and so staggered home with his load.

As soon as he got into the house Mrs Hak-Tak hurried from
the inner room to meet him.

'My dear husband,' she said, 'whatever have you got
there?'

'For a cooking pot it is too big; for a bath it is too small,'
said Mr Hak-Tak. 'I found it buried in our vegetable patch
and so far it has been useful in carrying my purse home for
me.'

'Alas,' said Mrs Hak-Tak, 'something smaller would have
done as well to hold any money we have or are likely to
have,' and she stooped over the pot and looked into its dark
inside.

As she stooped, her hairpin—for poor Mrs Hak-Tak had

only one hairpin for all her hair and it was made of carved bone—fell into the pot. She put in her hand to get it out again, and then she gave a loud cry which brought her husband running to her side.

'What is it?' he asked. 'Is there a viper in the pot?'

'Oh, my dear husband,' she cried, 'what can be the meaning of this? I put my hand into the pot to fetch out my hairpin and your purse, and look, I have brought out two hairpins and two purses, both exactly alike.'

'Open the purse. Open both purses,' said Mr Hak-Tak. 'One of them will certainly be empty.'

But not a bit of it. The new purse contained exactly the same number of coins as the old one—for that matter, no one could have said which was the old—and it meant, of course, that the Hak-Taks had exactly twice as much money in the evening as they had had in the morning.

'And two hairpins instead of one!' cried Mrs Hak-Tak, forgetting in her excitement to do up her hair which was streaming over her shoulders. 'There is something quite unusual about this pot.'

'Let us put in a sack of lentils and see what happens,' said Mr Hak-Tak, also becoming excited.

They heaved in the bag of lentils and when they pulled it out again—it was so big it almost filled the pot—they saw another bag of exactly the same size waiting to be pulled out in its turn. So now they had two bags of lentils instead of one.

'Put in the blanket,' said Mr Hak-Tak. 'We need another blanket for the cold weather.' And, sure enough, when the blanket came out, there lay another behind it.

'Put in my wadded coat,' said Mr Hak-Tak, 'and then when the cold weather comes there will be one for you as well as me. Let us put in everything we have in turn. What a pity we have no meat or tobacco, for it seems the pot cannot make anything without a pattern.'

Then Mrs Hak-Tak, who was a woman of great intelli-

gence, said, 'My dear husband, let us put in our purse again
and again and again. If we take two purses out each time we
put one in, we shall have enough money by to-morrow evening to buy everything we lack.'

'I'm afraid we may lose it this time,' said Mr Hak-Tak,
but in the end he agreed, and they dropped in the purse and
pulled out two, then they added the new money to the old
and popped it in again and pulled out the larger amount twice
over. After a while the floor was covered with old leather
purses and they decided just to throw the money in by itself.
It worked quite as well and saved trouble; every time, twice
as much money came out as went in, and every time they
added the new coins to the old and threw them in all together.
It took them hours to tire of this game, but at last Mrs Hak-
Tak said, 'My dear husband, there is no need for us to work
so hard. We shall see to it that the pot does not run away,
and we can always make more money as we want it. Let us
tie up what we have.'

It made a huge bundle in the extra blanket and the Hak-
Taks lay and looked at it for a long time before they slept,
and talked of all the things they would buy and the improve-
ments they would make in the cottage.

The next morning they rose early and Mr Hak-Tak filled a
wallet with money from the bundle and set off for the village
to buy more things in a morning than he had bought in fifty
whole years.

Mrs Hak-Tak saw him off and then she tidied up the cottage and put the rice on to boil and had another look at the
bundle of money and made herself a whole set of new hairpins from the pot, and about twenty candles instead of one
which was all they had possessed up to now. After that she
slept for a while, having been up so late the night before, but
just before the time when her husband should be back, she
awoke and went over to the pot. She dropped in a cabbage
leaf to make sure it was still working properly, and when

two leaves came out she sat down on the floor and put her arms round it.

'I do not know how you came to us, my dear pot,' she said, 'but you are the best friend we ever had.'

Then she knelt up to look inside it, at that moment her husband came to the door, and, turning quickly to see all the wonderful things he had brought, she overbalanced and fell into the pot.

Mr Hak-Tak put down his bundles and ran across and caught her by the ankles and pulled her out, but, Oh, mercy, no sooner had he set her carefully on the floor than he saw the kicking legs of another Mrs Hak-Tak in the pot! What was he to do? Well, he could not leave her there, so he caught her ankles and pulled, and another Mrs Hak-Tak so exactly like the first that no one could have told one from the other, stood beside them.

'Here's an extraordinary thing,' said Mr Hak-Tak, looking helplessly from one to the other.

'I'll not have another Mrs Hak-Tak in the house!' screamed the old Mrs Hak-Tak.

All was confusion. The old Mrs Hak-Tak shouted and wrung her hands and wept, Mr Hak-Tak was scarcely calmer, and the new Mrs Hak-Tak sat down on the floor as if she knew no more than they did what was to happen next.

'One wife is all I want,' said Mr Hak-Tak, 'but how could I have left her in the pot?'

'Put her back in again!' cried Mrs Hak-Tak.

'What? And draw out two more?' said her husband. 'If two wives are too many for me, what should I do with three? No! No! No!' He stepped back quickly as if he was stepping away from three wives and missing his footing, lo and behold, he fell into the pot!

Both Mrs Hak-Taks ran and each caught an ankle and pulled him out and set him on the floor, and there, Oh, mercy, was another pair of legs kicking in the pot. Soon another Mr Hak-

Tak, so exactly like the first that no one could have told one from the other, stood beside them.

Now the old Mr Hak-Tak liked the idea of his double no more than Mrs Hak-Tak had liked hers. He stormed and raged and scolded his wife for pulling him out of the pot, while the new Mr Hak-Tak sat down on the floor beside the new Mrs Hak-Tak and looked as if, like her, he did not know what was going to happen next.

The old Mrs Hak-Tak had a very good idea.

'Listen, my dear husband,' she said, 'now, do stop scolding and listen, for it is really a good thing that there is a new one of you as well as a new one of me. It means that you and I can go on in our usual way, and these new people, who are ourselves and yet not ourselves, can set up house next door to us.'

And that is what they did. The old Hak-Taks built themselves a fine new house with the money from the pot, and they built one just like it next door for the new couple. They lived together in the greatest friendliness, because as Mrs Hak-Tak said, 'The new Mrs Hak-Tak is really more than a sister to me, and the new Mr Hak-Tak is really more than a brother to you.'

The other neighbours were very surprised, both at the sudden wealth of the Hak-Taks and at the new couple who resembled them so strongly that they must, they thought, be very close relations of whom they had never heard before. They said, 'It looks as though the Hak-Taks, when they so unexpectedly became rich, decided to have two of everything, even of themselves, to enjoy their money more.'

From *The Treasure of Li-Po*, by Alice Ritchie

Jack Hannaford

Jack Hannaford was an old soldier who had been away so long, travelling from one place to another, that when he came home there wasn't a penny left in his pockets. His clothes were the worse for wear, and he hadn't had a proper meal for days.

He walked up hill and down again looking for work but there was none to be found for an old soldier.

At last he came to a farm. He knocked on the door and, as soon as the wife opened it, Jack Hannaford guessed she was a stupid woman. He was quite right. She was the most stupid woman for miles around, and what was more her husband was stupid too. Why, that very day he had handed her a bag of money.

'Here's ten pounds all in silver,' he had said. 'Take care of it while I'm away, there's a good wife!'

'I'll do that,' said she. 'It'll be safe enough here. No thieves'll find it now,' she added, stuffing it up the chimney. So the farmer rode happily off to market.

Soon after that Jack Hannaford knocked at the door.

'Who's that?' said the wife.

'Jack Hannaford, madam,' said the old soldier, bowing.

'Where have you come from?'

'Heaven.'

'Good gracious me!' said the wife. 'My first husband is there! Did you meet him?'

'I did.'

'How is he? What is he doing?' asked the wife.

'He's not too well; he mends shoes for the angels and saints, and has nothing to eat but cabbage soup.'

'Dear me, I thought he'd be having a fine time,' said she. 'Did he give you any message for me?'

'Yes, he did,' said Jack Hannaford. 'He said he was out of

leather and his pockets were empty, so would you please send him a few shillings.'

'He shall have all he needs, bless him,' said the wife, who was as kind as she was stupid. Then she pulled the bag of money from its hiding-place, and handed it to Jack Hannaford.

'There's ten pounds in silver in this bag. Give it to my old man and tell him to take what he needs from it. You can bring back the rest.'

'I'll do that,' said Jack Hannaford, and off he went as fast as his legs would carry him for fear the wife would change her mind.

When the farmer came home he asked for his bag of money.

'I gave it to an old soldier who came with a message from my old man in Heaven,' said she.

'You did what?' roared the farmer, unable to believe his ears.

'Well, that poor old man of mine is kept busy mending shoes for the angels and saints in Heaven, and he has no money left for food or leather,' she said, 'so of course I had to send him what I had.'

The farmer turned red with anger.

'You must be the most stupid woman in the world,' he roared.

'Then you're even more stupid than I am to leave your money with me!'

But the farmer didn't wait to listen to his wife; he jumped on his horse and rode after Jack Hannaford.

Now, the old soldier heard the sound of horse's hoofs, and guessed that the farmer was chasing him, and was bound to catch him. So he lay down on the ground and, shading his eyes with one hand, gazed up at the sky, pointing towards it with the other.

'Whatever are you doing that for?' asked the farmer, drawing up beside him.

'Good gracious me,' said Jack Hannaford. 'You should see what I see. It's a marvel, that's what it is, a marvel!'

'What is?' said the farmer. 'What are you talking about?'

'Look up there! A man is going straight up into the sky, just as though he was walking up a road.'

'Can you really see that?'

'I can.'

'Well, I can't see anything up there at all.'

'Can't you?' said Jack Hannaford. 'Well, get off your horse and lie down here.'

'All right,' said the farmer, 'but you'll have to hold my horse or she'll run away.'

'I'll do that,' said Jack Hannaford, readily taking the reins.

'I still can't see anything,' said the farmer, as he lay down.

'Shade your eyes with your hands and you'll soon see a man running away from you.'

And, sure enough, that is what he saw, for Jack Hannaford leapt on the horse and galloped away with it as well as the bag of money.

The farmer walked home.

'You're even more stupid than I am,' said his wife when she heard his story. 'I did one foolish thing, but you have done TWO!'

English Folk Tale

III

ANIMAL FABLES

The Hare and the Tortoise

One day a Hare met a Tortoise.

'Good day, Tortoise,' said he, 'where are you going?'

'Down to the field where the lettuces grow,' said the Tortoise.

'You'll have to move faster than that, or the white butter-flies will have eaten them first,' laughed the Hare. 'I've never seen anyone move so slowly as you do!'

'Is that so,' said the Tortoise. 'Well, I'll race you there any time!'

'Very well,' said the Hare. 'We'll start off at once. Ready, steady, GO!'

The Tortoise set off at his usual steady pace, and went on without looking back or wasting a moment.

Now, the Hare thought the race was a great joke. He laughed to think how ridiculous it was for *him* to race with a Tortoise of all animals.

'I'll just rest in the clover. If I start now I'll be there before poor old Tortoise is half-way. I can run across that field in no time!' So the Hare lay down. The clover was soft and the sun warm, and before long he was fast asleep.

The Tortoise plodded on very slowly, and he nibbled tender green shoots as he went along.

Suddenly the Hare woke up, and found the sun had already gone down behind the dark wood.

'I didn't mean to sleep as long as this,' he said to himself. 'Ah, well, I'll soon catch up with the Tortoise.'

But he was wrong. Although he ran as fast as his long legs could carry him, when he reached the other end of the field he found the Tortoise there already, waiting for him. The Tortoise had won the race after all!

Retold from Æsop

The Town Mouse and the Country Mouse

There was once a mouse who lived in the country all by himself. He was very comfortable in his little house, with a larder filled with food.

One day, when it was warm and sunny, he invited his friend, the Town Mouse, to visit him. The Town Mouse said he would be pleased to come, so the Country Mouse lined his house with fresh straw, and collected the best barley, nuts and peas he could find. Then he went to meet his friend.

'You are a lucky fellow,' said the Town Mouse, as they shook hands, 'the country looks beautiful, and the air is so fresh. You've no idea how stuffy it is in town.'

'You must be tired after your long journey,' said the Country Mouse, as he led his friend into his neat little house. 'Come and sit down. Supper is all ready for you.'

The Town Mouse found the straw hard and prickly, and he looked with disgust at the large pile of nuts and peas his generous host had set out for him. He thought of the creamy cheeses and chocolate cakes he was used to eating, and he picked at a nut here and a pea there, while his friend sat happily nibbling away at some barley.

'What do you do here to amuse yourself?' asked the Town Mouse, who was already feeling restless.

'I go out and gather any food I can find, I potter about until the Owl flies over, and then it's time to go to bed. You see, I've got to get up early before the farmhouse cat is about.'

'What a dull life! How do you put up with it?'

'It may sound dull to you but I'm quite happy.'

'My dear fellow, you don't know what you're missing! Believe me, you're wasting your time in this place. You must come back with me. I'll show you what fun life can be!'

So the Country Mouse agreed to go with his friend to the town.

It was dark when they arrived at the great big house where

the Town Mouse lived, but there in the dining-room they found a feast laid out on a long table. The Country Mouse had never seen such rich food before. He stood there staring, his little eyes bright with astonishment. There was cold chicken and hams and a plate of the most delicious cheeses, as well as creamy cakes and sweet biscuits of all shapes and sizes. There were jellies and creams and fruits and nuts, and goodness knows what else.

'Come along, my dear fellow,' said the Town Mouse. 'Just help yourself, and eat as much as you like. There's plenty more where this came from!'

But the Country Mouse nibbled a little of this and a little of that, and couldn't make up his mind what to choose out of so many tasty dishes.

Before he had time to taste anything properly, the door was flung open and in came a crowd of men and women dressed in fine clothes.

The Country Mouse had never seen so many people in one room, and the Town Mouse had to pull him to safety behind a curtain, where he stood shaking with fright.

'We'll stay here till they've gone,' said the Town Mouse, 'then we can finish our supper.'

But before long two pet dogs came running into the room and sniffing all over the floor.

'We'll have to go after all,' said the Town Mouse. 'Follow me.' And they scampered along the floor skirting till they came to the mouse-hole. In they ran to the dark dusty place under the floor-boards. And not a moment too soon, for they could hear the pet dogs yapping at the entrance to the mouse-hole.

'Sorry about this, my dear fellow,' said the Town Mouse. 'But don't worry. They'll all go to bed soon and then we'll have peace to eat before the house cat is up and about.'

'I won't stay for that,' said the Country Mouse. 'I've a long journey home so I'll set off at once.'

'You're not going already, are you? Why, you've not seen anything yet——!'

'I have, you know,' said the Country Mouse, 'and it has all been most interesting, and so kind of you to have me. I'll think of you when I'm having a dull time in the country. Good-bye!'

'Good-bye, dear fellow,' said the Town Mouse. 'So sorry you can't stay——!' But the Country Mouse was already out of sight.

Retold from Æsop

The Four Friends

There was once a tortoise, a rat, a raven and a gazelle. They were the greatest of friends and they all lived together in a forest.

One day the gazelle was running along enjoying herself when she was seen through the trees by a huntsman's hound. He chased her and on and on she ran, until she leapt into a snare and was trapped.

That night all the friends returned home except the gazelle. They made their supper but still the gazelle did not appear.

'What can have happened to her?' said the raven.

'Perhaps she has forgotten us,' said the rat, 'and found some other friends.'

'My dear rat, how can you say such a thing!' said the tortoise. 'I'm afraid she's had an accident. If I were a bird like you, my dear raven, I'd fly over the forest to find out what had happened to her.'

'A good idea, tortoise,' said the raven, and away he flew over the tree-tops until, there at the edge of the forest, he saw the poor gazelle entangled in a huntsman's snare.

'Have courage, dear gazelle,' he called to her. 'We'll soon set you free!'

Away he flew for he knew he could not help her on his own.

When the rat and the tortoise heard the news they were very sad.

'There is no time to be lost. We must release her before the huntsman finds her,' said the rat.

'I'll lead you to her,' said the raven.

'Then let us go at once,' said the tortoise.

'My dear tortoise,' said the rat, 'you go so slowly, we'll not reach her in time. It would be much better if you stayed and looked after the house, and made a nice warm supper for her.'

The tortoise said nothing for he knew perfectly well how slow he was, but when he saw the other two run off he felt so miserable he had to follow them.

'If only I hadn't got to carry my house with me wherever I go,' he grumbled, 'I'd be able to walk as fast as rat any day, I know I would.'

At last the other two friends reached the gazelle.

'Cheer up,' said the rat, 'we'll soon have you free!' And at once he started to gnaw the ropes that held her. And just in time, for as soon as he had freed her, along came the hunts- man. The rat scurried into a hole, the raven flew up into a tree and the gazelle ran off into the wood.

'Who has cut my snare and freed my gazelle?' cried the huntsman in anger and disappointment. He looked around and could see no trace of her. Then he caught sight of the tor- toise who had just arrived and was very flustered to find the huntsman instead of his three friends.

'Ah well, I'll just have to have this for my supper,' said the huntsman, picking up the tortoise and popping him into his bag.

When the raven saw this he flew to the gazelle and told

her what had happened. At once she ran from her hiding-
place, pretending to be lame. As soon as he saw her the huntsman threw his bag to one side and chased her. While he did
so, the rat came out of his hole and gnawed at the bag until
the tortoise was free.

That night, after they had all reached home safely, the
four friends, the tortoise, the rat, the raven and the gazelle,
sat down to supper. They had never felt so hungry or enjoyed a meal so much, and they made up their minds never to
wander far from each other again.

Retold from La Fontaine

The Bear says 'North'

One day, while Osmo the Bear was prowling about the forest,
he caught a grouse.

'Pretty good,' he thought to himself. 'Won't the other
animals be surprised when they hear old Osmo has caught a
grouse?'

He was very proud of his feat and he wanted all the world
to know of it. So, holding the grouse carefully in his teeth
without hurting it, he began parading it up and down the
forest paths.

'They'll certainly envy me this nice plump grouse,' he
thought. 'They won't be so ready to call me awkward and
lumbering after this!'

Presently Mikko the Fox sauntered by. He at once saw that
Osmo was showing off, and he made up his mind the Bear
should not get the admiration he wanted. So he pretended not
to see the grouse at all. Instead he pointed his nose upward
and sniffed.

'Um! um!' grunted Osmo, trying to attract attention to himself.

'Ah,' said Mikko in an offhand way, 'is that you, Osmo? Which way is the wind blowing to-day? Can you tell me?'

Osmo could not, of course, answer without opening his mouth, so he grunted, hoping Mikko would see the grouse, and understand why he couldn't speak. But the Fox didn't glance at him at all. With his nose still pointing upward, he kept sniffing the air.

'It seems to be from the south,' said he. 'It is from the south, isn't it Osmo?'

'Um! um!' repeated Osmo, growing more impatient every moment.

'Not from the south, you say? Then which way is it blowing?'

By this time the Bear was so cross with Mikko, he forgot all about his grouse, he just opened his mouth, and roared out, 'North!'

Of course the moment he opened his mouth the grouse flew away.

'Now, see what you've done!' he stormed angrily. 'You've made me lose my nice plump grouse!'

'I?' said Mikko. 'What had I to do with it?'

'You kept asking me about the wind until I opened my mouth—that's what you did!'

The Fox shrugged his shoulders.

'Why did you open your mouth then?'

'Well, you can't say "north" without opening your mouth, can you?' the Bear demanded.

The Fox laughed and laughed.

'See here, Osmo, don't blame me. Blame yourself. If I'd had the grouse in my mouth and you'd asked me about the wind, I'd never have said "north"!'

'What would you have said?' asked the Bear.

Mikko, the rascal, laughed harder than ever. Then he clenched his teeth together and said 'EAST'!

Finnish Folk Tale

The Cat and the Rat

There was once a time when the Cat and the Rat were friends and lived together on an island. There were birds in the trees for the Cat to eat and nuts and roots for the Rat.

One day the Rat said, 'I'm tired of living on this island. Let us go and find a village to live in. There you can have food without catching birds, and I can have food without digging in the ground for it.'

'That would be delightful,' said the Cat. 'But how are we going to cross this great water?'

'Nothing could be easier,' said the Rat. 'We'll carve a boat from a manioc root.'

So the Cat and the Rat dug up a large manioc root. The Rat gnawed and gnawed with his sharp teeth, until he had made a hollow large enough to hold the two friends. While he was busy at this, the Cat scratched and scratched to make the outside of the boat smooth.

Then the Cat and the Rat made two little paddles and set out in their boat.

It was farther across the great water than it had looked from their island. Also they had forgotten to put any food in the boat. Presently the Cat began to say, 'Caungu! Caungu! Caungu!' which means, 'I'm hungry! I'm hungry! I'm hungry!'

And the Rat began to say, 'Quee! Quee!' which means in his language, 'I'm hungry! I'm hungry!'

But that did not do any good. They grew hungrier and

hungrier. At last the Cat said, 'Caungu! Caungu!' very faintly, and curled herself up to sleep. And the Rat said, 'Quee! Quee!' very faintly, and curled himself up also, at the other end of the boat.

But while the Cat slept, the Rat stayed awake and thought. Suddenly he remembered that the boat was made of manioc root. He had eaten so much while he was gnawing out the hollow that he had not wanted any more for some time, but now he said, 'Good! I will eat a little more and make the hollow deeper.'

So he began—nibble, nibble, nibble!

'What is that noise?' exclaimed the Cat, waking at the sound.

But the Rat had shut his eyes and pretended he was fast asleep.

'I must have been dreaming,' said the Cat. She laid her head down on her paws and went to sleep again.

The Rat began again—nibble, nibble, nibble!

'What is that noise?' cried the Cat, waking up.

But the Rat just pretended to be fast asleep.

'What strange dreams I have!' said the Cat, as she curled herself up and went to sleep again.

Again the Rat began to nibble very fast. Nibble-nibble-nibble!

The noise wakened the Cat.

'What is that noise?' asked the Cat.

But again the Rat pretended to be sound asleep.

'My dreams are certainly very troublesome,' said the Cat, as she curled up and went to sleep once more with her paws folded over her eyes.

Then the Rat began nibbling again. This time he gnawed a hole right through the bottom of the boat, and the water began to come in.

'What is this?' cried the Cat, jumping up quickly.

'Quee! Quee! Quee!' squealed the Rat, perching on one end of the boat.

'Caungu! Caungu!' miaowed the Cat, climbing up on the other end, for she did not like the water at all.

'Quee, quee!'

'Caungu! Ca-ung-u-u!'

'Quee, quee!'

'You did this, you wicked creature!' screamed the Cat.

'I was so hungry!' squeaked the Rat, and then the boat began to sink, and there was no more time for talk. They had to swim for their lives.

'I am going to eat you,' said the Cat, glaring at the Rat as they swam.

'I deserve it,' squeaked the Rat, 'but don't eat me now or you'll be choked by the water. Wait until we reach the shore.'

'I will wait,' said the Cat, 'but when we reach the shore I will certainly eat you.'

At last they reached dry land.

'Now,' said the Cat, 'I will eat you.'

'I deserve it,' said the Rat, 'but I am too wet to be good for eating just now. Let me dry myself, while you dry your own beautiful coat. I shall be ready when you are.'

They sat down and began to dry their coats. The Cat was intent on making her beautiful coat very smooth and glossy. She did not see that the Rat was busy digging a hole.

'Are you ready?' asked the Cat at last, when every part of her coat was dry and glossy and smooth.

'Certainly,' said the Rat, and disappeared into the hole.

'You rascal!' cried the Cat, for the hole was too small for her to follow.

'Quee, quee!' said the Rat from the bottom of the hole.

'You'll never get out of that hole alive,' said the Cat. 'I'll stay here and wait for you, and when you come out I shall eat you.'

'What if I never come out?' said the Rat. 'Quee, quee!'

'Then you can stay in that hole and starve,' said the Cat.

She settled down in front of the hole with her nose on her paws, watching for the Rat to come out.

'Quee, quee!' said the Rat in the hole, and began to dig deeper.

All day long the Rat went on digging.

All day long the Cat watched beside the hole.

When night came, the Rat had dug down under a tree and had come up on the other side. He crept out of the other end of his tunnel and went on to the village, while the Cat still watched at her end.

From that day to this the Cat is never so fast asleep that she does not hear the gnawing of a Rat, and she is never tired of watching for the Rat to come out of a hole. And from that day to this the Rat knows that if there is a Cat in the village where he goes to steal grain, he will find the Cat waiting for him at the other end of his hole in the ground.

African Folk Tale

The Mouse and the Weasel

There was once a hungry wee Mouse who was so thin she could get in and out of the tiniest holes.

One day she found a basket full of corn. If only she could get into that basket she would not be hungry any more. At last she found a tiny weeny hole, and she squeezed and squeezed till she had squeezed herself right through the hole into the basket. There she was surrounded by lots of good corn.

So she ate and ate until she could eat no more. Then she decided it was time to go home.

But she had eaten so much and grown so fat that she could not squeeze her way out of the hole. She pushed and pulled.

She pulled and pushed, but it was no use. She was far too fat. She squeaked and cried until a Weasel heard her.

'What is the matter, wee Mouse?' said the Weasel, trying to peep through the tiny hole at the mouse inside the basket.

'Well, it is like this,' said the wee Mouse. 'I had grown so thin that I was able to squeeze through that tiny hole you are peeping through, but after I'd eaten enough of the corn here I grew very fat. Now I can't get out at all.'

'Well, it's no use crying,' said the Weasel, 'you won't get out that way.'

'I don't want to stay here for ever,' cried the wee Mouse.

'If you really want to get out you must stop eating,' said the Weasel, 'until you are as thin as you were when you went in through the hole.'

Then the wee Mouse began to cry harder than ever.

Poor wee Mouse.

Retold from Æsop

The Dog in the Manger

A dog once made his bed in a manger. When the horses came for their food, the dog stood up on top of the hay and snarled. 'Wow! Wow! Keep away from here!'

'We've been working hard all day,' said the horses, 'and now we're hungry, so you clear off our hay.'

'Wow, wow! Wow, wow!' barked the dog.

'You're keeping us from our dinner,' said the horses.

'Wow! Wow! It's not your dinner, it's my bed!' said the dog.

'Nonsense,' said the horses, 'it's put there for us to eat, and if we don't eat we'll not be able to work.'

'You shall NOT eat my bed,' growled the dog.

'Stupid dog, what is the use of a bed you can't sleep in? And you'll not have peace to sleep on our dinner, and that's flat!'

'I'll NOT allow you to eat the hay even if you don't allow me to sleep on it!' persisted the stupid dog.

And I don't know how this story ends, do you?

Retold from Æsop

The Proud Little Mouse

There was once a little mouse who was very proud of himself. He wondered what he could do to show how great he really was.

Now, one day, he was sleeping in a dark corner of a hut, when he heard a strange noise and woke up with a start. He looked about him but could see nothing. Then he crept quietly towards the door, where he saw a great fire burning.

'Oh dear, now I'm going to be burned up,' cried the little mouse. 'Whatever shall I do?'

The fire grew bigger and brighter every minute. The little mouse was very frightened and tried to think what he should do.

'Well, I'll burn up if I stay here,' he thought, 'so I might as well try to get out.'

So he made a dash through the flames and out of the door. He was very surprised to find that he was not burned at all. He looked himself over carefully but his fur was not even singed.

'Now I know I am really great,' said the little mouse, 'for fire does not burn me at all.'

He walked about proudly, whisking his little tail and thinking how great he was. Then he looked back. You can imagine his surprise when he saw there was no fire after all. What he had thought was fire was just the bright sunshine at the door.

'How stupid of me,' he said. 'Now I wonder what I can do to show I am really great.'

He looked about for a long time until he saw a high bank.

'I know what I'll do, I'll jump over that high bank,' he said. When he got to the bank it looked very high indeed.

'If I can jump over this bank,' he said, 'I *shall* be great.'

Hop, skip and a jump, the little mouse sprang as high as he could into the air and came down on the other side of the bank.

'Surely I am great when I can jump so high,' said he. But when he looked back he saw that the bank was not high at all, it was just a little heap of sand.

'I am silly,' cried the little mouse. 'I really must do something great now.'

He looked about him until he saw a lake.

'That lake is very big,' said he, for he could only see a little way across. 'If I swim across that lake all the animals will say I am great.'

So he swam and he swam. He grew so tired he could only swim slowly and he swam all day, but at last he reached the other side.

'Now,' said he, 'I am really great for I swam across that lake.' And he lay down for a good rest. He was so tired.

When he got up he turned to look at the lake, but there was no lake at all. It was just a puddle of water.

'Oh, dear, I am stupid,' said the little mouse sadly, but for all that he would not give up the idea that he was really great. Then he saw a tall pole in the distance. When he reached it, he walked all round it, but when he looked up he could not see the top of it.

'That pole is so high it must hold up the sky,' thought he.

'Now, if I gnaw through the pole the sky will fall down on to the earth and that will be the end of everything.'

First the little mouse dug a hole in the ground, and when it was finished he scurried into the hole to see if it was big enough to hold him. 'That's where I'll go when the sky falls down,' said he.

He started to nibble and gnaw the pole with his sharp little teeth, until he had nibbled and gnawed the pole right through. Then he ran as fast as he could into his little hole, and waited for the sky to fall down. He waited and waited but nothing happened, so he peeped out of his hole. There was the sky where it always was, as blue and bright as ever. As for the great pole on the ground, it was just a tall bare stalk.

'Oh dear me,' cried the little mouse, 'I really am ashamed of myself. I am so ashamed, I shall try to carry that great hill across the moor.'

When he reached the hill, the little mouse dug all round with his little claws, then he lifted one grain of earth across the moor. Back and forth he went every day, taking one grain at a time, until at long last he had carried the whole hill across the moor. And all the time he was so busy he had not had time to worry whether he was great or not.

Eskimo Folk Tale

How Rabbit fooled
the Elephant and the Whale

One day little Brother Rabbit was running along liperty, liperty, when he heard the Whale and the Elephant talking. And this is what they were saying:

'You are the biggest animal on land, Brother Elephant,' said the Whale, 'and I'm the biggest animal in the sea. If we

join forces, we can rule all the other animals in the world, and
have our own way about everything.'

'Very good, very good,' trumpeted the Elephant, 'that
suits me, Brother Whale. We'll do that.'

'You won't rule ME,' thought little Brother Rabbit, and
away he ran and fetched a very long, very strong rope. He
took out his big drum and hid it in the bushes. Then he walked
along the shore till he met the Whale.

'Brother Whale, you're the strongest animal in the sea,'
he said. 'Please will you come and help me pull my cow.
She's stuck in the mud a mile from here and I can't pull her
out.'

'I'll help you, little brother,' said the Whale, fairly bursting with pride.

'Then I'll tie the end of this rope to you,' said the Rabbit,
'and I'll tie the other end of it to my cow. When all is ready
I'll beat on my drum, then you'll know it is time to pull on the
rope. You'll have to pull very hard for my cow is very heavy
and she's stuck very deep in the mud.'

'Huf!' said the Whale. 'Just leave it to me. I'll have her
out in no time!'

So little Brother Rabbit tied the rope to the Whale and off
he ran liperty, liperty, till he came to the Elephant.

'Brother Elephant, you are the biggest animal on land,' he
said, 'please will you help me. My cow is stuck in the mud a
mile from here and I can't pull her out.'

'I'll help you! I'll pull her out!' trumpeted the Elephant.
'No trouble at all!'

'Then I'll tie the end of this rope to you,' said the Rabbit,
'the other end is already tied to my cow. But first I'll go back
and make sure it is secure, and when all is ready I'll beat on
my drum. When you hear that, pull! Pull as hard as you can
for my cow is very heavy!'

'Just leave it to me,' said the Elephant grandly, 'I could
pull twenty cows!'

'Of course you could,' said little Brother Rabbit, 'only be sure to pull gently at first, then harder and harder till you get her.'

When he had tied the rope tightly round the Elephant's trunk, Brother Rabbit ran off into the bushes. There he beat his drum.

The Whale began to pull, and the Elephant began to pull. They pulled and pulled till the rope tightened and was stretched as hard as could be.

'Goodness,' said the Elephant, 'this must be a heavy cow!'

'Gracious!' said the Whale. 'This cow is stuck mighty fast!' He drove his tail deep into the water and pulled and pulled. He pulled harder and the Elephant pulled harder.

Soon the Whale found himself sliding towards the land, for the Elephant had managed to turn the rope round his trunk. This made the Whale so cross with the 'cow' that he dived head-first into the water, right down to the bottom of the sea. That WAS a pull.

The Elephant was jerked off his feet, and came slipping and sliding down the beach, into the surf. He was terribly angry.

He braced himself with all his might, and pulled as hard as he could. Up came the Whale out of the water.

'Who's pulling me?' spouted the Whale.

'Who's pulling *me*?' trumpeted the Elephant.

AND THEN THEY SAW EACH OTHER.

'I'll teach you to fool me!' fumed the Whale.

'I'll teach you to play "cow"!' trumpeted the Elephant.

Then they began to pull again. This time the rope broke. The Whale turned a somersault, and the Elephant fell over backwards.

The Elephant wouldn't speak to the Whale, and the Whale wouldn't speak to the Elephant. So the pact between them was broken.

As for little Brother Rabbit, he sat in the bushes and laughed and laughed and laughed.

American Folk Tale

The Rabbit and the Crocodile

There was once a Crocodile who lived by the river. One day he lay sunning himself, when the Rabbit came along.

'How do you do, Crocodile?' said the Rabbit, edging up towards him. 'You seem to be taking life easy. You certainly have a fine time. All you do is to sleep, eat, bathe and enjoy yourself.'

'Go away, and let me alone,' grunted the Crocodile, who was sleepy. And he shut his eyes.

Close to the Crocodile's nose there grew a nice juicy clump of young lettuce leaves.

'How good those leaves do look,' thought the Rabbit. 'There they grow right under that old Crocodile's nose, and he never eats them. I wonder if I could just quickly gather some and then run?'

The Rabbit crept nearer, and nearer, and nearer, but just as he got closer to the lettuce leaves the Crocodile woke up.

'Get out of here!' he roared, and he snapped so savagely with his sharp, white teeth that the Rabbit ran as fast as he could and never stopped until he reached home.

He told his wife and children about the selfish old Crocodile, so full of dinner he could not keep awake, who would not allow a hungry little Rabbit to gather the leaves he did not want himself. When the little rabbits heard why there was no supper for them that night, they had a great deal to say about the Crocodile.

'That is all very well,' said Father Rabbit, 'but when a cat is the judge, the mouse gets no justice. We cannot expect anyone else to settle this matter, we must do it ourselves. I have a plan. Come, all of you, gather some dried grass and sticks, and I'll tell you what we'll do. We'll go and lay all these dried-up sticks and grasses in a circle round the Crocodile while he is asleep. THEN we will set them on fire. That'll give him a fine scare and chase him away from all those good lettuces!'

All the little rabbits wriggled with joy and kicked up their heels at the thought of what was going to happen. They gathered armfuls of dried grass, sticks and leaves, and they laid them in a circle round the Crocodile. They set fire to it and it began to blaze up and smoke.

The little rabbits hid themselves in the bushes and kept as quiet and as still as mice.

'Crackle — snap — crackle — crackle — snap — snap — snap!' went the fire. But the Crocodile did not wake up.

'Snap! snap! snap!' went the burning grass. But the Crocodile did not wake up.

'Crackle! crackle! crackle!' went the burning twigs. But still the Crocodile did not wake up.

The smoke became thicker and thicker, and blacker and blacker. At last the rabbits could not see the Crocodile at all, but they heard him cough in his sleep. Then he turned over and coughed again.

'Haugh! Haugh! What's the matter? I can't breathe!' grunted the Crocodile.

Then he coughed and coughed, choked and choked, and opened his mouth so wide that a red hot spark flew into it. Then he woke up.

He tried to get away from the fire, but whichever way he turned, there it was in front of him. All the time it was scorching his tail. Then he made one big jump right out of the circle of fire.

His hide was so thick that he was not burned at all, but he was very, very scared and he was very, very angry. When he heard all the squealing and laughter of the little rabbits in the bushes, he was so angry he could only just speak.

'Don't you ever come near the river again!' he shouted, as he waddled off as fast as he could to get into the cool water and put mud on his burned tail.

'Don't *you* ever dare to come up here on land again!' shrieked the rabbits. Then they set about gathering all the beautiful juicy green lettuce leaves.

From that day to this, the rabbits never go near a river if they can help it, and the Crocodile never goes far away from a river if he can help it. He does not like to be reminded of the time he was caught in a fire by a trick and the rabbits laughed at him. But news travels far and fast in the Jungle. The Crocodile never heard the end of it.

African Folk Tale

Who killed the Otter's Young?

One day the Otter went to the Mousedeer and said, 'Mousedeer, please will you look after my young while I go to fish in the river?'

'Yes, I will,' said the Mousedeer.

But when the Otter returned from the river with a fine catch of fish, he found all the young otters crushed flat.

'What happened?' he cried. 'Who killed my young ones, Mousedeer, while you were taking care of them?'

'I am very sorry,' said the Mousedeer, 'but as you know, I'm chief dancer of the war-dance, and when the Woodpecker came and sounded the war-gong, I danced. I forgot your children and trod on them.'

'We must go to King Solomon to see what he has to say about this,' said the Otter. 'You'll be punished!'

'Well, Mousedeer, did you kill the Otter's young?' asked the King.

'Yes, your Majesty,' said the Mousedeer, 'but I did not mean to.'

'How did it happen?' asked the King.

'Your Majesty knows I am the chief dancer of the war dance,' said the Mousedeer. 'Well, when the Woodpecker sounded the war-gong, I had to dance. As I danced I trod on the Otter's young.'

'Send for the Woodpecker,' said King Solomon.

'Did you sound the war-gong?' he asked the Woodpecker.

'Yes, your Majesty,' said the Woodpecker. 'I had to.'

'Why was that?' asked the King.

'Your Majesty knows that I am the chief beater of the war-gong. Well, I sounded the war-gong because I saw the Great Lizard wearing his sword.'

'Send for the Great Lizard,' said King Solomon.

'Why did you wear your sword?' he asked the Great Lizard.

'Your Majesty knows that I am the chief swordsman,' said the Great Lizard, 'so when the Tortoise came along wearing his coat of mail, I had to wear my sword.'

'Send for the Tortoise,' said the King.

'Why did you wear your coat of mail, Tortoise?' he asked.

'I put it on, your Majesty,' said the Tortoise, 'because I saw the King-crab carrying his pike.'

Then the King-crab was sent for.

'Why were you carrying your pike?' asked the King.

'Because, your Majesty,' said the King-crab, 'I saw that the Crayfish had shouldered his lance.'

Immediately the Crayfish was sent for.

'Why did you shoulder your lance, Crayfish?' asked the King.

'Because, your Majesty,' said the Crayfish, 'I saw the Otter coming down to the river to fish and hunt my young.'

'Oh,' said King Solomon, 'if that is the case, the Otter really killed his own young, and the Mousedeer cannot be blamed for it at all.'

Eastern Folk Tale

Who is in the Hare's House?

Once upon a time there was a Caterpillar who went into a Hare's house when the Hare was away from home.

When the Hare returned, he noticed marks on the ground all round the door of his house, and cried, 'Who is in *my* house?'

'The fiercest creature in the world!' replied the Caterpillar in a very loud voice. 'I can trample down elephants!'

The Hare trembled when he heard this and turned back down the road muttering to himself, 'What can a small creature like me do with one that can trample down elephants? It must be enormous!'

On the road he met a Fox.

'Come with me, Fox,' he said, 'and talk to the fierce creature who has taken possession of my house!'

'I'll do that,' said the Fox, who thought himself a brave fellow. So when they reached the Hare's house, the Fox shouted in his fiercest voice, 'Who is in the Hare's house?'

'The fiercest creature in the world!' replied the Caterpillar. 'I can trample down elephants!'

When he heard that, the Fox turned and trotted off down the road, saying, 'I'm sorry, Hare, I can't help you. That creature is far too fierce for me!'

Then the Hare met a Tiger and begged him to drive out the fierce creature who had taken possession of his house.

'I'll do that with pleasure,' said the Tiger grandly. 'Who is in the house of my friend, the Hare?' he roared.

'The fiercest creature in the world,' replied the Caterpillar in his loudest voice. 'I can trample down elephants!'

'Then he'll do the same to me,' said the Tiger to himself. He hurried away without so much as a word to the Hare.

Then the Hare met an Elephant and begged him to come and drive the fierce creature out of his house.

'Who is in the house of my good friend, the Hare?' trumpeted the Elephant. But when he heard the Caterpillar's reply, he made off as fast as he could, crying, 'I've no wish to be trampled!'

Now, a Frog was passing at the time and asked what all the fuss was about. The Hare told him all that had happened.

'I'll see what I can do to help,' said the Frog. So he went up to the Hare's house and opened the door and called 'Who is in the Hare's house?'

'The fiercest creature in the world—I can trample down elephants!'

'Nonsense!' said the Frog, and instead of running away as all the others had done, he went nearer and croaked in his loudest voice, 'And *I*, who am the strongest and the greatest jumper, have come to get YOU!'

When the Caterpillar heard this he trembled, and when he saw the Frog coming nearer and nearer, he called out in a tiny little voice, 'I am only a little Caterpillar and I don't mean any harm!'

It was just as well that the Caterpillar was able to run out of the back door, for the Frog could have eaten him up in no time.

African Folk Tale

The Turtle and the Wolf

Early one morning, when the ground was cool and damp, a Turtle came out of his home in the river. He crawled along hunting for things to eat. He found so many good things that he crawled farther and farther away from the river. If he had been a wise little turtle he would not have wandered so far from home, for River Turtles have to keep themselves damp and cool. If they become too dry, and if the sun is too hot, they die.

Now, while this little Turtle was crawling along slowly, the sun came up and shone down on him. He turned and started back for the river, but he travelled so slowly and the sun was so hot, he only got half-way there. Then he climbed into a shady hole and began to cry.

He cried so hard and so loud that a Wolf, who was passing near by, heard him. The Wolf's ears were not very sharp and he thought it was someone singing.

'I must find out who is singing,' said he, 'and get them to teach me that song.'

So the Wolf peeped into the hole and saw the Turtle with big tears in his eyes.

'Good-day,' said the Wolf, who didn't notice the tears, 'that was a nice song you were singing. Will you teach it to me?'

'I wasn't singing,' cried the Turtle.

'Oh, yes, you were. I heard you. I want to learn that song, and if you don't teach it to me, I'll swallow you whole!'

'That won't do you any good,' said the Turtle. 'I've a hard shell and that will hurt your throat!'

'Well, if you don't teach me to sing, I'll throw you into the hot sun!' said the Wolf.

'That won't hurt me,' said the Turtle. 'I'll just draw in under my shell!'

'Well, then,' said the Wolf, 'I'll throw you into the river if you don't sing!'

'Oh, please, Mr Wolf, don't throw me into the river,' said the Turtle. 'I can't sing at all, but you mustn't throw me in the river. I might drown!'

'Yes, I will!' said the Wolf. He picked up the Turtle and threw him, splash! into the river.

The little Turtle swam out under the water where the Wolf could not reach him. Then he stuck his head up out of the water.

'Thank you very much, Wolfy, for throwing me into the river! This is my home!'

And the old Wolf trotted home feeling very cross indeed.

African Folk Tale

The Fox and the Turkey

One day a hungry Fox went out to hunt. He had a good place to hunt in, for north of his den was a stretch of wood where wild turkeys and other animals lived. He was looking for something good to eat.

He hunted for a long time until he was tired. Suddenly he caught—what do you think?—a big fat Turkey. He was going to take the Turkey back to his den, when the Turkey said, 'Oh, Mr Fox, are you ill? You look so pale and tired out! Don't you think you should have a rest? You lie down and have a nap and I'll go down to your den and tell your wife to cook me for your supper. Poor fellow, you really do look sick!'

This sympathy made Mr Fox feel quite ill.

'That is very kind of you, Turkey,' said he. 'No tricks, mind. I'll be watching you.'

So the Turkey set off down the path to the Fox's den, and

the Fox watched him carefully until he saw him knock on the
den door, then he lay down under a tree and fell fast asleep.

When the Turkey reached the door of the Fox's den, he
knocked loudly on the door.

'Who's there?' called Mrs Fox.

'Just a friend with a message for you,' said the Turkey.

'Won't you come in?'

'No, thank you, I'm in a hurry. Mr Fox asked me to tell
you that he'll be home soon, and he wants you to have his
supper ready. He says cook up all those odds and ends of meat
you have.'

Then the Turkey ran off as fast as he could.

Mrs Fox got busy and cooked a large pot of all the bits and
pieces she had in the larder.

Presently Mr Fox came home. He smacked his lips at the
thought of the delicious turkey supper he was going to have.

Mrs Fox brought in a large pot and set it down on the table
before Mr Fox.

He bit off a large piece of meat and began to chew. He
chewed and he chewed and he chewed.

'This is the toughest turkey I've ever tasted,' he said. 'It
just tastes like all the bits and pieces of meat you could find.
It doesn't taste like turkey to me! What is wrong with it?'

'Turkey!' exclaimed Mrs Fox. 'I've no turkey! These *are*
the bits and pieces of meat I had in the larder. Someone
knocked at the door this morning. He said this is what you
wanted for your supper. So here it is!'

Well, didn't that old Fox choke and splutter and nearly fall
off his chair with rage when he heard what a trick the
Turkey had played on him. Mrs Fox choked and spluttered
too into her apron but, do you know, her choking sounded
more like laughing.

African Folk Tale

The Stone Monkey

Long, long ago, on top of the Flower and Fruit mountain, there lay a stone egg. It lay there on the grass until one day it split with a crack and out came a monkey of polished stone.

Soon the stone monkey was surrounded by a crowd of chattering monkeys. One of them came forward, spoke to the monkey and said, 'Will you be our king?'

'I will,' said the stone monkey, 'but first I will travel in search of wisdom.'

So he went down the mountain to the sea-shore where he made himself a raft and sailed away. He sailed on and on till he came to the other side of the ocean. He clambered ashore and went to the house of a magician.

'Will you teach me some magic?' he asked the magician.

'I will,' said the magician, 'I'll teach you to make yourself invisible, to fly into the sky and leap any number of miles in one jump.'

The monkey soon learned these tricks. He could do them with such ease that he thought himself no end of a fine fellow, and made up his mind to become Lord of the Skies.

Now the word went round about the monkey and his magical tricks and one day a prince went to the great Lord Buddha.

'Have you heard of this new king of the monkeys?' he said. 'He has learnt a lot of magical tricks and has been up to all sorts of mischief. He thinks he knows everything!'

'Does he indeed!'

'And what is more, he says he will turn the Lord of the Skies out of his palace and make himself Lord of the Skies instead. Will you help us, Lord Buddha, to deal with this monkey before he makes any more trouble?'

'I will do my best,' said the great Lord Buddha.

Off they went together to the Palace of the Skies. Here they found the stone monkey insulting everybody.

The Lord Buddha spoke to him quietly and said, 'What do you want, stone monkey?'

'I want to be the Lord of the Skies. I could manage things better than they are managed at present. See how I can jump!'

And the stone monkey jumped a great big jump. In a moment he was out of sight, and in another moment he was back again.

'Can *you* do that, Lord Buddha?' he asked.

The great Lord Buddha smiled.

'I'll make a bargain with you. You shall come outside the palace with me and stand on my hand. Then, if you can jump out of my hand, you shall be the Lord of the Skies. But if you cannot jump out of my hand, you will be sent down to earth.'

'Jump out of your hand, Lord Buddha? Why, I can easily do that!'

So they went outside the palace, the Lord Buddha put out his hand, and the stone monkey stepped on to it. He gave one big jump, and away he went out of sight.

On and on he went till he reached the end of the earth There he stopped and chuckled to himself.

'I'll soon be Lord of the Skies!' said he.

Then he saw five great pillars standing at the edge of the world, with nothing but an empty space beyond. He scratched a mark on one of the pillars.

'I'll bring the Lord Buddha here to see it for himself! Then he took another big jump, and in a moment he was back in the Lord Buddha's hand.

'When are you going to jump?' asked the Lord Buddha, when the monkey stepped down from his hand to the ground.

'I *have* jumped!' cried the monkey. 'I jumped to the very end of the world. If you want to see where I've been, you've only to get on to my back and I'll take you there. There are five red pillars at the edge of the world and I scratched a mark on one of them for you to see.'

'Look here, monkey,' said the Lord Buddha, holding out his hand. 'Look at this!'

The stone monkey looked. On one of the fingers of the Lord Buddha's hand was the very mark he had made on the red pillar.

'You see,' said the Lord Buddha, 'the whole world lies in my hand. When you jumped you thought yourself out of sight, but my hand was under you all the time. No, not even a stone monkey can ever get beyond my reach. Now, go down to earth and learn to be a real monkey.'

Eastern Legend

IV

STORIES ROUND THE YEAR

Persephone

Once upon a time there was a goddess of the cornfields, and her name was Demeter. Everyone believed that it was her magic that encouraged the brown seeds in the earth to send up green shoots. They said she had only to touch the corn for it to grow, and turn yellow and ripen under the ear, and she had only to lay her hand on a tree to be sure the blossoms would show, and the branches hang low with fruit before a year had passed.

All the creatures depended on Demeter for their food, and sometimes they called her their Earth Mother.

Now, Demeter had a daughter called Persephone, whom she loved better than anything else in the world. They went everywhere together. Demeter could not bear to be parted from her.

One day Persephone wandered up the hillside into a high meadow to gather wild herbs, when she saw a flower she had not seen before. She stretched out her hand to pick it, but instead she pulled the plant up by the roots. Then the earth opened up into a great cavern, and out of the cavern galloped four splendid black horses, drawing a golden chariot, and in the chariot stood a dark king wearing a golden crown. It was Hades, King of the Underworld.

Persephone was very frightened and turned to run away, but Hades caught her and lifted her up into the chariot.

'You must come with me,' he said, 'to be the Queen of the Underworld.'

'Let me go, let me go,' cried Persephone, but Hades only cracked his whip and galloped his horses back into the cavern, which closed behind them, leaving no trace of what had happened.

When Persephone did not return home, Demeter was very distressed. She wandered about the countryside without eating or drinking for nine days and nine nights; but she found no trace of Persephone, and no one could tell her where her daughter was or what had happened to her.

After many adventures, Demeter met a herdsman who told her that he had seen the earth open up and a chariot drawn by four black horses drive into the opening. He remembered because his own herd of swine had been swept into the earth too.

'Tell me,' said Demeter, 'was there anyone in the chariot?'

'There was,' said the herdsman. 'A dark chariot-driver, wearing a crown, and beside him was a pale, frightened girl.'

Demeter was in despair, for she knew now that Persephone had been carried off by Hades, the powerful god of the Underworld, and that there was little she could do to release her daughter.

She was so angry and distressed, that she wandered about the earth forbidding the corn to grow or ripen, or the plants to bear fruit.

Soon there was a famine, and all the creatures were starving, but Demeter refused to help until Persephone was allowed to return to her.

Zeus, the king of the gods and goddesses, promised her that she would have her daughter back if Persephone had not eaten any food in the Underworld. At the same time he ordered Hades to allow the girl to return home, and he sent his messenger, Hermes, to fetch her.

Hades knew he could not keep Persephone unless she ate some of his food, and he had been unable to persuade her to eat even a crumb of bread. So he went to her and said, 'You seem unhappy here, and your mother frets for you, so I have decided to send you home,' pretending it was his own idea.

At once Persephone smiled at Hades for the first time. She was so happy.

Hermes helped her into his chariot, but just as they were

leaving, one of Hades' gardeners held up a broken pomegranate.

'I saw Persephone eat three seeds from this fruit, your
Majesty!' said he.

The girl grew pale when she heard this, for she knew that
Hades now had power over her, and she wished with all her
heart she had not been tempted by the beautiful pink fruit.

Hades smiled and told his gardener to accompany Persephone as a witness.

You can imagine how delighted Demeter and Persephone were
to see each other again, but when Demeter heard about the
pomegranate seeds, she was very sad and dejected. Then she
said she would not help anything to grow unless her daughter
was returned to her for ever. On the other hand Hades was
equally determined not to lose Persephone. The gods were in
despair. It seemed that everything on the earth would perish.

At last they thought of an idea.

Because she had eaten the three pomegranate seeds,
Persephone was to stay with Hades as his Queen for three
months of every year, but she must be allowed to return to her
mother and the earth above for the remaining nine months.

Hades and Demeter both agreed to this plan, and so
Persephone stayed with her mother for nine months and while
she stayed, Demeter looked after all that grew in the earth.
She touched the corn and it grew, turned yellow and ripened,
and she laid her hands on the trees and they blossomed, and in
time their branches hung low with fruit.

But when Persephone had to return to the Underworld,
Demeter hid herself once more, and for three months nothing
grew. It was the first winter. But the men and animals on the
earth did not despair, for they knew Persephone would come
back and that for nine months all would be well again, and
they called these nine months, Spring, Summer and Autumn.

Greek Myth

Echo

There was once a nymph called Echo who liked to talk to her friends and tell them stories. Some of them grew tired of her chatter, but others loved to listen to her tales, for she was indeed a good story-teller.

Now, Echo and her friends were the maids of Queen Hera, the goddess of the Skies. She was a very strict mistress, and although they were happy, there were many things her nymphs were not allowed to do. They were not allowed to stay out late or go to some of the merry parties on Olympus. The Queen said they were far too young. There was one party they especially wanted to go to, but she would not hear of it. Then Echo had a plan.

'The Queen likes my stories,' she said to her friends.

'And you like telling them,' they teased.

'True enough,' admitted Echo, 'and that is why I've thought of a plan which may help you to go to the party without the Queen knowing you've gone.'

'What is it?' cried the nymphs. 'Tell us, Echo, please tell us your plan!'

'Well, to-night, after supper, I will stay and tell the Queen all my best stories,' said Echo, 'and she'll be so interested she won't notice you going to the party.'

'But she'll see we're not in our beds, and wait up for our return,' said the nymphs, 'and then there'll be trouble!'

'Don't worry—just leave it to me,' said Echo, 'I can keep the Queen interested all night with my stories!'

So, that night, Echo went to the Queen and said, 'Your Majesty, I have some new stories. Would you like to hear them?'

'Splendid,' said the Queen, 'come, sit down here beside me, and I will lie on my divan and listen.'

Echo sat on the floor beside the Queen, and told her one story after another. They were well told, and the Queen, who had had a tiring day, was only too pleased to have nothing to do but listen. Whenever she started to tell Echo it was time to go to bed, the nymph said, 'First let me tell you this story,' and so it went on until the Queen fell fast asleep.

It was early in the morning before those nymphs returned from the party, but Queen Hera did not hear them or notice that they had been away, and all would have been well if someone had not told her what had happened that night. Then she was more angry than she had ever been. She was most angry of all with Echo, and punished her much more severely than the others. It was the worst punishment she could give to a storyteller. She took away Echo's voice.

'Never again will you speak or be able to tell your wonderful tales,' said the Queen. 'From now on you shall be dumb. But, as you always liked to have the last word, you'll be allowed to repeat the last words of others.'

'Others,' cried poor Echo, trying to protest. But she could say no more, and in despair, she ran into the hills of Thespia, and wandered about, living on berries and sleeping under bushes.

One day she saw a handsome boy netting stags. She followed him through the forest, longing to speak to him but unable to say a word. He was very handsome indeed, and all who saw him loved him, and his name was Narcissus.

At last Narcissus heard a movement behind him in the trees, and turned to see who it was. He saw no one, so he called, 'Is anyone here?'

'Here!' repeated Echo.

'Come and show yourself then,' said Narcissus. 'Come!'

'Come!' answered Echo, running out to meet him, her arms outstretched.

When Narcissus saw Echo, thin and bedraggled, he turned his back on her.

'Go away,' he said, angry with disappointment. 'Go away, and leave me alone!'

'Alone,' cried poor Echo, as she ran off into the mountains and hid herself in a cave. There she stayed until she faded into the rocks, and all that remained of her was her voice.

And now, when we are in caves or mountains or glens, our voice seems to be repeated. We can hear it, far away. 'This place has an echo!' we call to each other. 'Echo!' We hear it again, and the sound is sad and lonely.

Greek Myth

Narcissus

One day Narcissus was wandering through a wood when he saw a beautiful clear pool. He was very thirsty, and as the water looked fresh and cool, he knelt down to take a drink.

When he leaned over the water he saw his reflection for the first time. (You see, there were no mirrors in those days.) Narcissus thought he had never seen such a beautiful face. He tried to touch it, but immediately it disappeared in the ripples of water his movement made, and only reappeared when the water was still.

Now, if Narcissus had had friends with him they would have told him he was only looking at his own reflection; instead he stayed, not daring to move for fear the face in the water would vanish.

He stayed there so long, that at last he became a flower. The flower still bears his name—Narcissus.

Greek Myth

Saint David

Long, long ago there was a prince in Wales called Sandde. One day an angel appeared at his side and said, 'To-morrow, down by the riverside, you will kill a stag, catch a fish and find a honeycomb. You must keep them in a safe place and give them to the son that will be born to you. The honeycomb is for courage, the fish for wisdom and the stag will help him to crush the serpent of evil.'

'I will do that,' promised Sandde, 'but when will my son be born?'

'In three years' time,' said the angel.

Well, next day, down by the river, Sandde saw a stag and killed it. Then he caught a fish and, sure enough, found a comb of honey nearby. So he put all three in a safe place—just as the angel had told him.

Three years passed and a son was born to Sandde and his wife, Nonna. The prince remembered his promise and gave his son the stag, the fish and the honeycomb that had been kept so carefully for him, and they called him David.

When he was being baptised, David dipped his small hand into the holy water and splashed it on to the blind eyes of the bishop who was baptising him. At once the old man was able to see. So everyone knew, right from the beginning, that David was a special person and different from other boys. Not that he set himself apart from them—he did not—and, because he did many things they were afraid to do, they admired him and made him leader.

When he grew up David became a monk. He gathered other young monks around him and together they built a monastery with their own hands. Some made books, writing and illus-trating them, while others worked outside, ploughing the fields and growing their food. They kept a great number of bees so that they had a good supply of honey for all the poor and sick people who came to them for help. One young monk, who looked after the bees, was asked to go to Ireland to work. He was sorry to leave his bees and they were so attached to him that they followed him on to the ship.

'Let me take the bees with me, brother David,' he pleaded.

'There are no bees in Ireland, there are not enough flowers,' said David, 'but with God's blessing, these will live there happily and their honey will enrich the land.' Then he blessed the bees. They sailed away with the young monk, and that is how bees first came to Ireland.

In those days Wales was constantly attacked and invaded by the Saxons. There were fierce battles and often the wounded were nursed back to health by the monks. They noticed that many of the wounds had been inflicted accidentally by their own side, in the confusion of battle, and naturally this greatly distressed David. One day there was news of a Saxon invasion and the Welsh soldiers mustered outside the monastery.

Now, the monks ate little meat, living mainly on vegetables, including the wild leeks that grew everywhere in Wales. Well, David and his monks gathered baskets full of these green leeks and took them to the Welsh captain.

'Tell each of your men to wear a leek in his helmet,' said David, 'so that in the confusion of the battle, he will know his friend from his foe.'

'I'll do that,' replied the captain. 'You and your good monks have saved the life of many a Welsh soldier. If the leeks save only one more they will have been worth the wearing!'

So the Welsh soldiers wore the leeks and, sure enough, when the battle was over, there were fewer casualties and none of them bore the marks of Welsh weapons. To this day Welshmen wear leeks or eat them with their dinner on Saint David's day and the leek has become the national emblem of Wales.

David was so well known as a preacher that people came from the length and breadth of the land to hear him. One day, as he stood preaching in the open air, there were so many people that some complained they could neither hear him nor see him. Then suddenly a white dove flew down and perched on his shoulder, the earth under his feet rose until it was a hill and his voice sounded loud and clear for all to hear. One can still see the church that was built on the top of that hill in his honour.

It is said that, wherever Saint David preached to a large crowd, this miracle was repeated and that is why there are so many hills in Wales. What is quite certain is the deep impression Saint David made on the Welsh people and the affection they feel for their national saint. His day is March 1st.

Saint Patrick

Once upon a time there was a boy called Patrick, and one day he was captured by pirates and taken over the sea to Ireland, where he was sold as a slave. His master was not an unkind man and he put Patrick in charge of his pigs. But the boy was very lonely away from his parents, his brothers and sisters. He longed to see them all again and, as he wandered over the green hillside herding the pigs, he wondered how he could escape, when he heard a voice say, 'Go, Patrick, the ship is waiting for you!'

Patrick was amazed for there was no one to be seen, and he thought his guardian angel must have spoken to him. So that night he made his way down to the beach, and sure enough, there was a ship ready to sail for Scotland.

Patrick begged the Captain to take him on board.

'Please let me sail to Scotland with you,' he said.

'Very well, then,' said the Captain, 'I'll take you. But if you're caught, I'll get into as much trouble as you will.'

At last Patrick reached his home. You can imagine how delighted his family were to see him again, and to hear all that had happened to him.

After a while, Patrick grew restless. He knew that, much

as he loved them, he could not stay with his family for ever. He wanted to become a priest, and return to Ireland to help the poor peasants he had seen there. It was a bold plan for a runaway slave to have but, after studying hard for several years, he not only became a priest, but he was given permission to sail to Ireland.

The first thing he did when he got there was to see his old master. At first the old man was very angry, but he admired Patrick's courage, and in the end they became good friends, and he helped the Saint in many ways.

The people listened to Patrick as he told them about the Christian faith, and soon he became so well known that the King of Ireland invited him to Court. But when the Queen became a Christian, the King was very angry, and made plans to get rid of him.

When Patrick left the Court, the King ordered his soldiers to waylay and kill him. The soldiers lay in ambush for Patrick, but no one passed except a herd of red deer. At last they returned to the King and told him what had happened. He was very troubled for he guessed that Patrick's God had protected him and his friends by disguising them as a herd of deer, and so they had escaped unharmed. After that the King did not try to hurt Patrick.

One day the people begged Patrick to drive away the snakes that infested the land. He said he would try, and taking a drum, he climbed to the top of a high hill, beating it as he went. The snakes of Ireland followed the sound of his drumming until they had all gathered about him on the hill top. Then he waved his staff towards the sea, and commanded them to throw themselves into the sea, which they did. And after that not one snake was seen in the fair land of Ireland.

Although the people listened to Patrick and loved him, they found it very difficult to understand all he tried to teach them. They could not understand this, and they could not understand that, but most of all they could not understand the

Holy Trinity. How could there be a Father, a Son and a Holy Spirit, all in one God? So Patrick picked a leaf from a wild flower, called a shamrock, and he showed them the three small leaves that made up the one large leaf, and at once they understood.

And so the people of Ireland chose Saint Patrick as their patron saint, and made the shamrock their national flower. Saint Patrick's Day is March 17th.

The Easter Hare

Long, long ago there was a village where the people were very poor. One Easter-time the mothers had no money to buy the presents of sweets they usually gave to their children on Easter Sunday. They were very sad for they knew how disappointed the children would be.

'What shall we do?' they asked each other, as they drew water from the well.

'We have plenty of eggs,' sighed one.

'The children are tired of eggs,' said another.

Then one of the mothers had an idea, and before dinner-time all the mothers in the village knew about it, but not a single child.

Early on Easter morning, the mothers left their homes and went into the woods with little baskets on their arms. It was quite impossible to see what they had in the baskets as they were covered with coloured cloths. When the mothers returned home, the cloths were tied about their heads like head-squares, and the baskets were filled with wild flowers.

'My mother went to pick flowers for Easter this morning,' said one child, as they all walked together to church.

'So did mine!' said another.

'And mine too!' said all the others, and laughed for they were happy and it was Easter Sunday.

When they came out of church, the children were told to go and play in the woods before dinner. Off they ran, laughing and talking. The girls picked flowers and the boys climbed trees, when someone shouted, 'Look what I've found!'

'A RED egg!'

'I've found a BLUE one!'

'Here's a nestful! All different colours!'

They ran about searching in the bushes and filling their pockets and hats.

'What kind of eggs are they?' they asked each other.

'They're too big for wild birds' eggs.'

'They're the same size as hens' eggs!'

'Hens don't lay eggs these bright colours, silly!' Just then a Hare ran out from behind a bush.

'They're Hares' eggs!' cried the children. 'The Hare laid the eggs! The Hare laid the eggs! Hurrah for the Easter Hare!'

German Legend

The Coming of the King

One day some children were playing in their playground when the newspaper boy rode past on his bicycle shouting, 'The King! The King is coming! Make way for the King!'

'Hurrah! Hurrah! The King is coming!' cried the children, and some jumped up and down, some turned cartwheels, and some even tried to stand on their heads, they were so excited.

Then they stood and looked at their playground. It was very untidy. Scraps of sweetie paper, empty ice-cream cartons, lolly sticks and broken toys lay about all over the place, just where the children had dropped them. They were very careless children.

'If the King looks over the wall he'll see how untidy and dirty our playground is, and I don't think he'll like it,' said one.

'He may stop us from playing here,' said another.

'Let us tidy it up and make it as nice as we can for the King when he comes,' said the littlest one.

So the children picked up all the scraps of sweetie paper, all the empty ice-cream cartons, all the lolly sticks and the broken toys.

Then one fetched a rake, another a hoe, while the littlest one brought a great big brush. They raked, they hoed and they brushed until they had an enormous heap of rubbish.

'What shall we do with it?' said one.

'We can't leave it here,' said another.

But the littlest one had already fetched the wheelbarrow to put the rubbish in.

'It is clean and tidy, but it does look bare,' sighed one.

'Let's fetch a seat and cover it with a red cloth, and lay a red carpet on the ground. Then perhaps the King will come into our playground and talk to us,' said another.

'We can gather flowers to make it look gay. I'm sure a King likes flowers,' said the littlest one.

So one fetched a seat and covered it with a bright red cloth, another brought a red carpet and laid it on the ground, while the littlest one and all the others gathered flowers, pussy willows and yellow catkins.

When it was ready, the playground looked so beautiful that the children stood and looked at it, and clapped their hands with delight.

They waited all day for the King, but he never came. They were just going home for tea when a man passed along the road and looked over the wall. He had a kind but very tired face, and his clothes were old and travel-worn.

'What a beautiful place,' said he as he stopped to look at the flowers. 'May I rest here for a while, children?'

The children opened the gate and led the man to the seat they had covered with the red cloth.

'Rest here,' they said. 'This is our playground. We made it ready for the King, but he did not come.'

'And now we mean to keep it as nice as this always,' said one.

'That is good,' said the man.

'We think pretty and clean is nicer than ugly and dirty,' said another.

'That is better,' said the man.

'And tired people can rest here,' said the littlest one.

'That is best of all,' said the man.

He looked at the children with such kind eyes that they told him all they knew. About the five little puppies in the barn, the four blue eggs in the blackbird's nest, and the three kittens the ginger cat had hidden in the wash-house. They told him about the twin lambs who grew fatter every day, and the new calf with the wobbly legs. The man listened and understood it all, and when he was rested he stood up and shook hands with them.

'Thank you, children. And now I must go on my way, and you must go home for your tea.'

The children stood by the wall and watched the man as he walked down the road in the evening sunlight.

'He looked very tired,' said one.

'But he was very kind,' said another.

'See how the sun shines on his hair,' said the littlest one. 'It looks like a crown of gold.'

From *The Golden Windows* by Laura E. Richards.

Saint George and the Dragon

Long, long ago there was a crusader knight called George who had so many strange adventures, and performed so many wonderful feats that it is impossible to count all the marvellous stories told about him. But there is no doubt that he was brave and valiant.

The story people remember best is the story of his fight with the dragon. Now, it happened that a fierce dragon was roaming the countryside, scorching the earth and killing any creature that came its way. At length and in desperation, the people made a pact with the dragon by which one of them was sacrificed each day, and in return he left the rest of them in peace.

Well, at last it was the turn of the young princess. Everyone was very sad, but it seemed there was nothing they could do to save her, and the poor girl had to go. As she stood there before the dragon, trembling with fright, she suddenly saw a handsome knight riding towards her, carrying a spear and a pennon — a red cross on a white ground. He stopped beside her, lifted her up into the saddle and rode with her to the safety of a high rock. There he left her while he rode out to fight the dragon.

It was an unequal combat, for the dragon was enormous. It was breathing great flames of fire and lashing at the earth with its tail.

For three days and three nights, Saint George fought the dragon. On the fourth day he was able to drive his sword into its weak spot which was just below its ear, and it sank to the ground with a terrible wail. The dragon was dead, the princess was safe, and the people were freed from the dreadful monster that had ruined their land.

Since the time of King Edward III, George has been the patron saint of England. His day is April 23rd.

What happened to Mustard

This is a story about Mustard, the little yellow cat, and about something that happened to him not very long ago.

One morning he was sitting on the grass in the front garden. He had been very busy washing himself, licking his paw and wiping it round and round his face. Now he was quite clean. He didn't know what to do next, so he just sat and watched the road beyond the front garden, waiting for something to happen.

Very soon something did happen. A great big van, the biggest van Mustard had ever seen, stopped outside the garden gate. It was a green van, with yellow letters painted on it, and it was even bigger than the coalman's lorry, and *that* was the biggest thing Mustard knew. Presently two men, wearing white aprons, got down from the driving seat at the front and walked round to the back of the van. Mustard couldn't quite see what they were doing but ... clank! ... clank! ... clank! ... clank! ... what a noise! The men pulled down the back of the van, for it was really a sort of door.

Mustard ran across the grass and climbed quickly up one of the trees by the gate so that he could see right into the van. It was almost empty. Only a few sacks and boxes were inside. The two men in white aprons opened the garden gate and walked up to the front door of the house.

'I wonder what they want?' thought Mustard. 'I've never seen them before.'

He sat on the branch of the tree and his green eyes watched and watched. They watched the men go back to the van and bring the sacks and boxes indoors. Mustard could hear the men's heavy boots clumping about the house. 'Clump! ... Clump! ... clump! ... clump!' they went. It sounded as if they were walking on floors which had no carpets on them.

'Goodness me!' said Mustard to himself. 'Look what they

are doing now! They are taking away the blue carpet from the hall and putting it into the big van. What *can* be happening?'

He watched the men bring out some more rolls of carpet. Then they brought out some chairs, then a table, then a sideboard, then a cupboard, and then . . . and *then* . . . they brought out Mustard's basket, Mustard's very own round basket with the brown cushion in it. And they put the basket into the van, with the carpets and the chairs and the table and the sideboard and the cupboard.

'Well!' said Mustard. 'My basket! Well!'

As soon as the men had gone inside the house again, Mustard jumped down from the tree and ran out of the front gate. He saw a wooden board which stretched like a hill from the ground to the floor of the big van. Up the hill he ran and into the van he pranced. This was fun.

'Miaouw! miaouw!' he laughed, showing his little pink tongue. 'Miaouw, miaouw.'

He ran round and round the inside of the big van, jumping on the chairs and on the table. And then, behind the cupboard, he found . . . his very own basket. He jumped into the basket and curled himself round on the soft brown cushion.

'A . . . a . . . a . . . ah! Mia-a-o-u-w!' he sighed. 'I *am* so tired.'

It was quite dark in that corner of the van behind the cupboard, and in a few minutes Mustard was fast asleep. He stayed asleep for a long time, and then suddenly, 'Clank! . . . clank! . . . clank! . . . clank!' What a noise! Mustard opened his eyes. Where *was* he? What was this strange, dark place full of tables and chairs and cupboards and rolls of carpet? Oh, yes! Of course! He was inside the big van. And the clank . . . clank . . . clank . . . clank must have been the noise the men made when they shut the van doors.

'Oh dear!' cried Mustard, sitting up in his basket. 'Oh, miaouw, miaouw! I'm shut in.'

Now he could hear the children calling him from the front garden.

'Mustard!' they called. 'Mustard, where are you?'

'Miaouw, miaouw!' cried the little yellow cat.

'Mustard! Come along! We're going in the car to the new house and we want to take you with us.'

'Miaouw! Here I am! Miaouw!' called Mustard, from the inside of the van.

But the children couldn't hear him. They were terribly worried, for they couldn't think where he could be.

'Honk! honk!' went the horn on the van. 'Honk! honk!' And the big, green van began to move slowly away, with the little yellow cat shut up inside it.

Mustard lay down again in his basket behind the cupboard. He didn't know where they were going, nor what was happening. But it was very comfortable on his nice brown cushion, and he was having a lovely ride.

After a little while, the van began to slow down. Then it stopped altogether.

'Clank!. . . clank!. . . clank!. . . clank!' What a noise! The men were opening the door at the back of the van. Mustard jumped out of his basket and ran towards them.

'Why, here's a little cat!' said one man.

'Oh, Mustard! Darling Mustard! He must have been in the moving van all the time. And we thought he was lost.'

'Miaouw!' cried Mustard happily.

'Come and see the new house, Mustard. Come along! This is where we're all going to live now.'

They picked him up and carried him into the house.

'We'll bring the little cat's basket indoors in a minute,' promised one of the white-aproned men.

The children said, 'Thank you very much,' and then they hugged Mustard more tightly than ever.

'What a clever little cat!' they said. 'He found the new house all by himself.'

'Miaouw!' said Mustard. And because he loved being hugged and stroked he purred as loudly as he could. Brr . . . brr . . . brr . . . brr. . . .

From *A Story a Day*, by Doris Rust

Pandora and the Box

Long, long ago, when the world was young, there were no troubles at all. Everyone was kind, beautiful and gay, and the sun always shone in a blue sky.

Now, there was one girl who was different, and her name was Pandora. She too was kind, beautiful and gay, but she was also *very* inquisitive. If Pandora saw a door, she wanted to open it. If she saw a wall, she wanted to look over it and see what was on the other side, and if she saw a drawer, she wanted to see what was inside it. Nobody minded, for everything was shared and there was nothing to hide.

One day Pandora was playing with her friend, Epimetheus, when she noticed a box that she had not seen before.

'What's in this box?' she asked.

'I don't know,' said Epimetheus. 'It's not to be opened.'

'Why not?' asked Pandora.

'I don't know "why". I just know that it must NEVER be opened.'

'Who said so?'

'The man who left it here. I don't know his name. He wore a cap of feathers and carried a staff with two serpents twisting round the end of it, and he had wings on his ankles. They were to help him to fly.'

'That must have been Mercury, the messenger of the gods,' said Pandora. 'He brought me here, so I expect the box was meant for me.'

'Well, you'll be told when you can open it. Leave it alone now, and come and play!' said Epimetheus. 'Come on, Pandora!' And he ran out into the sunshine.

But Pandora stayed and looked at the box. The more she looked the more she wondered what was inside. She looked at the carvings on the outside and at the curious fastening. It was not locked but tied with a knot of gold cord. She fingered the knot and she looked at its twists and turns. It could be untied without Epimetheus knowing, and retied after she had looked inside.

But when the box lay there unfastened, Pandora was afraid to raise the lid, and so she tried to tie the knot again, but the gold cord just refused to be tied, and from inside the box came a babble of tiny voices, making a most unpleasant sound. They were angry, quarrelsome voices, and she had not heard angry quarrelsome voices before.

'Let us out, Pandora!' they cried. 'Let us out! Open up the lid and let us out!'

This was too much for Pandora. If she had been frightened before, she was ten times more frightened now. So she raised the lid and peeped in.

As she did so, a black cloud hid the sun, and the room darkened. She could not see inside the box at all, but she felt a swarm of winged insects as they brushed past her, buzzing.

At that moment Epimetheus ran into the room. He had not seen a black cloud before, and he wondered what it was. Suddenly he let out a cry:

'I've been stung!'

Pandora let the lid fall with a crash. But it was too late. All around her, in the half light, buzzed a swarm of ugly little creatures. Some like hornets, some like bats, all looking like little demons. One landed on her forehead and would have stung her had Epimetheus not brushed it off.

'What are they?' she cried. 'What are they?'

'Troubles, troubles!' came the answer from somewhere. 'You have let out all the troubles of the world, Pandora!'

And that is what she had done. They were all around her, and she was afraid.

'Open the window, Epimetheus!' she cried. 'Open the window, and let them out!'

Epimetheus opened the window, and away they flew to tease and torment the world.

Then Pandora heard a little tap coming from inside the closed box, and she heard a little voice say, 'Please open up the lid and let me out!'

'Not I,' said Pandora. 'Enough trouble has come from the box already!'

'I know that,' said the little voice, 'but I have come to help you!'

'Shall I let the creature out?' Pandora asked Epimetheus.

'Do as you like!' snapped the boy, who, for the first time in his life, was in a bad temper.

'Please, Pandora,' pleaded the voice. 'Please let me out— I'm your only hope!'

'All right, I will,' said Pandora. But when she tried to raise the lid she found it was too heavy for her.

Then Epimetheus ran across the room to help her, and between them they raised the lid.

Out of the box came a light. When it shone on Pandora she felt happier, and when it shone on Epimetheus he was in a better temper.

'What are you?' cried Pandora.

'What is your name?' asked Epimetheus.

'Your name, your name?' cried the children.

'My name is HOPE!'

And away it flickered, out of the window, to help all the world.

Greek Myth

Clytie

Once upon a time there were water nymphs who lived in the streams and rivers. They liked swimming about under the water, and playing with the otters and water rats. Early every morning they came up out of the river and had great fun with these little creatures. But as soon as the sun began to rise, off they went, for they had been told they must never look at the sun. It would be too bright and too hot for them.

Now, there was a water nymph called Clytie who was very disobedient. She wanted to do whatever she was told she must *not* do. She was usually in trouble for one thing or another. Well, Clytie was curious to see what the sun looked like. She was always the last to return home, and every day she stayed on the river bank instead of diving into the water and swimming home like all her friends.

One morning she watched the sun grow bigger and bigger until one of its rays touched her. She was frightened by its brightness but it did not burn her. She had never before seen anything so beautiful.

Then she saw the Sun-god himself. He stood in a golden chariot drawn by four winged horses. Clytie was astonished. She sat there looking and looking at the Sun-god, as he drove his chariot slowly across the sky. When at last he disappeared behind the hills, everything grew cold and dark, and Clytie dived into the water and swam home.

She did not tell anyone where she had been all day. She knew she would not be allowed to go above water again if she did, but she thought of nothing but the Sun-god and his golden chariot. She did none of the things she was supposed to do, and when morning came she did not play with her friends. She just sat at the water's edge until sunrise; then she climbed up on to the river bank to watch for the Sun-god.

At last, far away in the east she saw him coming. And when

he was above her in the sky, she smiled and hoped he would smile back. But he was a great king and he did not see her.

Every day Clytie stood on the river bank watching him. Even when he had gone down behind the hills, she refused to return to her home under the water.

In the end, her feet became rooted to the spot where she stood, and her green dress became leaves, and her golden hair and face became a sun-flower.

Greek Myth

Arachne

There was once a girl called Arachne. She lived with her parents in a fishing village on the shores of the Mediterranean. They were poor, and while her mother was working in the fields or looking after the house, Arachne sat, all day long, spinning.

One day, her father, who was a fisherman, came home with a basketful of little shell fish, and with these fish he made a dye, a bright cerise red.

Now Arachne went out every evening to gather the wool left by the sheep on the rocks and bushes. Although she washed and carded it, it always remained a dirty cream colour. So when her father was able to dye the wool she had spun a brilliant cerise, Arachne could weave wonderful patterns into her cloth. Soon she was weaving tapestries, great big pictures of trees and flowers, animals and birds, and all so life-like that people from far away came to see them.

One day, when she was weaving the picture of a bowl of cherries into her tapestry, birds flew down and tried to peck them off they looked so real. These tapestries made Arachne famous and rich.

It is a pity that all this good fortune made Arachne proud and arrogant, for arrogance makes people do stupid things, and it was stupid of Arachne to defy a goddess. Well, this is how it happened. There was a crowd of people watching her as she worked, when one of them remarked that the goddess Minerva could not weave as well as Arachne, and that surely she must have been taught by the goddess herself.

Now, Arachne did not know that the goddess had indeed stood, unseen, beside her, guiding her hand. Perhaps if she had known this she would have thought twice before saying that she would enjoy a match with Minerva.

'Then we'll soon see who is the better weaver,' she said.

No sooner had she said this, than an old woman came forward wearing a grey cloak.

'Do not speak lightly of Minerva,' said the old woman.

'I shall say and do what I like,' said Arachne, furious with the old woman for interfering. But her anger turned into astonishment when the cloak fell from the old woman and the beautiful goddess, Minerva, stood in her place.

Arachne was frightened, but her fear was not as great as her pride, and she still insisted on having a weaving match.

So two frames were set up, and Minerva and Arachne each started to weave a tapestry.

Minerva's tapestry was a picture of the fate of boastful mortals like Arachne, while Arachne wove a picture of some of the foolish things the gods had done.

This made Minerva more angry than ever. She snatched the tapestry from Arachne, and tore it into little pieces.

Arachne was really frightened now, but it was too late. Minerva struck her on the forehead with her shuttle.

'As you think you are so good at spinning and weaving,' said the goddess, 'you shall spin and weave for the rest of your life.'

And at once Arachne shrank to a small creature no bigger than a bee. In her new shape, she ran and hid herself in a dark corner. She now had to earn her keep by spinning webs of fine, fine thread, in which she caught flies, just as her father had caught fish.

After that she was always called the Spinner. And from that day to this, Arachne's children weave their fine webs in dark corners and under bushes, and we call them spiders.

Greek Myth

King Midas and the Touch of Gold

Long, long ago there was a Greek king called Midas. One day, in return for a kindness, Bacchus, the Wine-god, promised the king anything he wished.

Now, nothing gave King Midas more pleasure than gold. He could not have enough of it. He had a vast collection of jewels and precious stones but, of all his treasures, he liked gold best. So he asked that whatever he touched would turn to gold.

'Do you think the touch of gold will bring you happiness?' asked Bacchus.

'How can it fail to do so?' replied the greedy king.

'Very well then,' said Bacchus, 'the touch of gold is yours.'

The king could scarcely believe his good fortune. He thought he must be the luckiest man on the earth. He could not wait to try his power, so he picked a branch from the nearest tree. Immediately it turned into pure gold. He could not believe it, so he touched a pebble and, sure enough, it at once changed into a nugget of gold. He picked an apple, and there was a golden apple in his hand. It was true, there was no doubt about it. He had the golden touch.

Then the king sat down to the meal that had been prepared for him. The corn was fresh, the grapes were sweet and juicy.

He felt quite hungry, but when he put a grape to his mouth it turned into a small hard ball of gold, and so it was with all the food he tried to eat. Even the water turned to gold when he tried to drink it.

Suddenly King Midas understood the meaning of the touch of gold and he was afraid.

When his children came running to meet him he told them to keep away from him, for now he dare not touch them. Then he realised that gold was not so important after all, in fact he now hated the sight of it. So he went to the god, Bacchus, and begged him to take this terrible gift from him.

Bacchus felt sorry for King Midas, for he knew he was a stupid rather than a bad king, and he told him to go and wash in the spring where the river Pactolus rises and that the fresh waters of that spring would wash away all traces of the golden touch.

King Midas did this and was freed from the strange magic, which seemed to flow into the spring, for to this day the river Pactolus flows over golden sands.

Greek Myth

King Midas and the Ass's Ears

You remember the story of King Midas and the touch of gold? Well, after he had washed away the touch of gold in the river, King Midas often visited his friend, Pan, the god of the shepherds, who lived in the woods near by.

Pan was a jolly fellow and quite unlike the other gods. He had pointed ears and horns, and the legs of a goat. All day long he played his reed pipes, and the music he made was so merry that all who heard it forgot their troubles and danced.

King Midas liked to listen to Pan's music, for then he

forgot his worries and danced like the rest. But no one enjoyed his music more than Pan himself.

'My pipes are sweeter than Apollo's lyre,' he boasted. Everyone laughed and said there should be a contest between them. To Pan's surprise, Apollo accepted the challenge, and Mulmus, the river god, agreed to be the judge.

On the day of the contest, Apollo, tall and handsome, arrived with his lyre. The music he made was so fine even the birds stopped singing to listen.

When it came to Pan's turn, he smiled as he lifted his pipes to his lips. He knew perfectly well that his simple music could not compete with Apollo's. He started to play one of his merry tunes when Mulmus, the judge, stopped him.

'We all like your music, Pan,' he said. 'It is gay and it makes us feel gay too, but it really cannot be compared with Apollo's fine music. I'm sure you will agree with me that Apollo is the better musician and the winner of the contest.'

'I agree, Mulmus,' said Pan good-naturedly. 'I accept your judgement.'

'Nonsense! Nonsense!' shouted King Midas, who really did prefer Pan's simple tunes, and found Apollo's too difficult to enjoy. 'The judgement is unfair. I protest! I say Pan is the better musician!'

Everyone at the contest laughed at this stupid outburst. Everyone except Apollo. He did not laugh. He was very angry indeed, and he stared scornfully at the ears of King Midas that had made such a foolish choice. Then slowly those ears began to grow until they were long and furry, like the ears of an ass.

Of course this caused great amusement, and King Midas ran off, trying to cover his ears with his hands. He knew that the gods had punished him for being stupid, and that made him all the more ashamed of his unsightly ears. So he covered them with a turban which he always wore, and in time people forgot about his ears.

One day, when the court barber was trimming the King's

hair, he caught sight of the long furry ears. He was so
surprised that he nearly clipped them with his scissors.
However, he was a wise man and did not mention it to anyone, although he longed to do so.

At last he could keep the information to himself no longer,
but instead of telling a neighbour, as most of us would have
done, he went to a lonely marsh, dug a little hole in the mud,
and whispered into the hole, 'King Midas has the ears of an
ass! King Midas has the ears of an ass!'

Then he covered up the hole and buried the secret. But
after a while, some reeds grew on that very spot, and whenever the wind blew, the reeds whispered, 'King Midas has the
ears of an ass! King Midas has the ears of an ass!'

And soon everyone knew, and now *you* know it too!

Greek Myth

The Rescue

Jenny and Jean were twins. They both had blue eyes, pink
cheeks and two brown pigtails tied up in red ribbons.

Jenny had a red woollen jersey, and so did Jean.

Jean had a pair of tartan pants and so did Jenny.

Jenny had red shoes and so did Jean.

In fact, they looked as alike as two peas, and sometimes
their mother could not tell one from the other. But they were
quite different really. Jean was quick and sharp as a needle,
while Jenny was slow and dreamy, and her mother had to tell
her twice before she would do what she was told. Not because she was naughty; she just did not listen. But Jean did it
quick as quick because she was Jean.

One day they went to the seaside for their summer holidays.
They stayed at a nice pink house beside the sea, and every

morning they went on to the beach. They took their buckets and spades and dug in the sand till Mother came down with their swimsuits and towels.

One morning Mother said, 'Come, children, the tide's in! I'll give you your swimming lesson.'

Jean was ready when Jenny came, trailing a long piece of seaweed, her pail full of treasures.

'Come on, slow coach,' called Mother.

Then Jean and Jenny pushed their brown pigtails into white rubber caps, and jumped about in their bright yellow swim-suits. Mother took Jenny's right hand and Jean's left hand, and away they ran together across the sands to the sea.

Jean loved the sea and she jumped up and down, splashed about and tried to float, but Jenny stood at the edge of the water, shivering and trying hard not to cry. She did not like the sea at all. It was too cold and too enormous altogether.

'I'll give Jean her lesson first, shall I?' said Mother. 'You jump about and keep yourself warm.' Jenny nodded, and did as she was told.

She watched Mother hold Jean's chin, and heard her say, 'Kick your legs up and down! That's right. Now paddle like a puppy!' Jenny wished she liked the sea and could learn to swim too.

Just then she heard a cry. She turned and saw a tiny boy struggling to get up out of the water. He must have been paddling for he was wearing his jersey and it was soaking wet.

'Mummy, Mummy! There's a wee boy in the water!' she screamed. But the sound of the wind and sea was so loud Mother did not hear her, and she was much too busy to notice that anything was wrong.

Jenny did not waste another moment. She ran into the sea to help the little boy. She tugged at his jersey, put her arms round him, and pulled and pulled and pulled. Although he was smaller than she was, he felt like a sack of potatoes, and she was afraid she would fall into the water on top of him.

'Help! Help!' she screamed as hard as she could.

Luckily a man heard her and came running to help them. He lifted Jenny and the little boy right up out of the water, before you could say 'Jack Robinson!'

Just then Mother and some other people noticed what was happening. They came running up with towels and very anxious faces.

'Whatever happened?' asked Mother.

'The tiny boy fell in the water,' said Jenny, her teeth chattering with cold.

'He might have been drowned if this brave lass hadn't gone to help him,' said the man.

Mother was busy rubbing Jenny with a towel, and the little boy's mother was rubbing him with a towel.

'But, darling, you don't like the sea,' said Mother to Jenny.

'Then she's a real heroine,' said the man, patting Jenny on the back.

When both children were dry, Mother said to the little boy, his mother and the man, 'Come and have a shivery bite and a nice hot drink. I've two full Thermos flasks so there is plenty for us all!'

Next day a great big box arrived for Jenny. She opened it and inside, what do you think there was? Not one doll, but two! They both had blue eyes, pink cheeks and brown pig-tails tied with red ribbon, but one had a red dress and the other had a blue dress.

'Oh, aren't they lovely!' said Jean. 'I like the one with the red dress best!'

'She's for you,' said Jenny. 'I like the one with the blue dress, and I think I'll call her Kate.'

Do you know, the next time they had a swimming lesson, Jenny was not afraid of the sea at all, and in a short time she was able to swim just as well as Jean.

Norah Montgomerie

My Naughty Little Sister and the Workmen

When my sister was a naughty little girl, she was very, very inquisitive. She was always looking and peeping into things that didn't belong to her. She used to open other people's cupboards and boxes just to find out what was inside.

Aren't you glad you're not inquisitive like that?

Well now, one day a lot of workmen came to dig up all the roads near our house, and my little sister was very interested in them. They were very nice men, but some of them had rather loud shouty voices sometimes. There were shovelling men, and picking men, and men with jumping-about things that went, 'ah-ah-ah-ah-ah-ah-aha-aaa,' and men who drank tea out of jam-pots, and men who cooked sausages over fires, and there was an old, old man who sat up all night when the other men had gone home, and who had a lot of coats and scarves to keep him warm.

There were lots of things for my little inquisitive sister to see, there were heaps of earth, and red lanterns for the old, old man to light at night time, and long poley things to keep the people from falling down the holes in the road, and workmen's huts, and many other things.

When the workmen were in our road, my little sister used to watch them every day. She used to lean over the gate and stare and stare, but when they went off to the next road she didn't see so much of them.

Well now, I will tell you about the inquisitive thing my little sister did one day, shall I?

Yes. Well, do you remember Bad Harry who was my little sister's best boy-friend? Now this Bad Harry came one day to ask my mother if my little sister could go round to his house to play with him, and as Bad Harry's house wasn't far away, and as there were no roads to cross, my mother said my little sister could go.

So my little sister put on her hat and her coat, and her

scarf and her gloves, because it was a nasty cold day, and went off with her best boy-friend to play with him.

They hurried along like good children until they came to the workmen in the next road, and then they went slow as slow, because there were so many things to see. They looked at this, and at that, and when they got past the workmen they found a very curious thing.

By the road there was a tall hedge, and under the tall hedge there was a mackintoshy bundle.

Now this mackintoshy bundle hadn't anything to do with Bad Harry, and it hadn't anything to do with my naughty little sister, yet, do you know, they were so inquisitive they stopped and looked at it.

They had such a good look at it that they had to get right under the hedge to see, and when they got very near it they found it was an old mackintosh wrapped round something or other inside.

Weren't they naughty? They should have gone straight home to Bad Harry's mother's house, shouldn't they? But they didn't. They stayed and looked at the mackintoshy bundle.

And they opened it. They really did. It wasn't their bundle, but they opened it wide under the hedge, and do you know what was inside it? I know you aren't an inquisitive meddle-some child, but would you like to know?

Well, inside the bundle there were lots and lots of parcels and packages tied up in red handkerchiefs, and brown paper, and newspaper, and instead of putting them back again like nice children, those little horrors started to open all those parcels, and inside those parcels there were lots of things to eat!

There were sandwiches, and cakes and meat pies and cold cooked fish, and eggs, and goodness knows what-all.

Weren't those bad children surprised? They couldn't think how all those sandwiches and things could have got into that old mackintosh.

Then Bad Harry said, 'Shall we eat some?' You remember he was a greedy lad. But my little sister said, 'No, it's picked-up food.' My little sister knew that my mother had told her never, never to eat picked-up food. You see she was good about *that*.

Only she was very bad after, because she said, 'I know, let's play with it.'

So they took out all those sandwiches and cakes, and meat-pies and cold cooked fish and eggs, and they laid them out across the path and made them into pretty patterns on the ground. Then Bad Harry threw a sandwich at my little sister and she threw a meat-pie at him, and they began to have a lovely game.

And then do you know what happened? A big roary voice called out, 'What are you doing with our dinners, you monkeys—you?' And there was a big workman coming towards them, looking so cross and angry that those two bad children screamed and screamed, and because the workman was so roary they turned and ran and ran back down the road, and the workman ran after them as cross as cross. Weren't they frightened?

When they got back to where the other workmen were digging, those children were more frightened than ever, because the big workman shouted to all the other workmen about what those naughty children had done with their dinners.

Yes, those poor workmen had put all their dinners under the hedge in the old mackintosh to keep them dry and safe until dinner-time. As well as being frightened, Bad Harry and my naughty little sister were very ashamed.

They were so ashamed that they did a most silly thing. When they heard the big workman telling the others about their dinners, those silly children ran and hid themselves in one of the pipes that the workmen were putting in the road.

My naughty little sister went first, and old Bad Harry went after her. Because my naughty little sister was so frightened she wriggled in and in the pipe, and Bad Harry came wriggling in after her, because he was frightened too.

And then a dreadful thing happened to my naughty little sister. That Bad Harry *stuck in the pipe* and he couldn't get any farther. He was quite a round fat boy, you see, and he stuck fast as fast in the pipe.

Then didn't those sillies howl and howl.

My little sister howled because she didn't want to go on and on down the roadmen's pipe on her own, and Bad Harry howled because he couldn't move at all.

It was all terrible, of course, but the roary workman rescued them very quickly. He couldn't reach Bad Harry with his arm, but he got a long hooky iron thing, and he hooked it in Bad Harry's belt, and he pulled and pulled, and presently he pulled Bad Harry out of the pipe. Wasn't it a good thing they had the hooky iron? And wasn't it a *very* good thing that Bad Harry had a strong belt on his coat?

When Bad Harry was out, my little sister wriggled back and back, and came out too, and when she saw all the poor workmen who wouldn't have any dinner, she cried and cried, and told them what a sorry girl she was.

She told the workmen that she and Bad Harry hadn't known the mackintoshy bundle was their dinners, and Bad Harry said he was sorry too, and they were really so truly ashamed that the big workman said, 'Well, never mind this time. It's pay-day to-day, so we can send the boy for fish and chips instead,' and he told my little sister not to cry any more.

So my little sister stopped crying, and she and Bad Harry said they would never, never meddle and be inquisitive again.

From *My Naughty Little Sister* by Dorothy Edwards

Home is best

There was once a Squirrel who lived in a wood. His home was an old oak tree. Up and down the tree, in and out of his hole he ran.

When summer was over, he made a cosy nest in the hole, and put all kinds of nuts in it so that he'd have plenty to eat in the winter, when there were no nuts to be found.

While he worked away at his winter store and home, he heard the birds chirping away to each other. They were all talking about the long journey they were going to make.

'Where are you going?' asked the Squirrel.

'To a far-away land where there is no winter,' said one.

'Where the trees do not lose their leaves!'

'Where there are plenty of flowers and nuts!'

'Where the sun shines warmly all day long,' said the rest.

'It sounds wonderful,' said the Squirrel. 'Could I go too?'

'Why not—just follow us over the blue hills.'

'When will you go?'

'Any day now,' said the birds. 'The swallows will go first, then the linnets will go, then the geese will go, and you can't miss them.'

'I'll think it over,' said the Squirrel, and went on building his nest. But when a cold east wind came, and the leaves began to fall, the Squirrel thought of the warm land where the sun shone warmly all day long, where there were plenty of flowers and nuts, where the trees did not lose their leaves, and where there was no winter.

One day the Squirrel made up his mind to follow the birds. On and on he went all day, but the blue hills still seemed as far away as ever, and the birds were soon out of sight.

'If only I had wings,' said he as he stopped to rest.

Just then a big Hawk flew down and picked up the Squirrel. It was going to carry him away and eat him, when another

Hawk had the same idea, and tried to snatch him from the first.

They began to fight over the Squirrel, and in the fight the first dropped him.

Down, down he fell, right on to the top of a big oak tree. The little Squirrel was quite dizzy, but soon he scrambled down the tree, out of sight of the birds.

And what do you think? In their fight, the Hawks had flown back to the Squirrel's wood and this was his very own oak tree.

He soon found his hole, and he crawled into his warm nest and ate some nuts. Then he curled up and went to sleep.

After that he always stayed at home for the winter.

From *Another Story Please!*, by Richard Wilson

Rip Van Winkle

Once upon a time there lived a man called Rip Van Winkle. He was the laziest man in the village. He just refused to work.

'You're a lazy good-for-nothing!' his wife scolded.

But Rip lay in the sun and went to sleep.

He didn't sleep all the time. Sometimes he sat under the trees in the village square and gossiped. The children gathered round him for he told them stories and mended their toys.

One day his wife said that there were no skins to make the children warm fur caps and gloves and jackets, and there was already a nip in the air.

Rip loved his children so he made a great effort to stir himself. He got out his gun, cleaned and oiled it, and slung it over his shoulder. He whistled to his dog, Wolf, and off he went up the mountain to shoot martins and squirrels. On and on he climbed until he came to a high wooded slope near the top of the mountain. He had never gone so far before.

'Wolf! Wolf! Come away, lad!' he called to his dog. 'We'll stop here and have a bite to eat.'

Wolf sat down beside his master and watched him open his knapsack. Suddenly the dog's fur stood on end and he gave a low whine.

'Rip Van Winkle! Rip Van Winkle!' called a voice.

Rip looked round and there, coming towards him, was an old, old man carrying a keg as big as himself.

'Rip Van Winkle,' said the old man, 'help me carry this keg.'

'I'll do that,' said Rip, 'it's far too heavy for you.' All the time he wondered how the old man knew his name and who he could be.

On and on they went, the little old man in front with Rip behind, the keg under one arm and his gun over his shoulder. At last they came to a glen Rip had not seen before. There, on a stretch of green grass, was a crowd of little old men playing skittles. They stopped their game and brought their empty flagons over to the keg. The flagons were filled, and they returned to their game.

There was still a little liquor left in the keg, so Rip drank it. At once he felt drowsy. His eyes closed and he fell into a deep sleep.

*   *   *

When Rip Van Winkle awoke, he found himself back on the mountain side, where he had first seen the little old man.

'Goodness,' said he, 'I must have been dreaming and asleep here all night.'

He was surprised to find how stiff he was. He could scarcely rise from the ground. Stranger still, he found he had a long white beard! That reminded him of the little old man with the keg. He called to his dog, but no dog came, and when he found his gun it was rusty and useless.

'Whatever can have happened to me?' he said. 'I'll get a poor welcome when I arrive home with no skins and a rusty gun.'

He scrambled down the mountain side, but the way had changed and it was difficult to find the path to the village.

The village had also changed. There were many more houses, rows and rows of them. He had never seen so many people and they wore such strange clothes. He didn't know any of them and they didn't know him. They all stared at him curiously, at his clothes and his rusty old gun.

'Are you looking for someone, old man?' they asked.

'I'm on my way home to my wife and family. My name's Rip Van Winkle.'

'We know plenty of Rip Van Winkles, old man,' they laughed. 'That's our nick-name for men who won't work! There was a man of that name here long, long ago, but he went off and never came back.'

'Don't torment the old man,' said a buxom woman with rosy cheeks. 'And let the name of my father alone.'

'You remind me of my youngest daughter, Judith,' Rip told her.

'My name is Judith,' said she. 'Now, come home with me, and I'll give you a bowl of soup. You look very tired.'

Rip felt tired, and he was very, very hungry. Slowly he began to realise that, somehow or other, many, many years had passed since he left home, although it seemed only yesterday. And this kind woman was indeed his little daughter, Judith.

Warmed by the good soup, Rip Van Winkle sat in his daughter's house, and told her and her family all that had happened to him that day on the mountain side. They said he must have been with the Little People, and he had been lucky to get away from them after drinking their wine, for few mortals returned home after staying with them. Rip

lived with his daughter, and people came from near and far
to hear his strange story.

Retold from Washington Irving

The Seven Sisters

Long ago there was a beautiful Moon-goddess called Diana.
Her favourite sport was hunting, and every night she rode
through the forest on her white horse, followed by her hounds
and her seven maids all dressed in white. They were the
seven daughters of King Atlas, and they ran like the wind
but, even so, Diana often left them far behind.

One night, a giant called Orion was out hunting, when he
caught sight of the seven sisters running through the trees.
They looked to him like a flock of beautiful white birds, and
at once he hoped to catch one of them.

When the sisters realised Orion was chasing them, they
were very frightened and ran off as fast as they could. On and
on they ran through the forest and over the mountains, and
all the time they heard the hunter coming nearer and nearer.
When they saw he was gaining ground, they called to Diana
to help them.

Then Orion saw seven beautiful white birds open out their
wings and fly up into the sky, out of his reach. Diana had
changed the seven sisters into white doves.

Higher and higher they flew till they became seven bright
stars. There they remained, and people called them the
Pleiades.

Orion could not forget the beautiful white birds, and
instead of hunting, he spent the rest of his life searching for
them. It is said that, at the end of his life, he was put into the
sky beside them. And sure enough, on clear nights, you can

see the three stars of his belt, and the stars that mark his head, shoulders, legs and sword. But the cluster of bright stars called the Pleiades, or Seven Sisters, still seem to be running away from him, and he never overtakes them as he chases them across the sky.

Greek Myth

Arion and the Dolphin

There was once a musician called Arion, who wandered about the country singing songs, and wherever he sang, people stopped to listen.

When the King of Corinth heard his music he invited Arion to live with him in the Royal Palace.

One day Arion received an invitation to compete at the music festival in Sicily.

'You must go,' said the king, 'for I am sure you will win the competition, and the prize is a bag of gold.'

'The gold does not interest me,' said Arion, 'but I would like to compete and of course I would like to win!'

'You may go in one of my ships,' said the king, 'but promise you'll return, for I shall miss your music.'

Arion promised to return and away he sailed in the king's ship over the sea to the island of Sicily.

All the best musicians in the world were there to compete. One by one they played their instruments and sang their songs, and then it was Arion's turn. He sang so beautifully that the King of Sicily awarded him the first prize, a bag of gold, and all his admirers gave him wonderful gifts of jewels and other treasure. They tried to persuade him to stay on in Sicily but Arion refused.

'I have promised the King of Corinth I shall return,' said

he, 'and his ship waits there in the harbour to carry me home.'

So the King of Sicily and all Arion's friends and admirers saw him off and waved him farewell.

Arion stood on the prow waving to them until they were out of sight, but when he turned to go to his cabin, he found himself surrounded by the captain and an angry crew. They had seen the gold and treasure Arion had carried on board, and had plotted among themselves how they could take it from him.

'You must die,' said the captain. 'It is the wish of the entire crew.'

'Why, what have I done to hurt you?'

'You are too rich,' said the captain.

'Spare my life, and I will give you the bag of gold and all the other treasures that were given to me,' pleaded Arion.

'No, we cannot do that, for when you reach Corinth you may change your mind, regret your gift, and make us return it,' said the captain. 'No, it is too dangerous. You must die!'

'Very well,' said Arion, 'I see that your minds are made up. But please, grant me my last wish. Allow me to sing one more song before I die.'

'You may do that,' said the captain, 'if, when the last note has been sung, you leap overboard, into the sea.'

Arion promised to do this and, dressed in his finest clothes, he stood on the prow of the ship and sang more sweetly than he had ever sung before. Then he took a great leap into the sea; and the ship sailed on.

Now, a school of dolphins had gathered round to listen to Arion's songs, for dolphins are very fond of music. When he leapt from the ship, one of them swam under him, caught him on its back, and saved him from drowning. Then the dolphin swam with Arion on its back and reached Corinth long before the ship.

The king was delighted to see Arion, but when he heard how the ship's crew had treated him, he was very angry indeed.

'I am astonished my sailors could behave so badly,' he said.

When, at last, the ship arrived in port, the king sent for the crew.

'Where is Arion?' he asked, pretending he did not know.

'He stayed in Sicily,' said those rascals. 'He was enjoying himself so much he refused to return with us, although we waited several days for him.'

'Is that so?' said the king frowning with anger.

Then Arion himself came into the room. He was wearing the same clothes in which he had leapt from the ship, and, when they saw him, the captain and the crew were terrified.

'A ghost! A ghost!' they cried out. 'Arion was drowned, and this must be his ghost!' And in their fright they confessed to the king all they had done to Arion. The king punished them, and ordered them to leave Greece for ever.

As for Arion, he stayed at Corinth and became one of the greatest musicians in all Greece.

Greek Legend

The Fire Makers

Long, long ago, the natives of the Australian bush, the black-fellas as we call them, had no fire. They used to eat their food raw or dried by the hot sun. They knew of no way to cook it.

One day a blackfella, called Bootoogah, was rubbing two pieces of wood together, when he saw a faint spark and a tiny wisp of smoke rise from them.

'Look, Goonur!' he said to his wife, 'see what comes when I rub two sticks together, a spark! Wouldn't it be good if we could make fire to cook our food and did not have to wait for the sun to dry it?'

'It would indeed,' said Goonur. She watched her husband rub the sticks together and saw the spark and wisp of smoke.

'Split your stick, Bootoogah,' she said, 'and let us put a tiny piece of dry grass in the opening. Then even a tiny spark may kindle a flame.'

'I'll try that,' said Bootoogah, who knew his wife was a wise young woman. Sure enough, after a lot of rubbing, there in the opening was a small flame. At once Goonur held a piece of dried bark to the flame, and the wood smouldered and burned. They had discovered the art of making fire. It was indeed a great day.

'We'll keep this a secret from the others,' said Bootoogah. 'We'll go into the Bingahwingul scrub to make our fires. There we can cook our food in secret.'

'We'll hide our fire-sticks in the open-mouthed seeds of the Bingahwinguls,' said Goonur, 'but one stick we'll always carry in our combee bag.'

After they had caught some fish, they took it to the Bingahwingul scrub. There they rubbed their sticks and made a fire with bark wood. Then they put their fish in the smouldering bark ash, and when they took it out it smelt and tasted better than anything they had eaten before. Instead of having to chew and chew and chew, this fish was so tender it seemed to melt in their mouths.

When they returned to the camp, they took some of their cooked fish with them. The other blackfellas noticed how different it looked from their sun-dried fish.

'What did you do to that fish?' they asked.

But Bootoogah and Goonur refused to tell them, and every day, after catching their fish, these two disappeared and returned later with their fish cooked and looking very different from that of the others. Always they refused to say how they had cooked it. So the tribe appointed two of their men, Boolooral and Quarrian, to follow them and find out what they did.

Next day after the fish was caught, Bootoogah and Goonur took their share and, as usual, disappeared with it into the

Bingahwingul scrub. Here the two men who had been
following them lost sight of them. Their tracks vanished in
the thick scrub and there was no sign of them. But there was
a high tree on the edge of the scrub, so the two men, Boolooral
and Quarrian, climbed it. From the top of the tree they could
see all there was to be seen for miles around.

They saw Bootoogah and Goonur throw down their load
of fish, open their combee bag, take out a stick, which they
rubbed, blew on and laid in the middle of a small heap of dried
twigs. At once a flame leapt from the heap and the fire-makers
fed it with small pieces of bark and stick. Then as the flames
died down, they placed their fish in the hot ashes.

So that was how they cooked their fish! They could
actually make fire! The two men in the tree were astonished.

They went back to the camp and told the tribe all they
had seen. There was great excitement. The tribe had long
wanted to find the way to make fire, for it seemed to them
that once they could do this, there was no end to the things
they could make. If only they could get hold of that combee
bag that held the secret fire-sticks. They knew Bootoogah and
Goonur would not give it up and they had no desire to hurt
them or take it from them by force. So they decided to hold a
Corrobboree, which is a sort of dance festival.

'Let it be the biggest and the best Corrobboree we've ever
had,' said one of the elders. 'We'll make those two so
interested in the dances they'll forget all about their precious
combee bag. While they're intent on the dancing, one of us
can seize the bag, and take out the fire-sticks. Then we can
have fires for the good of all. Beeargah shall be the one to do
this. He must pretend he is sick. He can tie a bandage round
his head and lie on the ground beside Bootoogah and Goonur
while they watch the dancing. He must watch like a hawk
for a chance to seize the bag and act quickly.'

'I'll do that,' agreed Beeargah.

Having made their plan, the tribe prepared for a great

Corrobboree. They invited the other tribes, especially the Bralgahs, who were celebrated for their wonderful dancing.

Everyone agreed to come and soon all were busy with the preparations. Each tribe determined to outdo the others in the brightness of their decoration for the Corrobboree.

As each tribe arrived they got a loud cheer from the rest. The Beeleers, the black cockatoo tribe, had bright splashes of orange paint on their black skins. The Pelican tribe had painted themselves white all over with just a little patch of black here and there where the white paint had rubbed off. The Black Diver tribe had merely polished their black skin until it shone like ebony.

Then, last of all, came the Bralgahs. They were very tall and dignified and held their heads high. They had painted their bodies grey and their heads a bright red. They were certainly very handsome.

Never before had the younger blackfellas seen such a splendid gathering.

Among the spectators were Bootoogah and his wife, Goonur, with her precious combee bag slung over her shoulder. They had decided not to join in the dancing for fear they might lose the bag, so they found a good place on a slope where they would be able to see all that was going on. They did not take much notice of Beeargah when he came and lay down on the ground beside them. He looked rather sick and appeared to be sleeping. Instead he watched them like a hawk.

At last his chance came. The Bralgahs started to dance. All eyes were on them, all except those of Beeargah; his were on that combee bag.

The Bralgahs were the most wonderful dancers of all. They advanced and retired, bowed, and then pirouetted round and round craning their necks and making such antics, as they repeated the pattern of their dance, that the audience rocked with laughter. Faster and faster they danced without stopping.

Bootoogah and Goonur were fascinated, and in their excitement forgot all about the combee bag and their precious fire-sticks. This was just the chance the cunning Beeargah had been waiting for, and, when the bag slipped unnoticed from Goonur's shoulder as she rocked with laughter, he seized it and ran off with it before she realised what had happened.

Beeargah opened the bag, pulled out a fire-stick, rubbed it and held it to the heap of dried grass ready near by. A thin tongue of flame shot up and spread from grass to grass.

By the time Bootoogah and Goonur had discovered their loss, it was too late. The fire had spread, and so had the secret of how it was made.

Australian Legend

The Crow and the Daylight

Long, long ago, when the world was young, there was no daylight in Alaska. It was dark all the time. The people of Alaska lived in the dark, managing as well as they could. They had only their seal-oil lamps for light.

In one village lived a crow. The people liked this crow, and thought he was very wise. He told them wonderful stories of all the things he had seen and done on his long journeys in distant lands.

One day he seemed very sad and did not speak at all. The people wondered what was troubling him.

'Crow, what makes you so sad?' they asked.

'I'm sad for all you people in Alaska,' said the crow, 'because you have no daylight.'

'What is daylight?' they asked. 'What is it like? We've never even heard of it.'

'Well,' said the crow, 'if you had daylight in Alaska, you could go anywhere and see everything.'

This seemed very wonderful to them.

'Please fetch us some daylight, dear crow,' they begged.

'I'm afraid that is impossible,' said the crow.

'Why is that?' asked the people.

'Well, I know where it is,' said the crow, 'but it would be far too difficult to bring it here.'

The people all crowded round and begged him to bring them some daylight.

'Oh, crow, you are so clever,' said their chief, 'we know you can do this for us.'

'Very well, I will go,' said the crow at last, 'and see what I can do.'

Next day, he spread his wings and flew towards the east. He flew on and on, in the dark, till his wings ached, but he never stopped.

After he had flown for many days, the sky gradually grew lighter, until at last daylight filled the whole sky.

Perching on a tree, he looked about him to find where the light came from. At last he saw it shining from a big snow-house in a village.

Now in the snow-house lived the chief of the village, and he had a beautiful daughter. She came out of the house every day to fetch water from the ice-hole in the river, the only place Eskimos can find fresh water in winter.

The crow slipped off his skin and hid it by the entrance of the house. Then he covered himself with magic dust, and said some magic words which sounded like this:

> 'Ya-ka-ty, ta-ka-ty, na-ka-ty!
> A tiny speck of dust I'll be,
> Then nobody will notice me!'

He sat on a sunbeam in a crack near the door, and waited for the chief's daughter. When she came back from the river, the crow, who looked just like a speck of dust, lighted on her dress and passed with her into the house where the daylight was. There was a small boy playing on the floor, surrounded by little toys of walrus ivory. They were tiny dogs, foxes, kayaks and little walrus heads. He kept putting the toys into the box and spilling them out again.

The chief watched his little son proudly, but did not notice the speck of dust that drifted down to the little boy's ear. (The dust was the crow, of course. Remember?)

Soon the child began to cry.

'What do you want, little son?' asked the chief.

'Ask for the daylight to play with,' whispered the crow into the little boy's ear. So the child asked for the daylight.

'Give him what he asks for,' said the chief to his daughter. She fetched a hunting bag, and took from it a small wooden box, out of which she took a bright shining ball, and gave it to the child.

He liked the ball and played with it for a long time. But the crow wanted to get hold of it, so he whispered in the child's ear, 'Ask for string to tie on it.'

'I want string on my ball,' demanded the little boy.

At once a piece of string was tied to the ball.

When the chief and his daughter went out, the crow whispered in the little boy's ear, 'Take your ball to the en-trance.'

So the little boy took his ball of daylight to the very place at the entrance where the crow had left his skin.

The speck of dust slipped back into the crow's skin, and became a real crow again. Seizing the string in his beak the crow flew away, leaving the child howling.

The cries brought the chief and his daughter and all the people of the village running to see what was wrong, and there, high in the sky, they saw the crow flying away with their precious daylight. They tried to shoot him down with their arrows, but he was too far away, and was soon out of sight.

When the crow reached the land of Alaska, he thought he would try the daylight to see how it worked. Passing over the first dark village, he scratched a little bit off the daylight. It fell on the village and gave it bright light.

At every village he came to he did the same, until he reached his very own village. Hovering over it, he broke the daylight into little bits, scattering them far and wide.

The people greeted him with shouts. They were so happy they danced and sang, and prepared a great feast in his honour. They were so grateful to him they couldn't thank him enough for bringing his gift of daylight.

To this very day the people of Alaska are grateful to the crow, and never try to shoot him.

Eskimo Folk Tale

The Piper and the Puca

In the old times, there was a half fool living in Dunmore, in the county Galway, and although he was excessively fond of music, he was unable to learn more than one tune, and that was the 'Black Rogue'. He used to get a good deal of money from the gentlemen, for they used to get sport out of him.

One night the piper was coming home from a house where there had been a dance, and he was half drunk. When he came to a little bridge that was up by his mother's house, he squeezed the pipes and began playing the 'Black Rogue.' The Puca came behind him and flung him up on his own back. There were long horns on the Puca, and the piper got a good grip of them, and then he said, 'Destruction on you, you nasty beast, let me home. I have a ten-penny piece in my pocket for my mother, and she wants snuff.'

'Never mind your mother,' said the Puca, 'but keep your hold. If you fall you'll break your neck and your pipes.' Then the Puca said to him, 'Play up for me the "Shan Van Vocht".'

'I don't know it,' said the piper.

'Never mind whether you do or not,' said the Puca. 'Play up, and I'll make you know.'

The piper put wind into his bag, and he played such music that made himself wonder.

'Upon my word, you're a fine music-master,' said the piper, then: 'but tell me where you're for bringing me?'

'There's a great feast in the house of the Banshee, on the top of Croagh Patric to-night,' said the Puca, 'and I'm for bringing you there to play music, and, take my word, you'll get the price of your trouble.'

'By my word, you'll save me a journey, then,' said the piper, 'for Father William put a journey to Croagh Patric on me, because I stole the white gander from him last Martinmas.'

The Puca rushed him across hills, bogs, and rough places till he brought him to the top of Croagh Patric. Then the Puca struck three blows with his foot, and a great door opened, and they passed together, into a fine room.

The piper saw a golden table in the middle of the room, and hundreds of old women sitting round it. The women rose up, and said, 'A hundred thousand welcomes to you, Puca of November! Who is this you have with you?'

'The best piper in Ireland,' said the Puca.

One of the old women struck a blow on the wall, and what should the piper see coming out, but the white gander which he had stolen from Father William.

'By my conscience, then,' says the piper, 'myself and my mother ate every taste of that gander, only one wing, and I gave that to Red Mary, and it's she told the priest I stole his gander.'

The gander cleaned the table, and carried it away, and the Puca said, 'Play up music for these ladies.'

The piper played up, and the old women began dancing, and they were dancing till they were tired. Then the Puca told them to pay the piper and every old woman drew out a gold piece, and gave it to him.

'By the tooth of Patric,' said he, 'I'm as rich as the son of a lord.'

'Come with me,' says the Puca, 'and I'll bring you home.'

They went out then, and just as he was going to ride on the Puca, the gander came up to him, and gave him a new set of pipes. The Puca was not long before he brought the piper to Dunmore, and he threw him off at the little bridge, and then he told him to go home, and says to him, 'You have two things now that you never had before—you have sense and music.'

The piper went home, and knocked at his mother's door saying, 'Let me in, I'm as rich as a lord, and I'm the best piper in Ireland.'

'You're drunk,' said the mother.

'No, indeed,' said the piper, 'I haven't drunk a drop.'

The mother let him in, and he gave her the gold pieces. 'Wait now,' says he, 'till you hear the music I'll play.'

He buckled on the pipes, but instead of music, there came a sound as if all the geese and ganders of Ireland were screeching together. He wakened all the neighbours, and they were all mocking him, until he put on the old pipes, and then he played melodious music for them; and after that he told them all he had gone through that night.

The next morning, when his mother went to look at the gold pieces, there was nothing there but the leaves of a plant.

The piper went to the priest and told him his story, but the priest would not believe a word from him, until he put the pipes on him, and then the screeching of the geese and the ganders began.

'Leave my sight, you thief,' says the priest.

But nothing would do the piper until he would put the old pipes on him to show the priest that his story was true.

He buckled on the old pipes, and he played melodious music, and from that day till the day of his death, there was never a piper in the county Galway was as good as he was.

Retold by Douglas Hyde, from *Irish Fairy and Folk Tales*, by W. B. Yeats

A Teeny-Weeny Tale

Once upon a time there was a teeny-weeny woman who lived all by herself in a teeny-weeny house.

One day she went for a teeny-weeny walk. She had not gone far when she came to a teeny-weeny gate, so she opened the teeny-weeny gate and went into a teeny-weeny wood, and what should she find but a teeny-weeny bone under a teeny-weeny tree.

'I'll make a teeny-weeny pot of soup from this teeny-weeny bone,' said the teeny-weeny woman to her teeny-weeny self. So she put the teeny-weeny bone into her teeny-weeny pocket, and went out of the teeny-weeny wood to her teeny-weeny house. She put the teeny-weeny bone in her teeny-weeny cupboard, and then she went to her teeny-weeny bed.

But she had not been long in her teeny-weeny bed when she heard a teeny-weeny voice come from the teeny-weeny cupboard, and the teeny-weeny voice said:

'Give me back my bone!'

When she heard this, the teeny-weeny woman was a teeny-weeny bit frightened. She hid under her teeny-weeny bedclothes, and went to sleep. Suddenly, the teeny weeny woman woke to hear the teeny-weeny voice coming from the teeny-weeny cupboard again, and it said a teeny-weeny bit louder :

'Give me back my bone!'

This made the teeny-weeny woman more frightened than ever, and she hid her teeny-weeny self a teeny-weeny bit further under her teeny-weeny bedclothes. But she could not go to sleep, and after a teeny-weeny while she heard that teeny-weeny voice come from the teeny-weeny cupboard, but this time the teeny-weeny voice was a teeny-weeny bit louder, and it said :

'GIVE ME BACK MY BONE!'

This made the teeny-weeny woman nearly jump out of her teeny-weeny skin, but she poked her teeny-weeny head out of the teeny-weeny bedclothes and said in her loudest voice :

'TAKE IT!'

English Folk Tale, for Halloween, October 31st

Saint Andrew

Saint Andrew is Scotland's patron saint. He was a fisherman like his father and his brother Simon Peter, before he followed Our Lord and became one of his Apostles.

One day Andrew set out on a journey across the sea to tell the people of a little northern island, called Britain, about the new faith, Christianity. He sailed round the coast of this island till he came to the northern shores of Scotland. The country-side looked so wild and deserted he nearly sailed away. Instead he landed and explored the bleak hills inland.

At last he came to a great castle of grey stone. He could see the flicker of candle-light through the slits in the wall so,

although there was no sign of life anywhere, he knew someone must be living there.

Sure enough, the door was opened to him and he was
surprised to find how comfortable and pleasant it was inside.
A king welcomed him, and soon the entire court gathered
round him, eager to find out who he was and where he came
from. When he had answered all their questions, it was his
turn to ask about them.

At once they became very quiet and sad. The king told him
they had offended one of their gods. This God had then
changed his six beautiful daughters into six swans. It seemed
that nothing could be done to save them. They were doomed
to swim for ever in the river that flowed past the castle.

Saint Andrew listened patiently to their story, but he told
them they should not believe in such witchcraft, and that
such things would not happen if they worshipped the true
God.

The king and his court were very angry when they heard
this, and the pagan knights challenged Andrew to fight with
them in combat.

One by one they rode against him and, one by one, he
defeated them, until the king called a halt to the fighting.

Kneeling before Saint Andrew, the king vowed he would
become a Christian. As he made the vow, six swans flew
from the river and alighted on the ground before him.
Immediately they were changed back to their human forms.
The six princesses stretched out their arms to greet their
father, the king.

When the people saw this miracle, they were amazed and
said that the god of Saint Andrew must indeed be the true
God. They gathered round to listen to him and, before long,
the entire country was converted to Christianity.

Saint Andrew did not stay in Scotland for the rest of his
life. After a while he returned to the Mediterranean to
continue his work there. Many years later he died for his

faith, and a monk, called Regulus, brought his body back to Scotland and buried it on the east coast of Scotland. The place where he was buried was named after him. A great cathedral and university were built there, and a fine town grew up around them both, called St Andrews. His day is November the 30th.

The Talking Cat

Once in another time, my friends, a great change came into Tante Odette's life although she was already an old woman who thought she had finished with such nonsense as changing one's habits.

It all happened because of a great change that came over Chouchou. The grey cat was a good companion because he seemed quite content to live on bread crusts and cabbage soup. Tante Odette kept a pot of soup boiling on the back of the stove. She added a little more water and a few more cabbage leaves to it each day. In this way, she always had soup on hand and never had to throw any of it away.

She baked her own bread in her outdoor oven once a week, on Tuesday. If the bread grew stale by Saturday or Sunday, she softened it up in the cabbage soup. So nothing was wasted.

As Tante Odette worked at her loom every evening, Chouchou would lie on the little rug by the stove and steadily stare at her with his big green eyes.

'If only you could talk,' Tante Odette would say, 'what company you would be for me!'

One autumn evening, Tante Odette was busy at her loom. Her stubby fingers flew among the threads like pigeons. Thump, thump went the loom.

Suddenly there was a thump, thump that didn't come from the loom. It came from the door.

The old woman took the lamp from the low table and went to the door. She opened it slowly. The light from the lamp shone on a queer old man who had the unmistakable look of the woods. He wore a bright red sash around his waist and a black crow feather in his woollen cap. He had a bushy moustache like a home-made broom and a brown crinkled face.

'Pierre Leblanc, at your service,' said the old man, making a deep bow.

'What do you want?' asked Tante Odette sharply. 'I can't stand here all night with the door open. It wastes heat and firewood.'

'I seek shelter and work,' answered Pierre Leblanc. 'I am getting too old to trap for furs or work in the lumber camps, I would like a job on just such a cosy little place as this.'

'I don't need any help,' snapped Tante Odette. 'I am quite able to do everything by myself. And I have my cat.'

She was beginning to close the door, but the man put his gnarled hand against it. He was staring at Chouchou.

'A very smart cat he looks to be,' he said. 'Why don't you ask him if you should take me in? After all, you need pay me nothing but a roof over my head and a little food.'

Tante Odette's eyes grew bigger.

'How ridiculous!' she said. 'A cat can't talk. I only wish——'

To her great surprise, Chouchou began to talk.

'Oh, indeed I can,' he told her, 'if the matter is important enough. This Pierre Leblanc looks to me like a very fine man and a good worker. You should take him in.'

Tante Odette stood with her mouth open for two minutes before she could make any sound come out of it. At last she said, 'Then come in. It is so rare for a cat to be able to talk that I'm sure one should listen to him when he does.'

The old man walked close to the stove and stretched his fingers towards it. He looked at the pot of soup bubbling on the back.

Chouchou spoke again.

'Pierre looks hungry,' he said. 'Offer him some soup—a big deep bowl of it.'

'Oh, dear,' sighed Tante Odette, 'at this rate, our soup won't last out the week. But if you say so, Chouchou.'

Pierre sat down at the wooden table and gulped down the soup like a starved wolf. When he had finished, Tante Odette pointed to the loft where he would sleep. Then she took the big grey cat on her lap.

'This is the most amazing thing that you should begin talking after all these years. Whatever came over you?'

But Chouchou had nothing more to say. He covered his nose with the tip of his tail, and there was not another word out of him all night.

Tante Odette decided that the cat's advice had been good. No longer did she have to go to the barn and feed the beasts. And no more skunks crawled into her oven because Pierre saw to it that the door was kept closed. He was indeed a good worker. He seemed quite satisfied with his bed in the loft and his bowls of soup and chunks of bread.

Only Chouchou seemed to have grown dissatisfied since his arrival.

'Why do you feed Pierre nothing but cabbage soup and bread?' he asked one day. 'A working man needs more food than that. How about head cheeses and pork pie?'

Tante Odette was startled, but Pierre went on drinking his soup.

'But meat is scarce and costs money,' she told the cat.

'Pouf!' said the cat. 'It is well worth it. Even I am getting a little tired of cabbage soup. A nice pork pie for dinner to-morrow would fill all the empty cracks inside me.'

So when Pierre went out to the barn to water the beasts,

Tante Odette stealthily lifted the lid of the chest, fished out a torn sock and pulled a few coins out of it. She jumped in surprise when she raised her head and saw Pierre standing in the open doorway watching her.

'I forgot the pail,' said Pierre. 'I will draw some water from the well while I am about it.'

The old woman hastily dropped the lid of the chest and got the pail from behind the stove.

'After Pierre has done his chores,' said Chouchou, 'he will be glad to go to the store and buy meat for you.'

Tante Odette frowned at the cat.

'But I am the thriftiest shopper in the parish,' she said. 'I can bring old Henri Dupuis down a few pennies on every-thing I buy.'

'Pierre is a good shopper too,' said Chouchou. 'In all Canada, there is not a better judge of meat. Perhaps he will even see something that you would not have thought to buy. Send him to the store.'

It turned out that the old man was just as good a shopper as Chouchou had said. He returned from the village with a pinkish piece of pork, a freshly dressed pig's head, a bag of candy, and some tobacco for himself.

'But my money,' said Tante Odette. 'Did you spend all of it?'

'What is money for but to spend?' asked Chouchou from his rug by the stove. 'Can you eat money or smoke it in a pipe?'

'No,' said Tante Odette.

'Can you put it over your shoulders to keep you warm?'

'No.'

'Would it burn in the stove to cook your food?'

'Oh, no, indeed!'

Chouchou closed his eyes.

'Then what good is money?' he asked. 'The sooner one gets rid of it the better.'

Tante Odette's troubled face smoothed.

'I never saw it that way before,' she agreed. 'Of course, you are right, Chouchou. And you are right too, Pierre, for choosing such fine food.'

But when Pierre went out to get cabbage from the shed, Tante Odette walked over to the chest again and counted her coins.

'I have a small fortune, Chouchou,' she said. 'Now tell me again why these coins are no good.'

But Chouchou had nothing more to say about the matter.

One Tuesday when Pierre Leblanc was cutting down trees in the wood and Tante Odette was baking her loaves of bread in the outdoor oven, a stranger came galloping down the road on a one-eyed horse. He stopped in front of the white fence. He politely dismounted and went over to Tante Odette.

The old woman saw at a glance that he was a man of the woods. His blouse was checked and his cap red. Matching it was a red sash tied round his waist. He looked very much like Pierre Leblanc.

'Can you tell me, madame,' he asked, 'if a man named Pierre Leblanc works here?'

'Yes, he does,' answered Tante Odette, 'and a very good worker he is too.'

The stranger did not look satisfied.

'Of course, Canada is full of Pierre Leblancs,' he said. 'It is a very common name. Does this Pierre Leblanc wear a red sash like mine?'

'So he does,' said Tante Odette.

'On the other hand,' said the man, 'many Pierre Leblancs wear red sashes. Does he have a moustache like a home-made broom?'

'Yes, indeed,' said the woman.

'But there must be many Pierre Leblancs with red sashes and moustaches like brooms,' continued the stranger. 'This

Pierre Leblanc who now works for you, can he throw his voice?'

'Throw his voice!' cried Tante Odette. 'What witchcraft is that?'

'Haven't you heard of such a gift?' asked the man. 'But of course only few have it—and probably only one Pierre Leblanc in a thousand. This Pierre with you, can he throw his voice behind trees and in boxes and up in the roof so it sounds as though someone else is talking?'

'My faith, no!' cried the woman in horror. 'I wouldn't have such a one in my house. He would be better company for the *loup-garou*, that evil one who can change into many shapes.'

The man laughed heartily.

'My Pierre Leblanc could catch the *loup-garou* in a wolf trap and lead him around on a chain. He is that clever. That is why I am trying to find him. I want him to go trapping with me in the woods this winter. One says that never have there been so many foxes. I need Pierre, for he is smarter than any fox.'

The creak of wheels caused them both to turn around. Pierre Leblanc was driving the ox team in from the woods. He stared at the man standing beside Tante Odette. Then both men began bouncing on their feet and whooping in their throats. They hugged each other. They kissed each other on the cheek.

'Good old Pierre!'

'Georges, my friend, where have you kept yourself all summer? How did you find me?'

Tante Odette left them whooping and hugging. She walked into the house with a worried look on her face. She sat down at her loom. Finally she stopped weaving and turned to Chouchou.

'I am a little dizzy, Chouchou,' she said. 'This *loup-garou* voice has upset me. What do you make of it?'

Chouchou said nothing.

'Is he maybe in league with the *loup-garou*?'

Chouchou said nothing. Tante Odette angrily threw the shuttle at him.

'Where is your tongue?' she demanded. 'Have you no words for me when I need them most?'

But if a cat will not speak, who has got his tongue?

Pierre came walking in.

'Such a man,' he roared gleefully. 'Only the woods are big enough for him.'

'Are you going away with him?' asked the woman, not knowing whether she wanted him to say 'yes' or 'no'. If only Chouchou hadn't been so stubborn.

'That makes a problem,' said Pierre. 'If I go into the woods this winter, it will be cold and I will work like an ox. But there will be money in my pocket after the furs are sold. If I stay here I will be warm and comfortable but——'

He pulled his pockets inside out. Nothing fell from them.

'What is this business about your being able to throw your voice to other places?' asked Tante Odette.

'Did Georges say I could do that?'

Tante Odette nodded.

'Ha! Ha!' laughed Pierre. 'What a joker Georges is!'

'But perhaps it is true,' insisted the woman.

'If you really want to know why not ask Chouchou?' said Pierre. 'He would not lie. Can I throw my voice, Chouchou?'

Chouchou sank down on his haunches and purred.

'Of course not!' he answered. 'Whoever heard of such nonsense?'

Tante Odette sighed in relief. Then she remembered that this did not fix everything.

'Will you go with him?' she asked Pierre. 'I have made it very comfortable for you here. And now it is only for supper that we have cabbage soup.'

Chouchou spoke up.

'Tante Odette, how can you expect such a good man as Pierre Leblanc to work for food and shelter only? If you would pay him a coin from time to time, he would be quite satisfied to stay.'

'But I can't afford that,' said the woman.

'Of course you can,' insisted Chouchou. 'You have a small fortune in the old sock in your chest. Remember what I told you about money?'

'Tell me again,' said Tante Odette. 'It is hard to hold on to such a thought for long.'

'Money is to spend,' repeated the cat. 'Can it carry hay and water to the beasts? Can it cut down trees for firewood? Can it dig paths through the snow when winter comes?'

'I have caught it again,' said Tante Odette. 'If you will stay with me, Pierre, I will pay you a coin from time to time.'

Pierre smiled and bowed.

'Then I shall be very happy to stay here with you and your wise cat,' he decided. 'Now I will unload my wood and pile it in a neat stack by the door.'

He briskly stamped out. Tante Odette sat down at her loom again.

'We have made a good bargain, haven't we, Chouchou?' She smiled contentedly.

But Chouchou tickled his nose with his tail and said nothing.

From *The Talking Cat and other stories*, by Natalie Savage Carlson

Father Christmas and the Carpenter

There was once a carpenter called Anderson. He was a good father and he had a lot of children.

One Christmas Eve, while his wife and children were decorating the Christmas tree, Anderson crept out to his wood shed. He had a surprise for them all; he was going to dress up as Father Christmas, load a sack of presents on to his sledge and go and knock on the front door. But as he pulled the loaded sledge out of the wood-shed, he slipped and fell across the sack of presents. This set the sledge moving, because the ground sloped from the sledge down to the road, and Anderson had no time even to shout 'Way there!' before he crashed into another sledge which was coming down the road.

'I'm very sorry,' said Anderson.

'Don't mention it; I couldn't stop myself,' said the other man. Like Anderson, he was dressed in Father Christmas clothes and had a sack on his sledge.

'We seem to have the same idea,' said Anderson. 'I see you're all dressed up like me.' He laughed and shook the other man by the hand. 'My name is Anderson.'

'Glad to meet you,' said the other. 'I'm Father Christmas.'

'Ha, ha!' laughed Anderson. 'You will have your little joke, and quite right too on Christmas Eve.'

'That's what I thought,' said the other man, 'and if you will agree we can change places to-night, and that will be a better joke still; I'll take the presents along to *your* children if you'll go and visit *mine*. But you must take off that costume.'

Anderson looked a bit puzzled. 'What am I to dress up in then?'

'You don't need to dress up at all,' said the other. 'My children see Father Christmas all the year round, but they've never seen a real carpenter. I told them last Christmas that if they were good this year I'd try and get a carpenter to come and see them while I went round with presents for human children.'

'So he really *is* Father Christmas,' thought Anderson to himself. Out loud he said, 'All right, if you really want me to, I will. The only thing is, I haven't any presents for your children.'

'Presents?' said Father Christmas. 'Aren't you a carpenter?'

'Yes, of course.'

'Well, then, all you have to do is to take along a few pieces of wood, and some nails. You have a knife, I suppose?' Anderson said he had and went to look for the things in his workshop.

'Just follow my footsteps in the snow; they'll lead you to my house in the forest,' said Father Christmas. 'Then I'll take your sack and sledge and go and knock on your door.'

'Righto!' said the carpenter.

Then Father Christmas went to knock on Anderson's door, and the carpenter trudged through the snow in Father Christmas's footsteps. They led him into the forest, past two pine-trees, a large boulder and a tree-stump. There peeping out from behind the stump were three little faces with red caps on.

'He's here! He's here!' shouted the Christmas children as they scampered in front of him to a fallen tree, lying with its roots in the air. When Anderson followed them round to the other side of the roots he found Mother Christmas standing there waiting for him.

'Here he is, Mum! He's the carpenter Dad promised us! Look at him! Isn't he tall!' The children were all shouting at once.

'Now, now, children,' said Mother Christmas. 'Anybody would think you'd never seen a human being before.'

'We've never seen a proper *carpenter* before!' shouted the children. 'Come on in, Mr Carpenter!'

Pulling a branch aside, Mother Christmas led the way into the house. Anderson had to bend his long back double and crawl on his hands and knees. But once in, he found he could straighten up. The room had a mud floor, but it was very cosy, with tree stumps for chairs, and beds made of moss with covers of plaited grass. In the smallest bed lay the Christmas baby and in the far corner sat a very old Grandfather Christmas, his red cap nodding up and down.

'Have you got a knife? Did you bring some wood and some nails?' The children pulled at Anderson's sleeve and wanted to know everything at once.

'Now, children,' said Mother Christmas, 'let the carpenter sit down before you start pestering him.'

'Has anyone come to see me?' croaked old Grandfather Christmas.

Mother Christmas shouted in his ear. 'It's Anderson, the carpenter!' She explained that Grandfather was so old he never went out any more. 'He'd be pleased if you would come over and shake hands with him.'

So Anderson took the old man's hand which was as hard as a piece of bark.

'Come and sit here, Mr Carpenter!' called the children.

The eldest one spoke first. 'Do you know what I want you to make for me? A toboggan. Can you do that—a little one, I mean?'

'I'll try,' said Anderson, and it didn't take long before he had a smart toboggan just ready to fly over the snow.

'Now it's my turn,' said the little girl who had pigtails sticking straight out from her head. 'I want a doll's bed.'

'Have you any dolls?' asked Anderson.

'No, but I borrow the field-mice sometimes, and I can play with baby squirrels as much as I like. They love being dolls. Please make me a doll's bed.'

So the carpenter made her a doll's bed. Then he asked the smaller boy what he would like. But he was very shy and could only whisper, 'Don't know.'

''Course he knows!' said his sister. 'He said it just before you came. Go on, tell the carpenter.'

'A top,' whispered the little boy.

'That's easy,' said the carpenter, and in no time at all he had made a top.

'And now you must make something for Mum!' said the

children. Mother Christmas had been watching, but all the
time she held something behind her back.

'Shush, children, don't keep bothering the carpenter,' she
said.

'That's all right,' said Anderson. 'What would you like
me to make?'

Mother Christmas brought out the thing she was holding;
it was a wooden ladle, very worn, with a crack in it.

'Could you mend this for me, d'you think?' she asked.

'Hm, hm!' said Anderson, scratching his head with his
carpenter's pencil. 'I think I'd better make you a new one.'
And he quickly cut a new ladle for Mother Christmas. Then
he found a long twisted root with a crook at one end and
started stripping it with his knife. But although the children
asked him and asked him he wouldn't tell them what it was
going to be. When it was finished he held it up; it was a very
distinguished-looking walking stick.

'Here you are, Grandpa!' he shouted to the old man, and
handed him the stick. Then he gathered up all the chips and
made a wonderful little bird with wings outspread to hang
over the baby's cot.

'How pretty!' exclaimed Mother Christmas and all the
children. 'Thank the carpenter nicely now. We'll certainly
never forget this Christmas Eve, will we?'

'Thank you, Mr Carpenter, thank you very much!'
shouted the children.

Grandfather Christmas himself came stumping across the
room leaning on his new stick. 'It's grand!' he said. 'It's just
grand!'

There was the sound of feet stamping the snow off outside
the door, and Anderson knew it was time for him to go. He
said good-bye all round and wished them a Happy Christmas.
Then he crawled through the narrow opening under the
fallen tree. Father Christmas was waiting for him. He had
the sledge and the empty sack with him.

'Thank you for your help, Anderson,' he said. 'What did the youngsters say when they saw you?'

'Oh, they seemed very pleased. Now they're just waiting for you to come home and see their new toys. How did you get on at my house? Was little Peter frightened of you?'

'Not a bit,' said Father Christmas. 'He thought I was you. "Sit on Dadda's knee," he kept saying.'

'Well, I must go back to them,' said Anderson, and said good-bye to Father Christmas.

When he got home, the first thing he said to the children was, 'Can I see the presents you got from Father Christmas?'

But the children laughed. 'Silly! You've seen them already—when you were Father Christmas; you unpacked them all for us!'

'What would you say if I told you I had been with Father Christmas's family all this time?'

But the children laughed again. 'You wouldn't say anything so silly!' they said, and they didn't believe him. So the carpenter came to me and asked me to write down the story, which I did.

From *Mrs Pepperpot Again*, by Alf Prøysen

Babushka and the Three Wise Men

Once upon a time, three Wise Men were travelling across the country with gifts for the great King who was soon to be born. Tired and hungry, they stopped at a little cottage and asked for food and shelter. The good Babushka opened her door wide and told them to make themselves comfortable by the fire while she prepared a meal for them. The three Wise Men thanked her and accepted her hospitality.

As they ate the meal she had made for them, they told her

that they were following a star which would lead them to the place where the King of Kings was to be born, and that they were carrying gifts for Him. Babushka listened to them.

'How I would like to greet the Little One too,' she said.

'Come with us then,' said the three Wise Men. 'We shall leave as soon as the stars are bright in the sky.'

'I can't leave my cottage until I have cleaned and swept it, and then of course I will have to prepare for the journey. But I will come as soon as I'm ready.'

When the stars were bright in the sky, the three Wise Men said it was time for them to go but, as Babushka was not ready, they had to leave without her.

After they had gone Babushka cleared away the meal, washed up, and bustled about the house until everything was as neat and tidy as she could make it. Then she searched for gifts to take to the Little One, for she was sure she could not go empty-handed.

After that she scrubbed her face until it shone and took out her best Sunday clothes, and dressed herself very carefully, for was she not going to visit the King of Kings?

When she was quite sure everything was in good order, she locked the door of her cottage and set out along the road the Wise Men had taken.

But the star that had guided them had moved across the sky and was nowhere to be seen, and soon poor Babushka was lost. She tried this road and she tried that.

'I wish I had gone when I had the chance,' she sighed 'I could have tidied the house some other time.'

But it was too late, there was no sign to tell her which way to go, and although she wandered on and on she never found the stable where the King was born.

*   *   *

On Christmas morning, in Russia, when the children find toys and sweets in their stockings, they say, 'See, what Babushka has left me!'

For they believe she is still wandering about on Christmas Eve, searching for the Little One in every house where there are children, and that she leaves gifts in all their stockings just to be sure she does not miss Him.

Russian Legend

The Story of the Christmas Rose

Long, long ago there was a Robber family who lived in the Great Forest. Robber Father had stolen sheep and the Bishop had made him an outlaw. So the Robber family went into the forest and there they lived in the shelter of a deep cave, for they had nowhere else to go. Robber Father hunted for food, while Robber Mother and their five children gathered berries to eat, ferns for their beds and wood for the fire.

Sometimes Robber Mother took the children into the village to beg, but they looked so rough and wild with their unkempt hair and their ragged clothes, people were afraid of them and locked their doors when they saw them coming. Sometimes the people left a bundle of old clothes or a parcel of food outside the door for Robber Mother to collect. But not once did they ask her in or even say a word of greeting, as they did to any stranger. This made Robber Mother furious. She scowled and muttered to herself, even when her sack was full, and looked more fierce than ever.

One warm summer day, as she trudged home, her sack slung over her shoulder, Robber Mother saw that a little door in the monastery wall had been left open. She stopped and peeped in. There she saw a beautiful garden filled with bright flowers. Honeysuckle, red roses and white jasmine covered the grey stone walls, and she had never seen so many butterflies. She put down her sack and walked into the garden. She bent down to smell the pink roses and smiled.

You can imagine how surprised the monastery gardener was when he saw the rough Robber Mother in his beautiful garden.

'Hi there!' he shouted. 'You can't come in here, this is the Abbot's private garden. No women are allowed in here. Be off with you!'

Robber Mother looked up and scowled fiercely.

'I'm doing no harm,' she snapped, 'and I'll go when I've found what I'm looking for.'

'You'll go right now, my good woman,' shouted the gardener, 'or I'll throw you out!'

'Just you try!' laughed Robber Mother, who was much bigger than the gardener and probably stronger too.

This made the gardener very angry. He went off and fetched two fat monks who tried to put her out. But she bit and kicked and screamed, and made such a noise that the old Abbot came hurrying out to see what all the fuss was about.

'This woman won't leave your garden, Lord Abbot,' said one of the monks.

'Leave her to me, brothers, I will deal with her,' said the Abbot and turning to Robber Mother, he said, 'I expect you have never seen such a fine garden, my good woman. Do you want to pick some of the flowers?'

'I do not,' said Robber Mother. 'This is a fine garden, but it cannot compare with the one we have in the Great Forest every Christmas.'

'Is that so?' laughed the Abbot. His garden was his pride and joy and was said to be the finest in the land. But Robber Mother said angrily,

'I'm not joking, Lord Abbot, I know what I'm saying. Every Christmas Eve, part of the Great Forest near our cave is transformed into a wonderful garden to celebrate the birth of the Christ Child. We who live in the forest see it every year. In that garden flowers of all the seasons grow together at the same time, and there are flowers there I would not dare to touch, they are so beautiful. They have frail silver petals and pale gold stamens. We call them Christmas roses. I do not see them in your garden.'

The old Abbot listened to Robber Mother. He remembered hearing, as a child, how part of the Great Forest was transformed into a beautiful garden on Christmas Eve. He had longed to see it and then he had forgotten all about it. So he smiled kindly at Robber Mother.

'I have heard of your garden,' he said, 'and I would like to see it. Would you send one of your children to guide me to the spot next Christmas Eve?'

'How can we be sure you will not drive us away from our cave if we show you where it is?' said Robber Mother.

'I would not do that,' said the Abbot. 'I would rather ask my Lord Bishop to grant your husband a free pardon in return for your kindness.'

'You would do that?' asked Robber Mother eagerly.

'Yes, I shall ask,' said the old Abbot, 'but whether my Lord Bishop will grant my request I do not know.'

'I trust you,' said Robber Mother, 'and my eldest boy will wait for you next Christmas Eve and guide you through the Great Forest to our cave. He will wait for you by the old oak. But you must promise you will bring only one companion with you—this gardener here.'

'I promise,' said the Abbot, and after he had blessed the Robber Mother, she left the garden quietly and returned home.

The Abbot went to the Bishop and told him all that had happened, and the story of the Christmas garden. 'If God allows the Robber family to see this miracle there must be some good in them. Will you not give the Robber Father a free pardon and a chance to live and work like our people? As it is, their children are growing up rough and wild. If we

are not careful we shall have a young Robber gang up there
in the Great Forest, and then there will be trouble.'

'There is some truth in what you say, good father Abbot,'
said the Bishop. 'Not that I believe this story of the Christmas
garden. However, you can go and look for it if you wish,
and if you bring me back one of those silver and gold flowers,
I'll grant the Robber a free pardon with pleasure.'

Well, Christmas Eve came at last. The good old Abbot
asked his gardener to go with him into the Great Forest,
and there, under the old oak, waited the eldest Robber Son.
The gardener muttered angrily under his breath as they followed the boy through the dark forest. He had not wanted to
leave his warm home on Christmas Eve. He thought of his
cosy chair beside the fire, and he wished he was sitting in it,
watching his wife pluck the turkey and his children decorate
the Christmas tree. He did not believe in the Christmas garden
and thought the whole expedition was stupid. However, he
dared not disobey his old master and he was too fond of him
to do so.

On and on they tramped through the snow till they came
to a cave. They followed the boy through an opening into a
cavern where Robber Mother was sitting beside a log fire.
The Robber children sprawled about the floor playing with
small stones, while Robber Father lay stretched out on a pile
of dried bracken.

'Sit down by the fire and warm yourself, Lord Abbot,'
said Robber Mother. 'You can sleep if you're tired. I'll keep
watch and I'll wake you when it is time to see what you have
come to see.'

'I'll keep watch too,' said the gardener, who still did not
trust the Robber family.

The old Abbot thanked the woman and stretched himself
on the ground beside the fire and fell asleep. He was so
tired.

He had not slept long when he woke to hear the chimes of

the Christmas bells. The gardener helped him to his feet and they followed the Robber family to the entrance of the cave.

'It is extraordinary to be able to hear the Christmas bells here in the forest. I wouldn't have thought it possible,' said the Abbot.

'Ah well, everything looks the same as ever out here,' grumbled the gardener, who was still in a bad temper.

It was true, the forest was as dark and gloomy as before, but instead of an icy wind, they felt a warm gentle breeze and a strange stirring all about them. Suddenly the bells stopped ringing. And then it happened.

The darkness turned into a pink dawn. The snow melted from the ground, leaving emerald shoots that grew before their eyes. Ferns sent up their fronds, curled like a bishop's staff, and spring flowers carpeted the earth. Trees burst into leaf and then into blossom. Butterflies and birds darted from tree to tree, and there was a soft hum of insects.

The Robber children laughed and rolled in the grass while Robber Mother and Robber Father stared wide-eyed and smiling. They too seemed transformed. And there, at his feet, the Abbot saw the silver and gold flower of the Christmas rose. He was filled with happiness and he knelt down and thanked God for allowing him to see such a miracle.

This seemed to make the gardener more angry than ever.

'This is no miracle,' he said in a loud voice, 'this is witch-craft and the work of the devil!'

As he said this darkness fell and an icy wind blew snow through the forest. The Robber family ran shivering into the cave, but the old Abbot stumbled forward on his face, clutching at the earth as he fell. The garden vanished, leaving the forest as dark and gloomy as ever.

The gardener hoisted the Abbot on to his back and carried him back to the monastery. There he was laid on his bed.

The monks all marvelled at the radiant smile on his still face. At least he had died with a happy heart, they told each other.

Now, the old Abbot was found to have the root of a plant clutched in one hand. It was given to the gardener who planted it carefully in the Abbot's garden. Every day he went to see if it was growing, but although there were green leaves there were no signs of a flower in the spring, nor in the summer, and autumn passed and there was not even a bud to be seen. The gardener wondered if it would ever flower.

Then on Christmas morning, when the ground was sprinkled with snow, the gardener saw a beautiful cluster of silvery white flowers growing from the plant, their frail petals surrounding the pale golden stamens. He had seen the flower only once before, in that Christmas garden of the Great Forest. It must be the Christmas rose, and the good Abbot had managed to pluck one after all.

At once the gardener knew what he must do. He picked three of the white flowers and took them to the Bishop.

'My Lord Bishop,' said the gardener, 'our father Abbot sends you these flowers as he promised.' Then he told the Bishop about the wonderful Christmas garden and all that had happened in the Great Forest that Christmas Eve.

'The good Abbot kept his promise and I shall keep mine,' said the Bishop, and he wrote a free pardon for the Robber Father there and then.

The gardener took the pardon to the Robber Father but when he reached the cave he found the entrance barred against him.

'Go away!' roared Robber Father. 'Thanks to you there was no wonderful garden here this Christmas Eve. Go away, unless you want a fight!'

'You're right, it was my fault; I had no faith. I was wrong but you must allow me to deliver your free pardon from the

Bishop. You are free, and from now on you may return to the village and live and work among the people.'

And so it was that the Robber family left the Great Forest and were able to enjoy Christmas in their own home, with all their friends around them.

Scandinavian Legend

V

HEROES AND HEROINES

Robert Bruce

When Bruce, King of Scotland, was getting the worst
Of the war he was waging with Edward the First;
When most of his friends had been captured or slain,
And the sky over Scotland looked very like rain;

When he spent his days hiding in bushes and trees,
Getting thorns in his fingers and cuts on his knees;
And when nothing could lighten the gloom he was feeling—
He lay in a hovel and looked at the ceiling.

He stared at the ceiling with thoughts that were black,
Till a spidery spider came out of a crack,
A spidery spider all bulging with thread,
Which she started to spin on the beam overhead.

She spun the web once, but the spider-thread broke;
She spun the thread twice—Bruce's interest woke;
She spun the web three times with pluck unavailing;
She spun the thread four times but still went on failing.

She spun the web five times—'God bless me!' cried Bruce,
'Yon spidery spider must see it's no use!
O spidery spider, it's plain as a pike
We two are as like as two peas are alike!'

She spun the web six times—'How now!' cried the Scot,
'Don't you know when you're beaten?' The spider did not,
But calmly proceeded, as patient as ever,
To start on an obstinate seventh endeavour.

She hung and she swung and she swayed in the air,
While Bruce for the Spider recited a prayer—
Then he whooped with delight and sprang to his feet,
For from one beam to another the web hung complete!

With hope he was filled and with courage he burned.
'O spider!' he said, 'What a lesson I've learned!
Dear Scotland! Of English invaders I'll rid it!'
Then Bruce sallied forth and at Bannockburn did it!

From *Heroes and Heroines*, by Eleanor and Herbert Farjeon

Lady Godiva

Long, long ago in the old town of Coventry, there ruled a
powerful tyrant called Lord Leofric. He did nothing to help
his people, instead he took as much from them as he could,
leaving them poor and unhappy, and without help when they
were sick or in trouble.

Now, this powerful lord had a young wife, the Lady
Godiva, who was as kind as she was beautiful, and everyone
loved her. It distressed her to see how poor and neglected the
people of Coventry were, and she did all she could to help
them. She begged her husband to have pity on them, but he
laughed at her.

'Go back to your needlework, good wife,' said he, 'and
don't bother your head about such things.'

'Please, my lord, give me just one bag of gold,' she pleaded,
'and I will help these people.'

'It is easy enough for you to ask me to give you money,' he
said, 'but I doubt if you would really do anything difficult on
their behalf.'

'I would, I would!' she said.

'Then ride naked through the streets of Coventry,' he
sneered, 'and you shall have a bag of gold for these poor people
of yours!'

The Lady Godiva at once sent a messenger to the poor people
of Coventry, asking them to close their shutters and to stay

indoors while she rode naked through the streets of Coventry for their sakes.

And they all, every man, woman and child, did as she asked them.

Then she took the pins from her long yellow hair, and let it fall loose about her shoulders, and she took off all her clothes. Her long yellow hair hung down like a cape, covering her completely as she rode, mounted on her white mare, through the silent streets of Coventry. All the shutters were closed and the doors locked, and there was not a soul to be seen.

There was just one man who did not keep his word, and his name was Tom. He peeped through a chink in his shutters and he saw the Lady Godiva, her long hair hanging about her like a cape, riding on her white mare. He was the first Peeping Tom!

When Lord Leofric saw that his wife was seriously willing to help the people, his heart softened. He kept his word and gave her the bag of gold. And she used it to help the sick and the poor. And this is why the people of Coventry still remember the Lady Godiva.

English Legend

Our Lady's Juggler

Long, long ago there was a young juggler who wandered from one fair to another delighting the country folk of France with his amazing antics and clever tricks.

As soon as he rolled out his piece of carpet on the ground a crowd gathered round. His favourite tricks were played with six bright copper balls which he kept moving in the air with his hands or his feet, as he turned somersaults or stood on his head. This pleased the children, who clapped, jumping up and down, begging him to do it again and again, while their parents threw money into his cap.

If the weather was good, the young juggler slept and ate well but, during the winter months and on wet days, it was a different story. No one wanted to stand about in the cold and wet, watching a juggler—not even the children. At such times he had often to go without food and sleep where he could, not that he grumbled. He loved juggling and did it as well as he could, trying to improve his tricks and invent new ones. Whenever he passed a church he would go in and pray to Mary, the Mother of God, thanking her if the day had gone well and asking her help when he was in trouble.

One day, as he walked along the road, the young juggler overtook a monk. As they were going in the same direction, they went along together.

'What do you do for a living, my son?' asked the monk.

'I'm a juggler, brother monk,' replied the young man. 'Sometimes I make a living and sometimes I do not; but it is my life and I wouldn't change it for any other. I think it is the finest in the world!'

'That is where you are wrong, my son,' said the monk. 'The best life is one spent in prayer as is ours at the monastery.'

'That is true,' said the young man thoughtfully. 'Much as I love my work, I'd gladly give it up if I could be a monk, but what chance is there of that for an ignorant fellow like me? Juggling is the only thing I can do well.'

The monk looked at the young man's honest face and recognised his simple goodness.

'If you are serious about it I will take you to our monastery; then if you really like the life there, you will be allowed to join us, first as a novice and then a monk.'

The young juggler found the monastery a wonderful place —everything was so bright and clean. Every day he was kept busy in the garden and the kitchen but, after a while, he longed to juggle again.

None of his brother monks seemed to be interested. They were much too engrossed in their own work which they offered up to the glory of God. The monastery was dedicated to Our Lady, and the monks used their talents to enrich it. One of them was an artist. He painted great murals on the walls depicting scenes in the life of Our Lady, another wrote music and conducted the choir in her praise. Another wrote poems and the words of the hymns that were sung, and yet another carved her image in stone and in wood.

The young juggler wished he had some talent he could use. Instead he hung about sadly watching the others practise theirs. He became thin and moody for he felt there was nothing he could do to honour the Mother of God.

One day he had an idea. While all the other monks were busy working at their painting, their music and their sculpture, the young juggler went alone to the Lady Chapel. There, in front of the statue of Our Lady, he unrolled his carpet, took out his six copper balls and began to juggle.

At first he was stiff and could not keep the balls in the air for long but, after a while, his skill returned and soon he was performing the most difficult feats. He did not stop until the bell rang for the midday meal. Then he bowed gravely to Our Lady, rolled up his carpet, put away the six copper balls and joined the other monks in the refectory.

At once they noticed his bright eyes and rosy cheeks.

'You must have been working hard in the garden, brother,' they said. 'It has done you good. Why, you've got back your bright smile. Does this mean you're going to be happy with us after all?'

'I think it does,' said the young man, but he was far too shy to tell them he had been juggling all morning, for he was sure they would laugh at him if he did.

So he kept it a secret until one of the monks found that the young novice was not working in the garden when he disappeared every morning, nor was he in the kitchen or any of the other likely places. He was nowhere to be seen. The monk was worried and went to the Abbot. Together they searched the workshops and the grounds, but he was nowhere to be found.

As they passed the Lady Chapel, they heard a noise. It was unusual for anyone to be in the chapel at this time, so they went quietly in to see who was there. Suddenly they stopped and gasped for, there in front of the statue of Our Lady, was the young novice. He had removed his habit and cowl and wore only his undergarments.

They watched, shocked but fascinated, as the young man juggled so cleverly with six bright copper balls, while he turned somersaults or stood on his head and did other extraordinary tricks. He was so absorbed in what he was doing he noticed neither the two monks nor the sweat that poured down his face.

'He must be stopped at once,' said the Abbot. 'This is an outrage!'

At that moment the dinner bell sounded. The juggler caught all six balls and held them as he bowed low before the statue.

'O Holy Mother of God!' he prayed, 'please accept these humble feats performed in your honour!'

And, to the astonishment of the monks, Our Lady bent forward, gently wiping the sweat from the juggler's brow.

'A miracle!' whispered the monk.

'Such simple faith is a miracle,' said the Abbot, who had been greatly moved by what he had seen. 'Come, brother, we have intruded long enough. We must allow our young novice to finish his prayers.'

After that, although the monks knew where he was and what he was doing, they made no attempt to interfere.

'We must not forget that each of us should offer to God what he can do best, no matter what that may be,' commented the Abbot.

French Legend

William Tell

Long ago there was a man called William Tell. He was a brave man and a great hunter, indeed he was the best shot with a cross-bow in the whole of Switzerland.

Now, at that time, Switzerland was ruled by a cruel tyrant called Gessler. One day, Gessler placed his hat on a high pole in the market square, and he ordered everyone who passed to bow to it.

It happened that William Tell had not heard of this, and when he passed the pole, he did not even notice the hat.

'Halt!' shouted the soldier on guard. 'Why do you not bow to your master's hat?'

'Why should I?' asked William Tell.

'Because your ruler, Herr Gessler, orders you to do so.'

'I don't care who orders me,' said Tell. 'I'll never bow to a hat!'

'Then you must come along with me,' said the soldier.

'I'll do nothing of the sort,' said Tell.

Just then Gessler himself rode up with a company of soldiers.

'What is all the fuss about?' he asked.

'This man, William Tell, will not bow to your hat, sir,' said the guard.

'So you are William Tell,' said Gessler, riding up to him. 'They tell me you're a fine shot, the finest in the land. Well, my man, is that true?'

'I have shot and won many times,' said Tell quietly.

'I have a mind to try your skill,' said Gessler, 'and I promise you, if you can hit the mark I set, you shall go free.'

'I will be glad to shoot for you,' said Tell. 'Where is the target?'

'Is this your son?' asked Gessler, pointing to the boy standing beside William Tell.

'It is.'

'Then let the lad stand in front of that oak tree. Place an apple on his head. If you can hit the apple you may go free,' said Gessler with a sneer.

'I will not shoot at my son,' said Tell. 'I will not do it.'

'Father, I will stand up straight and still,' said the boy. 'Do not worry. You never miss a target. I know you will hit the apple.'

And the brave lad took the apple from Gessler, walked over to the oak tree and stood before it. Then he carefully placed the apple on his own head.

'Now, father, I'm ready,' he said.

William Tell picked two arrows. He put one in his belt, and the other he fitted to his bow. Taking careful aim, he loosed the string.

The arrow flew straight to the target, and split the apple in two. And the boy ran to his father, who took him in his arms.

Gessler turned to William Tell. 'Why did you put a second arrow in your belt?'

Tell looked straight at Gessler.

'The second arrow was for your heart if the first had harmed as much as a hair of my son's head,' he said.

Gessler shook with rage at these bold words. Turning to his soldiers he said, 'Seize this man and take him to my castle across the lake.'

And before William Tell could move, the soldiers seized him and pushed him into a boat.

As they rowed across the lake, a great storm arose. The waves dashed against the boat, and it grew so dark they could not see where they were going. At last one of the soldiers said to Tell, 'You know this lake better than we do. If we untie you, will you guide us to the shore?'

'I will,' said Tell. So he took charge of the boat and soon brought it close to a narrow point of land.

Before he could be stopped, he seized his bow and jumped ashore, pushing the boat back into the lake.

'Hi! Come back!' shouted the soldiers. But Tell was already out of sight, hidden by the trees and rocks.

It did not take him long to climb to his mountain home, where he and his family were free from Gessler's power.

Not long afterwards, the whole nation went to war against this enemy. Gessler was killed, and the people, led by William Tell, became free.

Swiss Legend

Grace Darling

A long time ago, when your great, great, great grandmother was a little girl, there lived with her father, in a lighthouse, a girl called Grace Darling. The lighthouse was on the rocks of a lonely island called Farne off the Northumberland coast and Grace's father was the lighthouse-keeper.

Every night he trimmed the great lamp and saw that everything was bright, clean and in good order. He knew that all ships sailing along the coast would look out for his light, for it told them where they were and to be careful of the rocks.

One night there was a terrible storm, with thunder and lightning. As the gale blew and howled, the rain poured down out of the sky. Mr Darling looked anxiously out to sea, and then he saw two rockets, distress signals from a ship in trouble.

There was no telephone in those days and Mr Darling knew there was no time to lose.

'What shall I do?' he said to his daughter. 'There's no time to get help and I can't possibly launch our small lifeboat on my own in this sea.'

'I'll help you launch her, Dad,' said Grace. 'I've done it many times!'

'Not in weather like this, you haven't!'

'Well, we can't stay here and do nothing, can we?' said his daughter, already hitching up her long skirts and pulling on her oil-skins.

Together they managed to launch the lifeboat, and together they managed to row out to the sinking ship. At last they reached her and were in time to help nine of.the crew into the lifeboat and save them from drowning. Between them, Grace and her father rowed the rescued men back to the lighthouse, and there Grace made them change their wet clothes and drink the hot toddy she had made them.

The ship that was wrecked that night was called *The Forfarshire*. She had been sailing from Hull to Dundee, and those of her crew who were saved never forgot Grace Darling. She became the toast of sailors and fisherman all up and down the east coast of Great Britain.

Alexander Selkirk

There was once a strange Scotsman called Alexander Selkirk. He didn't like this and he didn't like that, and he couldn't agree with anyone at all.

One day he decided to go to sea. But it was just the same there. He didn't like this and he didn't like that and he could not get on with the captain no matter how hard he tried. So when the ship was passing a deserted island, Alexander Selkirk said to the captain, 'Would you mind putting me off on that island?' and the captain said, 'With the greatest of pleasure! There's no one there for you to disagree with, so you'll be quite happy!'

So he was left on the island with a case of food to keep him from starving for a week or two. But as the ship sailed out of sight, Alexander Selkirk wondered if he was going to miss his arguments with the captain and the crew.

He walked round the island and found it was not as deserted as he had thought. There were rats and there were cats, there were humming birds and some nice shaggy goats which he liked best of all.

There were many plants and trees, so, what with peppers, dates and pumpkins, and all the different little fish he caught, he found there was plenty to eat.

The goats became his special friends and gave him fresh milk every day.

He built himself a little house of reeds and lined it with grasses. When his clothes became worn, he made new ones from goat-skins. There was always so much to do he did not have time to feel homesick. He found the cats, the goats and the monkeys more amusing than the men he had known, and none of them disagreed with him about anything at all. He sang to them and even taught the cats and the goats to dance, they had become so tame. He felt very happy. He was the king of the castle! He was monarch of all he surveyed.

He stayed on his island for four years. Then one day he was looking out to sea, when he saw the smoke of a ship on the horizon. Suddenly he longed to see men and his home once more. So he gathered some dried sticks and lit a large bonfire on the shore, to attract the attention of the ship.

The crew saw the bonfire, and took Alexander off the island and carried him over the seas to Scotland.

He was glad to see his mother and father, and to tell them of all the strange adventures he had had on his island. But as he grew old he longed for his island and for his friends the cats, the goats and the monkeys, and he wished he had never left it.

Alexander Selkirk's experiences on his island were later used by Daniel Defoe as the basis for his book *Robinson Crusoe*.

Hans, the Hero of Haarlem

Holland is a very flat country. Part of it is lower than the sea, and the people have built walls all round the land to keep the sea from coming in and flooding everything. These walls are called dykes, and the people of Holland would have a poor life without them.

Now, in this part of Holland there is a town called Haarlem, and everyone who goes there is told the story of Hans, the little boy who once saved the town from the sea.

Hans lived in Haarlem with his father, mother and younger brother. His father was a fisherman, like most of the men, and Hans hoped to be a fisherman, too, when he grew up.

Well, one day, Hans and his small brother wandered away, playing beside the dykes. He ran along the top of a dyke, looking down at the water lapping against it on the other side.

'I want to run along the top too,' worried his little brother. 'Please let me up!'

'No, you stay down there,' said Hans. 'You're too small to come up here, you'd fall off.'

So his brother had to run along below, and he was not too pleased about it. He ran his hand along the side of the dyke, muttering to himself about the meanness of elder brothers, when suddenly he stopped.

'Look, there's a wee hole here!' he said, fingering the dyke. 'It's a wee hole. The water is trickling through!'

'Where?' asked Hans, who had been thinking of something else.

'Here, Hans, in the dyke!'

Without another word, Hans slipped off the wall, and was down beside his brother, staring at the dyke. Sure enough, water was seeping through a tiny hole in the lower part of the dyke. He knew what this meant, and that there was not a moment to lose.

'Whatever shall we do?' he said, looking toward the town. There was no one to be seen on that flat stretch of land. If they ran for help, it would be too late. The tide was in, and already the hole was bigger.

'You must run for help,' said Hans, 'and I'll stop the hole with my finger.'

So his little brother ran back to the town, while Hans knelt down and stuck his finger into the hole. It fitted exactly, just like a plug, and the water stopped coming through.

Hans watched his brother grow smaller and smaller, until at last he was out of sight.

His arm began to ache and he was so cold he could scarcely move, and still there was no sign of anyone coming. He heard the water lapping against the dyke on the other side, and he grew frightened. He wanted to take his finger from the hole and run home, but he knew that if he did this, the water would come rushing in through the hole and the dykes would collapse, and soon the flat countryside would be flooded.

'I'll *not* give in,' said he.

At that moment, he heard a shout. There away in the distance, he could see men coming. They carried pickaxes and shovels and spades, and as they came nearer he saw that one of them was his father.

Soon they were beside him. And while some mended the breach in the dyke, others rubbed him and gave him a warm drink from their flasks.

'You've saved Haarlem,' they said.

When the dyke was safe, Hans' father lifted him on to his shoulder and they carried him back to Haarlem like a hero.

Reputed Dutch Legend

Little Abe Lincoln

Long ago, there was a boy called Abe Lincoln. He lived with his mother and father in a log cabin, built on a hillside in the backwoods of America, far away from a town.

One cold winter day, Abe pulled on his deer-skin leggings and bear-skin moccasins, his thick woollen coat and his new fur cap. Away he went whizzing down the hill to deliver a message to a neighbour.

As he waited in the neighbour's house for a reply, he picked up a book and started to read. There were not many books in those days, but Abe loved reading. His mother was often mad with him for reading so much, but when the neighbour saw him reading he said, 'Why, Abe, got your nose in a book as usual!'

'This is the most exciting book I've ever read.'

'Then take it home with you,' said the man, 'and bring it back when you've read it.'

'Oh, sir, may I?' said Abe.

'Of course you can, son,' said the man. 'Just you bring it back in good shape, that's all I ask.'

'I'll take care of it, sir, sure I will,' said Abe.

'Then take it, and don't forget this message for your father.'

Abe stuck the book under his thick woollen jacket, and ran off home. It was a stiff climb up the hill to his home, but Abe did not mind. He thought of the book.

When he reached home he had to fetch in logs for the fire, and milk the cow. By the time he had done that his mother had his supper ready.

After supper he took out his book, but his mother said. 'Time you were off to bed, son, or you'll not get up in time to milk the cows.'

So Abe had to go to bed without reading his book. He climbed the ladder to his little room and put the book carefully on a shelf beside his bed. It was no good trying to read in bed, there was not enough light, but as soon as he woke up next morning he took his book to the little skylight, and read until his father called him.

One morning Abe woke, shivering with cold. He stretched out his hand for his book as usual, and laid it on his bedcover while he tried to pull the blankets up round his shoulders. It was so cold. When he picked up his book he was horrified to find it was soaking wet, and already the pages were stuck together. Then he saw that, during the night, the light snow had blown in through the cracks between the logs, and on to his bedcover. He had put his precious book right into the middle of the snow.

He tried to dry the pages, one by one, but it was no use. The damage had been done, and the more he tried to separate the pages the more they stuck together. What would the kind neighbour say? Abe found it difficult to eat any breakfast that morning, he had such a lump in his throat.

As soon as his work was finished, Abe set off down the hill to the neighbour's house. Sadly he handed back the book and told the man what had happened. When he saw how sorry Abe was, the man patted him on the shoulder, saying, 'Don't worry. The pages will soon dry, and the book will be almost as good as before. Would you like to have it for your very own?'

'I would indeed,' said Abe.

'Then you can work three days for me. After that the book will be yours.'

'To keep?' asked Abe.

'Naturally,' said the man, 'you will have earned it.'

So Abe was able to finish reading his book.

Years later, when Abe was a great man and President of the United States of America, he used to tell the story of his first book.

'That book,' he would say, 'was the story of George Washington, and I think it helped me to become President.'

Appleseed John

There was once a man called John Chapman who worked all his life in the fields, ploughing and planting and raising a good crop. He enjoyed his work and when he grew old he soon became tired of just sitting in the sunshine watching other folk ploughing and planting.

One morning as he sat, peeling an apple, he had an idea; and, after he had eaten the apple, he went home and took his strong cane walking stick, slung an empty bag over his bent shoulders and set out on a long journey.

Over the meadows and through the lanes he walked, stopping to speak to the small wild animals who were not afraid as he went by. At every farm he stopped and rapped on the door. And when someone came and opened the door and asked, 'What do you want, my good man?' what do you think he said? 'Just a few apples.' That was all he asked for. Now, the farmers had so many apples that summer, they were glad to give some away, and soon old John's bag was full, right to the very top.

When he was hungry he ate berries that grew in the woods, but not his apples—oh, no!

At last he came to a place where there were no farms and nothing had been planted on the land. There he sat down, took out his jack-knife, and carefully cut the core from every apple in the bag. With his cane he drilled deep holes in the earth, and into every hole he dropped an apple core. When his bag was empty he hurried on to the next village to ask for more apples.

Soon all the farmers knew him and they called him Apple-seed John. They gave him their best apples to plant, the 'Pippins' and the 'Seek no Furthers'. They gave him cuttings from their pear trees, plum trees and peach trees, and they gave him a corner of the settle nearest the fire and a bed when he stopped with them for the night.

He was always welcome for he had a bright smile, and the children liked to listen to his stories. He told them of all the things he had seen on his travels—the Red Indians with their bright-coloured blankets and feathers, the animals, the wolves, the hares and the little shy roe deer. No one even wanted Appleseed John to leave, but he would never stay longer than one night. With his bag over his shoulder, his cuttings under his arm, he hurried on, cane in hand, to plant young orchards by every river and lonely pasture.

Soon these apple seeds grew and sent up green shoots. They grew in the wind and the sun until they were trees, covered first with blossoms and then with ripe fruit, until all the empty places in the country were full of orchards.

Old Appleseed John died, but the children who had listened to his stories grew to be fathers, and then grandfathers, and as they sat under the trees, they would say to their grand-children, 'This orchard was planted by Appleseed John.' And then they would tell them this story as I have told it to you.

American legend about John Chapman (1774-1845)

Buffalo Bill

Buffalo Bill was a Cowboy who could ride faster and shoot straighter than anyone else in the Wild West. Some said he lived in his saddle, and that he never changed out of his long riding boots, leather-fringed breeches and red check shirt. Certainly he was seldom seen without his Cowpuncher hat and two guns stuck in his belt.

The things that Cowboy did! He not only herded cattle, but he drove the wild buffalo right off the prairies where they had done so much damage. It was because of this he was called Buffalo Bill, king of the Cowboys.

Buffalo Bill was more at ease in the saddle than out of it, which was not surprising, for he had been riding since he was a small boy. Indeed, his first job was that of a rider with the famous Pony Express. This was a team of riders who carried mail, in relays, between Missouri and Sacramento in California. It was a long tough journey, much of it over high mountain ranges, and the life would have been adventurous enough for any boy; but, when the American Civil War broke out, Buffalo Bill joined the Northern Army as a scout.

He was still only twenty-one years old when the Civil War ended, and it was then that he volunteered to hunt buffalo. It is said that he killed over 4,000 of these enormous animals and that he made a fortune selling their carcasses to the Kansas Pacific Railway for meat.

By the time Buffalo Bill was a middle-aged man, everything was much quieter, and most of Buffalo Bill's friends were for settling down and having a nice easy time. But not so Buffalo Bill! If he could no longer gallop after wild boar and Red Indians, then he'd show the young folk how it was done.

He organised an enormous Circus, and there, in comfortable seats and at a safe distance, people could see Cowboys riding, shooting and lassoing wild boar and Red Injuns, and all for one shilling! As long as there are Cowboys I'm sure Buffalo Bill will be remembered.

VI

ONCE UPON A TIME

The Rat Princess

Once upon a time there was a Rat Princess who lived with her mother, the Rat Queen, and her father, the Rat King. They all lived together in a ricefield.

The Rat King and the Rat Queen thought their daughter was the most beautiful rat in the whole world and they would allow no one to play with her.

When she grew up they were determined she should marry the most powerful person on the earth or in the sky, for no one else would be good enough.

So they went to the Oldest and Wisest Rat and said, 'Tell us, who is the most powerful person in the world?'

The Oldest and Wisest Rat thought for a while and said, 'The Sun is the most powerful, for he makes the rice grow and ripen, yes, the Sun is the one.'

So the Rat King went to find the Sun. He climbed a mountain, ran along a rainbow, and at last he came to the Sun.

'What do you want, little brother?' asked the Sun.

'I come to offer you the hand of my daughter, the Rat Princess, in marriage, for you are most powerful in the whole world, O Sun, and no one else is good enough.'

'Ho! ho! ho!' laughed the Sun. 'You are kind, little brother, but if that is the case, the Princess is not for me. The Cloud is more powerful, for when he passes me I cannot shine.'

'Oh, indeed,' said the Rat King, 'then you'll not do.' And away he went, along the Sun's rays, till he came to the Cloud.

'What do you want, little brother?' sighed the Cloud.

'I come to offer you the hand of my daughter, the Rat Princess, in marriage, for you are the most powerful in the whole world, O Cloud, and no one else is good enough.'

'You are kind, little brother,' sighed the Cloud, 'but if that is the case, the Princess is not for me, for the Wind is far more powerful. When he blows, I must go wherever he sends me.'

'Oh, indeed,' said the Rat King, 'then you'll not do.'

Away he went till he came to the Wind's home at the very edge of the world.

'What do you want, little brother?' asked the Wind.

'I come to offer you the hand of my daughter, the Rat Princess, in marriage, for you are the most powerful in the whole world, O Wind, and no one else is good enough.'

'Ha! ha! ha!' laughed the Wind in a loud gusty roar. 'You are kind, little brother, but if that's the case, then the Princess is not for me. The Great Wall that man made is much stronger than I am. I cannot move him no matter how hard I blow.'

'Oh, indeed,' said the Rat King, 'then you'll not do,' and away he went, back to earth and across the mountains till he came to the Great Wall of China.

'What do you want, little brother?' asked the Great Wall.

'I come to offer the hand of my daughter in marriage, for you are the most powerful one in the whole world, O Wall of China, and no one else is good enough.'

'Ugh, ugh, ugh,' grumbled the Great Wall, 'you are very kind, but if that's the case, the Princess is not for me. I'm not the most powerful. The Grey Rat, who lives under me, is much stronger, for when he gnaws and gnaws at me, I crumble. And one of these days I shall fall down altogether!'

So, after searching the wide world for the most powerful person, the Rat King had to marry his beautiful daughter to an ordinary Rat after all.

But the Princess did not mind, in fact she was very pleased, for *she* had wanted to marry the Grey Rat all the time.

Eastern Folk Tale

The Cock and the Handmill

There once lived an old man and his wife. They were so poor, they had not even a scrap of bread to eat. So they went out into the woods, gathered acorns and ate them at home for their supper.

As they ate, an acorn rolled off the table, across the floor, down a crack in the floorboards, right into the cellar below.

After a while this acorn began to sprout. It grew and it grew until it was a young oak tree, as high as the cellar ceiling.

The old woman noticed this, and said to the old man, 'Husband, you must cut a hole in the floor, and let the oak tree up through the cellar ceiling. If it grows much more, we'll be able to pick our acorns at home, instead of having to go out into the woods to gather them.'

So the old man cut a hole in the floor to let the oak through and it grew and it grew until it was as high as the roof.

Then the old man cut a hole in the roof to let the oak tree through; and it grew and it grew until it reached the sky.

Soon the old man and his wife had eaten all the acorns they could reach, so the old man took a bag and climbed up the tree. He climbed and he climbed until he reached the sky.

He was walking across the sky, when he saw a Cock with a beautiful golden comb, and beside the Cock was a Handmill. The old man did not take long to make up his mind, he just grabbed the Cock and the Handmill, and climbed down the oak tree into his cottage.

'Well, wife, when are we going to have our dinner?' said the old man, after he had given her the Cock and the Handmill.

'Wait a bit,' said the old woman. 'I want to try this Hand-mill.' And she took the Handmill and began to grind.

She gave one turn. A pancake fell out!

She gave another turn. A pie fell out!

Then she gave another turn, and a PANCAKE and a PIE
fell out!

The old man and the old woman ate and ate, and had as many
pancakes and pies as they liked. They soon forgot they once
had to eat acorns. They shared their food with the Cock, who
lived with them as their friend, and they were never hungry.

One day a very rich man was riding that way, when he
stopped at the cottage.

'Have you anything for me to eat, old woman?' he called
out. 'I'm feeling peckish!'

'I can only give you pancakes and pies, sir,' said she.

'That'll do fine,' said the very rich man as he tied his horse
to the gate, and walked into the cottage.

There he saw the old woman turning her Handmill, and at
every turn out fell a pie and a pancake.

'My, but these are good!' said he after he had gobbled up
about ten of each. 'I'd like to buy that Handmill of yours!
How much do you want for it?'

'I'll never sell it, sir,' said the old woman. 'Never!'

'Ah, well,' said he. 'If that's the case, just bring me out
some water for my horse.'

While the old woman was going to fetch the water, the rich
man took the Handmill, hid it in his jacket and rode off with it.

When the old man and woman found that their precious
Handmill had gone they were very sad. They did not know
how they would manage without it.

'Don't worry,' said the Cock with the golden comb, 'I'll
fetch back your Handmill.'

Up into the sky he flew and on till he came to the rich
man's house. There he perched on the roof and crowed:

> 'Cock-a-doodle-doo!
> Give us back our mill!
> Cock-a-doodle-doo!
> Give us back our Handmill!'

When the rich man heard the Cock he was furious and said
to his servants, 'Catch that Cock and throw him down the
well!'

So they caught the Cock and threw him down the well,
but the Cock sat at the bottom of the well and said:

> 'Drink up water, little beak!
> Drink up water, little mouth!'

He drank and drank until there was no water left in the well.
Then he flew out of the well, perched just outside the rich
man's window and crowed:

> 'Cock-a-doodle-doo!
> Give us back our mill!
> Cock-a-doodle-doo!
> Give us back our Handmill!'

When the rich man heard this he was more furious than ever,
and he shouted to his servants to take the Cock and put him
in the kitchen stove.

So they took the Cock and put him in the kitchen stove, and
at once he said:

> 'Pour out water, little beak!
> Pour out water, little mouth!'

The water soon put out the fire in the kitchen stove. Then the
Cock flew out of the stove into the rich man's dining room,
and perched on the side-board and crowed:

> 'Cock-a-doodle-doo!
> Give us back our mill!
> Cock-a-doodle-doo!
> GIVE US BACK OUR HANDMILL!'

Now the rich man was entertaining many guests and feast-
ing them on pancakes and pies. When they heard the Cock
with the golden comb, they were so frightened they ran off in
all directions, the rich man after them.

So the Cock with the golden comb took the Handmill and
flew with it back to the old man and woman.

Russian Folk Tale

Peter, Paul and Espen

Once upon a time there were three brothers called Peter, Paul
and Espen. One day they were walking through a wood when
they heard a strange sound.

'What is that?' asked Espen.

'Just a woodman chopping down a tree, silly!' said Peter
and Paul. They thought they knew everything and laughed
at their younger brother, for they thought he was a dull
lad.

'Haven't you heard a woodchopper before?' they teased.

'This sounds different,' said Espen. 'I'm going to find out
what it is.'

Away he went far into the wood till he saw an axe chopping at a tree all on its own.

'Good morning, axe,' said Espen. 'What are you doing
here, all by yourself?'

'I'm waiting for you,' said the axe.

'Well, here I am,' said Espen, and he took the axe and
tucked it under his belt. Then he hurried on to catch up with
his brothers. They had not gone very far when they heard a
strange tapping sound.

'What is that?' asked Espen.

'Just a stonecutter working with a pickaxe, silly,' said
Peter and Paul. 'Haven't you heard a pickaxe before?'

'This sounds different,' said Espen, 'I'm going to see for myself.'

He went into the far wood till he saw a pickaxe tapping at a rock all by itself.

'Good morning,' said Espen. 'What are you doing here, all by yourself?'

'I'm waiting for you,' said the pickaxe.

'Well, here I am,' said Espen. He took the pickaxe, and slinging it over his shoulder, hurried off to catch up with his brothers.

They had not gone very far when they came to a brook.

'I wonder where this brook comes from,' said Espen.

'Have you never seen a brook before, silly?' laughed Peter and Paul.

'Of course I have,' said Espen, 'but I mean to find out where this one comes from.' So away he went.

He followed the brook till it grew narrower and narrower, and smaller and smaller, till it was a mere trickle from a walnut shell.

'Good morning, brook,' said Espen. 'What are you doing here all by yourself?'

'Waiting for you,' said the brook.

So Espen took the walnut shell, plugged it with moss and stuffed it in his pocket. But, although he hurried as fast as he could, he was unable to catch up with his brothers.

Peter and Paul reached the city before Espen was even within sight of it, and they went straight to the palace.

Now the king was very worried about a tree that grew in front of his palace. The tree had grown so big it kept all the daylight from the palace, making it dark and gloomy.

Curiously enough, every time a branch was cut, three more, three times as large, grew in its place. The tree grew larger and larger, and not only that, the palace was built on a great rock with no water near at hand.

The king had offered half his kingdom to the man who could cut down the tree and dig a well in its place.

Every day men came and tried to cut down the tree and dig the well, but they all failed and were sent to a faraway island in disgrace. Among them were Espen's two brothers, Peter and Paul. When Espen reached the city, they had already gone. However, he was determined to cut the tree down himself.

He took his axe from his belt, put it at the foot of the tree and said:

'Chop away, my little axe, chop away!'

The axe chopped, and chopped, and chopped till it had chopped that tree right down. Then he took up his pickaxe, placed it against the rock, and said:

'Dig away, my pickaxe, dig away!'

In a short time the pickaxe had dug a deep, deep hole. Espen took the walnut shell from his pocket and dropped it into the hole. Immediately water bubbled up as high as a fountain, and there was a fine spring of fresh water, all that was needed at the palace.

The king was so pleased when he saw what Espen had done that he gave him half his kingdom, and Espen lived there happily ever after.

Norwegian Folk Tale

Jock and his Bagpipes

Once upon a time there were two brothers, one called John and the other called Jock.

One day John said to his mother, 'Mother, I'm going away to seek my fortune.'

'Very well, my son,' said she. 'Take this sieve to the well. Fetch some water in it, and I'll make you a bannock. If you fetch a lot of water, you'll get a large bannock, but if you fetch a little water, you'll get a wee one.'

So John took the sieve to the well. There he saw a wee bird sitting on the hillside. When it saw John with the sieve, the wee bird said:

> 'Stuff it with moss!
> Clog it with clay!
> Then you can carry
> The water away!'

'Oh, you stupid!' said John. 'Do you think I'm going to do as you tell me? No, no!'

So the water ran out of the sieve, and he took home only a little water. His mother baked a wee bannock for him, and away he went to seek his fortune.

After a while, the wee bird came to him again and said, 'Give me a piece of your bannock, and I'll give you a feather from my wing to make bagpipes.'

'I'll not,' said John. 'It's all your fault I've such a wee bannock. Why, it's not enough for myself!'

So the bird flew away, and John went farther and farther than I can say. When he came to the King's house, he went in and asked for work.

'What can you do?' said the house-keepers.

'I can sweep a floor, take out ashes, wash dishes and keep cows,' said he.

'Can you keep hares?'

'I don't know,' said John, 'but I'll try.'

They told him that if he looked after the hares, and brought them all safely home at night, he could wed the King's daughter. If he did not bring them all home, he'd be banished from the land for ever.

So, in the morning, John set out with four and twenty hares, and one that was lame. He was very hungry, for he had only had a wee bannock, so he caught the lame hare, roasted it and ate it. When the other hares saw this, they all ran away.

When he returned that night without any hares, the King was very angry and banished him from the land for ever.

Now, John's brother, Jock, went to his mother.

'Mother,' said he, 'I'm going away to seek my fortune.'

'Very well,' said she. 'Take this sieve to the well, and fetch home some water. If you bring a lot of water, you shall have a large bannock, but if you bring home a little water, you'll get a wee one.'

So Jock took the sieve to the well, and there he saw a wee bird sitting on the hillside. When it saw Jock with the sieve, it said:

> 'Stuff it with moss!
> Clog it with clay!
> Then you can carry
> The water away!'

'Ay, my bonnie bird,' said Jock, 'I'll do that.'

So he stuffed the sieve with moss and clogged it with clay, and he was able to take home a lot of water. His mother baked him a great big bannock, and away he went to seek his fortune.

After a while, the bird came to him again.

'Give me a piece of your bannock,' it said, 'and I'll give you a feather from my wing to make bagpipes.'

'Ay, my bonnie bird,' said Jock, 'I will, for it was you who helped me to get such a large bannock,' and he gave the bird a piece of the bannock.

'Pull a feather from my wing,' said the bird, 'and make the bagpipes.'

'No, no! I'll not pull a feather, for it will hurt you.'

'Just do as I tell you,' said the bird.

So Jock pulled a feather from its wing, made the bagpipes, and went along playing a merry tune.

He went far and far and farther than I can tell. When he came to the King's house, he went in and asked for work.

'What can you do?' asked the house-keepers.

'I can sweep floors, take out ashes, wash dishes and keep cows,' said Jock.

'Can you look after hares?' asked the house-keepers.

'I don't know,' said Jock, 'but I'll try.'

They told him that if he could look after the hares, take them out in the morning and bring them all safely home at night, he would win the King's daughter. But if he did not bring them all home, he would be banished from the land for ever.

Well, next morning, Jock set out with four-and-twenty hares and one that was lame. He took them over the hills and played them such a merry tune on his pipes that they danced round him all day and never left his side. And all day he carried the lame hare because it could not walk.

That night he returned to the palace with four-and-twenty hares running beside him and the lame one under his arm.

The house-keepers were pleased, and the King was so pleased he gave Jock his daughter to be his bride. And he played her such merry tunes on his pipes that they lived happily ever after.

Scottish Folk Tale from *The Well at the World's End* by Norah and William Montgomerie.

The Three Brothers

A man had three sons and he was fond of them all. He had no money, but the house in which he lived was a good one.

'To which of my three boys shall I leave my house?' thought the old man. 'They have all been good sons to me and I want to be fair to them in every way.'

Maybe you think the simplest thing would have been to sell the house and then divide the money among the three brothers. It would have been simpler but nobody wanted to do this. The house had been in their family for many years. Not only the three brothers but their father, their grandfather, and their great-grandfather had been born in it. It was their home. They knew it and they loved every room, every window, every nook and cranny of it, and they could not bear to sell it to a stranger.

So the old man had to think of a way out, and he did.

He called to his three sons and said, 'This is the way we'll do it. All of you must go out into the world and learn a trade after his own heart and learn it well. In one year we we will meet here together. He who has learned his trade best shall have the house. Do you all agree?'

'Yes,' said the sons, 'that is fair enough.'

The eldest said, 'I think I will become a blacksmith. That is the work I like best.'

'And I,' said the second, 'have always wanted to be a barber. That's what I'll set out to be.'

'And I,' said the third, 'would like to be a fencing master.'

They agreed to return at the appointed time, and then they all went their separate ways.

The eldest son became such a good blacksmith that he was soon hired to shoe the king's own horses.

'Well,' said he to himself, 'I don't see how I can fail to win. I'll surely get the house.'

The barber learned his trade so well that he was soon shaving all kinds of grand people like earls and lords and dukes.

'This isn't a bad start,' said he to himself. 'The house is a good as mine now, I think.'

The youngest son endured many a blow while he was learning to fence, but he never winced or whimpered, although he seemed to progress slowly.

'If you're going to be discouraged,' said he to himself, 'you will never get the house.'

At last the year was up and they all returned to their father's house, but although each had become a master of his own particular trade or art, none could think of a good way to prove it.

They were all sitting on a bench in front of the house, talking it over, when a rabbit came running over the field.

'Aye,' said the barber, 'that's as good as though I had called him.'

He took his mug and soap and quickly whipped up a lather while the rabbit was running towards them. Then just as the rabbit ran past at top speed, he lathered the little creature's chin and shaved it, leaving just enough fur to make a nice little pointed beard. Although the rabbit had been running as fast as he could he was not hurt or cut in any way.

'That pleases me,' said the father. 'Unless the others do better, the house will surely go to you.'

Just then there was a buzzing in the air. The blacksmith looked up and said:

'Ah! A gnat! That's just the thing for me.'

And so, while the gnat was flying, the smith quickly fitted it with little golden horseshoes, one for each foot and each shoe fastened with twenty-seven tiny nails. All this time the gnat had been flying around, and all was finished in a flash.

'You're a real fellow,' said the father. 'You've done your work as well as your brother. At this rate I won't know which of you should get the house.'

In the meantime dark clouds had been gathering in the sky and now a few drops of rain began to fall.

The youngest son sprang up and said, 'I couldn't have wished for anything better! Now I'll show you what I have learned.'

He stood before them, and drawing out his sword, he

swung it in criss-cross strokes above his head and was so clever about it that not a drop of rain fell on him.

Yet harder fell the rain, faster and faster, until it seemed as though it were being poured by tubfuls from the sky. Still his sword circled, swished and swirled. All around him everything was wet, but he himself was dry as though he had been standing under a roof.

When the father saw this he was astonished and said, 'You have accomplished the greatest feat of all. The house is yours.'

But the young fencer did not want the house all to himself.

He shared it with the others, and there they all lived happily together for the rest of their lives.

    Retold from Grimm

The Tailor and the Three Beasts

There was once a tailor of Galway, and he set out on a journey to the King's court in Dublin.

He had not gone far when he met a white horse.

'Good-day to you!' said the tailor.

'Good-day to you!' said the white horse. 'Where are you going?'

'I'm going to Dublin to build a castle for the King. If I can do this the King will give me his daughter as a wife.'

'How is that?' said the horse.

'Well, three enormous giants live in a wood near Dublin, and every time the King builds a castle, these giants come and knock it down.'

'If you can build a castle, you can surely make me a hole,' said the horse, 'where I can hide from the farmer and the miller. I am tired of working for them.'

'I'll do that,' said the tailor.

He put down his bag, took out his shovel and spade, and made a hole.

'Go into the hole,' said he, 'to see if it fits.'

The white horse went into the hole, but he could not get out of it when he tried.

'Make a path,' said he, 'so that I can come out of the hole when I'm hungry.'

'I will not,' said the tailor. 'You remain there till I return. Then I'll lift you out.'

The tailor went on until he met a fox.

'Good-day to you!' said the tailor.

'Good-day to you!' said the fox. 'Where are you going?'

'I'm going to Dublin to build a castle for the King.'

'Would you build me a hiding-place?' said the fox. 'I'm tired of being hunted.'

'I'll do that,' said the tailor.

He put down his bag and took out his axe and saw. With the wood from a tree he made a crate for the fox.

'Go into the crate and see if it fits,' said he.

The fox went into the crate, and the tailor let down a shutter. When the fox tried to get out again he found he could not.

'Lift up the shutter,' said he, 'so that I can get out whenever I wish.'

'I will not,' said the tailor, 'You remain here until I return, then I'll let you out.'

The tailor went on till he met a lion.

'Good-day to you!' said the tailor.

'Good-day to you!' said the lion. 'Where are you going?'

'I'm going to Dublin to build a castle for the King.'

'Would you make me a plough?' said the lion. 'I need to plough if I'm to grow some food to eat in the winter.'

'I'll do that,' said the tailor.

He took out his axe and saw, and he made a plough.

He also made a hole in the beam of it, and a peg to fit the hole.

'See if the plough fits you,' said he.

The lion was harnessed to the plough. When he was not looking, the tailor put the lion's tail into the hole, clapped in the peg and the lion was caught.

'Let me go now, there's a good fellow,' said the lion, 'and I'll show you how well I can plough.'

'I will not,' said the tailor. 'You'll stay here until I return. Then I'll let you go.'

Away went the tailor till he came to Dublin.

Next day, with the help of twenty workmen, he started to build the castle. At the end of the day the work was far on but before the men went home to rest, the tailor told them to fix a great boulder at the top of the scaffolding, which could crash below when given a push. When this was done and the men had all left, the tailor hid himself behind the boulder and waited for the giants.

As soon as it was dark, the giants came out of the wood to knock down the work. Just as they got ready to tear every-thing down, the tailor pushed the boulder and down it went crashing on top of them. It only killed one of the giants, but that frightened the other two. Away they ran and did not return that night.

The King and the people were very surprised the building was still there in the morning. It was the first time it had happened.

All day long the tailor and his workmen worked as they had never worked before and by evening they had managed to put the roof on the castle. Before they went home the men fixed an even bigger boulder above the building. When they had left, the tailor hid himself as before and waited for the giants.

As soon as it was dark, the two giants strode out of the woods to tear down the building. They were just about to strike, when the tailor pushed the huge boulder. Down it went, crashing on top of them. It only killed one of them, but the other was so frightened he never returned, and the building went on until the castle was finished.

It was a very fine castle and the King was pleased with it.

'You have done well. Here is your reward,' said he, hand- ing the tailor a bag of gold.

'Thank you,' said the tailor, 'but you promised me your daughter as well.'

'You cannot have my daughter until the third giant has been killed,' said the King.

So the tailor went to the third giant and asked him if he wanted a servant.

'I do,' said the giant, 'but he must be able to do all that I can do myself.'

'Anything you can do I can do also,' said the tailor.

'We'll soon see about that,' said the giant.

While they sat at dinner, the giant said:

'I can drink a gallon of boiling broth. Can you?'

'I can,' said the tailor, 'and I'll show you how at supper.'

Before supper the tailor got a sheepskin, sewed it into a bag, and hid it under his shirt and jacket.

At supper, a gallon of boiling broth was put before the giant, and a gallon of boiling broth was put before the tailor.

'You drink yours first!' said the tailor.

'Your turn now!' said the giant, when his own broth was finished.

'All right,' said the tailor, and he carefully poured the boiling broth into the skin bag hidden under his jacket. He poured and poured and poured until it was all in, and the giant thought he was drinking it.

'I didn't think you'd manage to do that,' growled the giant.

'That's nothing,' said the tailor. 'I'll now do something you will not dare to do.'

'Nonsense!' said the giant. 'What are you going to do?'

'Make a hole and let the broth out again!' said the tailor.

'Do it yourself first,' said the giant.

'All right,' said the tailor, and he gave the front of his jacket a prod with a knife, and the broth came pouring out of the skin bag beneath.

'Now you do that,' said he.

'I will,' said the giant, giving himself such a prod with a knife that he was dead before he knew what had happened.

And that was the way the tailor killed the third giant.

Then he went to the King and told him that the giant was dead, and if he was not given the Princess for his wife he'd knock the castle down as quickly as he had built it up.

The King was afraid so he told his daughter she must go with the tailor and marry him.

After the tailor and his bride had gone, the King began to miss his daughter and wished he had not let her go. He called his men together and told them to follow the couple and bring back his daughter for he could not bear to be without her.

The King's men rode on until they came to the lion, still caught in his plough.

'Did the tailor and his bride pass this way?' asked the men.

'They did,' said the lion, 'and if you release me I'll catch them for you. I'm swifter than you.'

So the men released the lion, and away they all went after the tailor and his bride, till they came to the fox, still caught in the crate.

'Did the tailor and his bride pass this way?' they asked.

'They did,' said the fox, 'and if you'll let me out, I'll catch them. I'm swifter than you.'

So they set the fox free, and away they all went, till they came to the white horse, still trapped in the hole.

'Did you see the tailor and his bride pass this way?' they asked.

'I did,' said the white horse, 'and if you help me out of this hole I'll catch them for you. I'm swifter than you.'

So they pulled the white horse out of the hole, and away they went, the lion, the fox, the white horse and the King's men, till at last they caught up with the young couple.

When the tailor saw them coming, he said to his bride:

'Do not be afraid, just stay by these trees. I'll soon send them away.'

Then to her surprise he sat cross-legged on the ground. When the lion saw this, he suddenly stopped running.

'I'll not go near him,' said he. 'That's the way he sat when he made the plough that held me fast for so long!'

'I'll not go near him,' said the fox. 'That's the way he sat when he made the crate that kept me prisoner!'

'I'll not go near him,' said the white horse. 'That's the way he sat when he made the hole that I couldn't get out of, after I'd got into it!' And he turned and galloped back the way he had come. And so did the fox. And so did the lion.

And when they saw this, the King's men were afraid and they too turned and went all the way back to Dublin.

Then the tailor took his bride home to Galway where they lived happily ever after.

Irish Folk Tale

'The Owl was a Baker's Daughter'

Once upon a time and long, long ago, the country people were so poor they could not afford to buy baker's bread, so they gathered up their own grain, ground it into flour, and made dough. They took the dough to the baker who baked it in his large oven, charging them a few pence for the service.

Now, there was one baker who, helped by his daughter, used to break small pieces of dough off each loaf as he pushed

it into the oven. With the small pieces he made rolls which he
sold to the rich folk. In this way he and his daughter became
richer and richer, while the poor people wondered why their
loaves came out of the oven smaller and smaller.

'Why are our loaves so much smaller after you have baked
them in your oven?' they complained. 'We think you're
stealing bits off them!'

'Nonsense,' said the baker, 'it's the bad flour you use. Now,
if you bought my flour, you'd soon see the difference!'

'You know we can't afford your flour,' they said.

'Very well, take your dough elsewhere,' said the greedy
old baker, knowing perfectly well they couldn't do that
either, because there wasn't another baker for miles and miles
around.

So they just had to put up with their small loaves, and
they grew hungrier while the baker and his daughter grew
rich.

Then one day a strange thing happened. All of a sudden,
that greedy old baker turned into a grey bird, and flew off,
calling: 'Cuck! Cuck! Cuckoo!' while his greedy daughter
was changed into a white owl, and looked as though a bag
of flour had been poured over her.

Although the greedy old baker had been changed into a
cuckoo, he never changed his ways. He is just as dishonest as
a bird as he was when a baker. He never bothers to build a
nest for his wife, but tells her to lay her eggs in the nests of
other birds, leaving them to hatch them, and care for the
chicks, while she flies off, carefree and singing, 'Cuckoo!
Cuckoo!'

But his daughter, changed into a Barn Owl, was sorry for
what she had done. Now she flies about the granaries and
barns, catching all the mice and rats, who would like to eat
up all the grain stored there.

English Folk Tale

Snow-white and the Seven Dwarfs

Once upon a time, in winter when the snowflakes were falling, a Queen sat sewing at a window. As she sewed she looked out at the snow on the black ebony of the window frame. She pricked her finger with her needle, and three little drops of blood fell on the snow.

'I would like a child,' thought the Queen, 'as white as snow, as red as blood and as black as ebony.'

Well, soon after that she had a little daughter with skin as white as snow, lips as red as blood and hair as black as ebony. She was called Snow-white.

After one year, the Queen died and the King married again. The new Queen was beautiful, but she was proud and vain. She had a magic mirror, and when she looked at herself in it, she would say:

> 'Mirror, mirror, in my hand,
> Who is the fairest in the land?'

The magic mirror would answer:

> 'Fairest Queen, 'tis very true
> There is none as fair as you!'

Then the Queen would be happy for she knew the mirror always spoke the truth.

As for Snow-white, she grew more beautiful every day and, when the Queen asked her mirror:

> 'Mirror, mirror, in my hand,
> Who is the fairest in the land?'

the mirror answered:

> 'My Lady Queen, is fair, 'tis true,
> But little Snow-white is fairer than you.'

When she heard that, the Queen was very angry, and from

that moment she looked at Snow-white with hatred. She planned how she might get rid of her, called her huntsman, and said, 'Take the child into the forest and kill her, for I cannot endure the sight of her.'

The huntsman did as he was told and took Snow-white out into the forest, but she wept and said, 'Dear huntsman, spare my life! I'll run into the forest and never return, I promise you!'

She looked so young and beautiful the huntsman had pity on her, and let her go.

Away she ran into the forest till she came to a little house. She tapped on the door, but no one answered, so she opened the door and peeped in. Everything looked so neat and warm she just stepped inside to rest herself.

It was one of the cosiest rooms she had ever seen. There was a little table covered with a white table cloth, and on it were laid seven little plates, seven knives and forks, and seven glass tumblers of wine. Round the table were seven little chairs, and against the wall were seven little beds, each covered with a white quilt.

Snow-white was very hungry and thirsty, so she drank a little wine from each tumbler and ate a little bread from each plate. Then, as she was very tired, she tried all the beds, one by one. They were either too long or too short, too hard or too soft, too high or too low, until she came to the seventh bed. It was so comfortable that as soon as she lay down on it she fell fast asleep.

In the evening, the owners of the house returned home. They were the seven dwarfs who worked in the mountain, digging for gold. They lit their seven little lamps and soon they saw that things were not as they had left them.

'Who has been sitting on my chair?' asked the first.

'Who has been eating off my plate?' said the second.

'Who has been using my knife?' said the third.

'Who has been using my fork?' said the fourth.

'Who has been eating my bread?' said the fifth.

'Who has been drinking my wine?' said the sixth.

'Here she is,' said the seventh, 'sleeping in my bed!'

They shone their lamps on Snow-white and gasped, 'Good gracious, what a beautiful child!'

Just then Snow-white awoke and when she saw the seven dwarfs looking down at her she was very frightened.

'Don't be afraid,' they said kindly. 'Just tell us your name.'

'I'm called Snow-white,' she replied, and then she told them all that had happened to her.

'You are safe here, Snow-white,' they said kindly. 'If you'll take care of our house, keep everything neat and tidy, cook our meals, wash and sew and knit for us, you can stay here as long as you like and have all that you want.'

So she lived happily with them keeping their house in good order.

Every morning the dwarfs went off to the mountain to dig for gold, and every evening they came home to a neat and clean house, their clothes washed and mended, and a nice hot meal ready on the table. All the same they did not like leaving Snow-white alone in the house all day.

'Don't allow anyone in while we're away,' they said. 'Your stepmother will soon find out you're here and she'll try again to harm you, so mind you take care.'

Now, back in the palace, the wicked Queen took her mirror and said:

> 'Mirror, mirror, in my hand,
> Who is the fairest in the land?'

The mirror answered:

> 'My Lady Queen, you are fair, 'tis true,
> But little Snow-white is fairer than you,
> For over the hills where seven dwarfs dwell
> Little Snow-white is alive and well.'

When she heard this the Queen was very angry. She knew now that the huntsman had deceived her.

She wondered how she could get rid of Snow-white. At last she thought of a plan. She stained her face and dressed herself up as a pedlar woman. In this disguise she went over the hills to the house where the seven dwarfs lived, and knocked on the door.

'Pretty things to wear! Pretty things to sell!' she cried.

Snow-white looked out of the window and called, 'Good-day, good-wife! What have you to sell?'

'Fine silks and stay laces of every colour! Come, open the door, my dear, and see for yourself.' And the pedlar woman held up a pair of bright laces.

'Surely I can let this old woman in,' thought Snow-white. So she unlocked the door, and when she saw the pretty laces she forgot all the good dwarfs had told her.

'Goodness, how untidy you look, my dear. Come, I'll lace you up neatly.'

Snow-white, suspecting no harm, stood and allowed the old woman to thread her bodice with bright new laces. But she laced so quickly and so tightly that it took Snow-white's breath away, and she fell lifeless to the ground.

When the seven dwarfs returned home that night they found little Snow-white lying still on the floor. They lifted her up gently and at once saw how tightly her bodice was laced, so they cut the laces and she began to breathe a little. Gradually the colour returned to her cheeks and they knew she was alive. When the dwarfs heard what had happened they said, 'The old pedlar woman was the wicked Queen, you may be sure of that. Now you must take care and let in *no one* while we are away.'

As soon as the Queen reached home she looked in her mirror and said:

> 'Mirror, mirror, in my hand,
> Who is the fairest in the land?'

The mirror answered:

> 'My Lady Queen, you are fair, 'tis true,
> But Snow-white is fairer far than you,
> For over the hills where seven dwarfs dwell
> Little Snow-white is alive and well.'

At this the Queen shook with rage for she knew the mirror spoke the truth, and she would get no peace while Snow-white lived.

So she made a poisoned comb, and disguised herself as an old woman, and away she went over the hills to the house of the seven dwarfs. She knocked at the door and called,

'Fine combs to sell! Fine combs to sell!'

Snow-white looked out of the window.

'Go away, old woman!' she cried. 'I mustn't let anyone in!'

'I did not ask you to let me in, my dear. Surely you may look. How do you like this?' and she held up the poisoned comb.

Snow-white had never seen such a pretty comb before. It shone like gold, and jewels were set in the handle. She liked it so much she forgot all that the good dwarfs had told her, and ran to open the door.

'It is beautiful!' she said.

'I'll show you how well it combs the hair.'

Before Snow-white realised what was happening, the old woman ran the comb through her hair. The poison worked at once and the poor girl fell senseless to the ground.

'You're really done for this time, my beauty!' said the Queen as she hurried back to the palace.

Fortunately the dwarfs returned home early. They saw Snow-white lying on the floor, and noticed the bright comb in her hair. The moment they pulled the comb out, she came to life, and told them all that had happened. Once more they warned her to be on her guard and open the door to no one.

When the Queen reached home she asked her mirror:

> 'Mirror, mirror, in my hand,
> Who is the fairest in the land?'

And the mirror answered:

> 'My Lady Queen, you are fair, 'tis true,
> But Snow-white is fairer far than you,
> For over the hills where seven dwarfs dwell,
> Little Snow-white is alive and well.'

And when she heard this she was in a great rage. Secretly she made a poisoned apple which looked so delicious that whoever saw it would want to eat it. Then the wicked Queen disguised herself as a farmer's wife. Away she went over the hills to the house of the seven dwarfs, and knocked on their door.

'I cannot open the door,' said Snow-white, looking out of the window. 'The dwarfs have forbidden it.'

'Never mind, I'll sell my apples elsewhere,' answered the old woman. 'But I'll give you one, for you're a pretty child.'

'Oh no,' said Snow-white, 'I dare not take anything.'

'Then share it with me,' and the old woman took the finest apple from her basket and cut it in two, and offered Snow-white the rosy half.

When she saw the woman eat the other piece, Snow-white took the red half and ate it. As soon as she took the first bite she fell dead on the ground, for the red half had been poisoned.

'Ha, ha!' laughed the Queen. 'White as snow, red as blood, black as ebony! The Dwarfs will not be able to wake you this time.' She could hardly wait to look in her mirror and ask the usual question.

This time the mirror answered:

> 'My Lady Queen, now 'tis true,
> There is none as fair as you.'

At last the wicked Queen was satisfied.

When the dwarfs returned home that night they found Snow-white lying dead on the floor and they could not bring her to life, no matter what they did. She looked so beautiful they could not bear to part with her, so they made a glass case and put her in it, and wrote her name in gold upon the lid.

They took the glass case to the top of the mountain, and took it in turn to watch over it. There she remained, white as snow, red as blood, black as ebony and as beautiful as ever.

Now, one day a King's son rode into the forest, past the dwarf's house and on up the mountain. There, in a glass case, her name written in gold on the lid, he saw Snow-white, and fell in love with her.

'Give me this treasure,' said the Prince to the dwarf on guard, 'and I will give you whatever you wish.'

'We would not part with it for all the gold in the world,' said the dwarf.

Again and again the Prince pleaded with the dwarfs and at last they agreed to let him have it.

As his men carried the glass case, they stumbled and jolted it so violently that the piece of apple was jerked out of Snow-white's mouth, and before long she opened her eyes and sat up alive and well.

'Wherever am I?' she said.

'You are with me,' said the Prince, 'and I will take care of you.' He told her all that had happened and asked her if she would go with him to his father's palace and be his Princess.

Snow-white gladly went with him, and the wedding was prepared.

Now, the wicked Queen was invited to the wedding. She dressed herself in her finest clothes, and little did she know who the bride really was.

When she went to her mirror and asked:

> 'Mirror, mirror, in my hand,
> Who is the fairest in the land?'

the mirror answered:

> 'My Lady Queen, you are fair, 'tis true,
> But this young Bride is fairer than you.'

Hearing this, the wicked Queen, mad with rage, ran out into the dark forest and was heard of no more.

Snow-white and her Prince were married and lived happily ever after.

Retold from Grimm

Tinga-ling-BOME!

Tinga-ling-BOME!
Tinga-ling-BOME!
A fire broke out in the little goat's home.
A pailful of water was brought by the hen
To pour on the little goat's home, and then
The Cock with the Golden Comb hurried along.
He was bringing a ladder and singing a song:
'Tinga-ling-BOME!
Tinga-ling-BOME!
We'll put out the fire in the little goat's home!'

Index of Titles and Authors

Acknowledgments

The publishers have made every effort to trace the ownership of the copyright material in this book. It is their belief that the necessary permissions from publishers, authors and authorised agents have been obtained, but in the event of any question arising as to the use of any material, the publishers, while expressing regret for any error unconsciously made, will be pleased to make the necessary correction in future editions of this book.

Thanks are due to the following for permission to reprint copyright material: Mrs Diana Denney for her story 'The Good Hen and the Bad Hen' from *William and the Lorry*, published by Faber & Faber Ltd; Faber & Faber Ltd for 'Too Timid, Too Bold and Just About Right' from *Nursery Tales* by Diana Ross, for 'What happened to Mustard' from *A Story a Day* by Doris Rust, for 'The Riddle-me-ree' from *Adventures of Tim Rabbit* by Alison Uttley, and for 'The House that suits you will not suit me' from *The*

Golden Hen by Diana Ross; Harper & Brothers for 'The Talking Cat' from *The Talking Cat* by Natalie Savage Carlson, copyright 1952 by Natalie Savage Carlson; George G. Harrap & Company Ltd for 'The Bear says "North"' from *The Mighty Mikko* by Parker Filmore; David Higham Associates for 'Robert the Bruce' from *Heroes and Heroines* by Eleanor and Herbert Farjeon, published by Gollancz; the Hogarth Press for 'Two of Everything' from *The Treasure of Li-Po* by Alice Ritchie, and for 'The Wee Bannock' and 'Jock and his Bagpipes' both from *The Well at the World's End* by Norah and William Montgomerie; Houghton Mifflin Company for 'Soap! Soap! Soap!' from *Grandfather Tales* collected and retold by Richard Chase; the Hutchinson Publishing Group for 'Father Christmas and the Carpenter' from *Mrs Pepperpot Again* by Alf Prøysen; Methuen & Company Ltd for 'The Red Hat' from *Next Time Stories* by Donald Bisset, and for 'My Naughty Little Sister and the Workmen' from *My Naughty Little Sister* by Dorothy Edwards; Thomas Nelson & Sons for 'Home is Best' from *Another Story Please!* by Richard Wilson; Prentice-Hall, Inc, for 'The Pedlar and his Caps' from *Storytelling* by Ruth Tooze, reprinted by permission; the Syndics of the Cambridge University Press for 'Who killed the Otter's Young?' from *Fables and Folk Tales from an Eastern Forest* by Walter Skeat; the Trustees of Dr Douglas Hyde's Estate for 'The Piper and the Puca' from *Irish Fairy and Folk Tales* edited by W. B. Yeats; the Trustee of the author's estate for Laura E. Richards' 'The Coming of the King' from *The Golden Windows*; Basil Blackwell, Oxford, for 'Tinga-ling-BOME!' from *Picture Tales from the Russian;* and Robert Bright for his story 'The Travels of Ching'.